QUEEN's CALL

ANITA RENAGHAN

Cover Design by Denise Collie www.deedesign.com

©2019 by Anita Renaghan

anitarenaghan.com

Kitchen Entertainment

ISBN-13: 978-1-7335671-0-7

DEDICATION

To my Godmother, Aunt Ellen, who is not long for this world. Your encouragement will continue to resonate as I write my works, and the thought of your smile will help light my way on this path.

Chapter 1
Stone Future

The ground shook and dust fell from the cracks in the stone ceiling, and Mandetta knew that the Anthracites were tearing their monstrous charcoal bodies from the ground. In a few minutes, King Hawker would call for Mandetta and her mother to go and ring the kasic bell and call the Anthracites back toward the castle. King Hawker, the man who had slain her father, commanded her now, and Mandetta felt the sting of loss and of change and tried not to cry. The ground shook again and Mandetta readied the bell and bow and waited for the King to call.

Mandetta's mother didn't seem to notice the ground shake as she walked her twentieth lap around the small apartment. This wasn't her large suite of rooms. They had been moved to two small rooms the moment the men had returned from their outing. The men had returned, but her husband had not.

Her husband, the Monarch of Cormicks, was dead, and she could hardly believe it. She wanted to fall down and cry, but there was no time to mourn. Tears now wouldn't have been for him as much as for the loss of her stature in Cormicks. Her husband had treated her well most of the time though, and she had enjoyed watching her children grow.

Her three boys, two of age and one of ten years, had talked of fighting. They were going to challenge the newcomer and fight for the throne. She encouraged the boys to move forward with any plan that they could hatch, although they would get no help from the counselors or anyone they had counted as friends before. She would mourn for her sons as well, but better to let them fall fighting with hope than brought to inevitable slaughter.

Her oldest was Mandetta, her eighteen year old daughter who was of age to be married, but there would be no offers from her suitors and no one would come to their defense. The Monarch hadn't wanted real competition, so her daughter had only been called on by the counselor's sons. They were all the plotting, weak, and petty weasels that their fathers were.

She knew that there was no hope for the family. This man, although a foreigner, would surely kill his predecessor's family, her family. She had no doubt that she and her children would all be dead within the week. She understood this; her own husband had killed the family of his predecessor, sparing one, and then killing her once the language of the Anthracites had been passed on. And that is what this King Hawker would do, no doubt at the urging of the counselors. With their white robes and baldheads and quiet deliberation, they would do away with her entire family.

She had considered bringing the Anthracites in to crush the castle. Revenge would suit her. But for all of her anger, there was a part of her that wanted Mandetta to live. They would have to keep one of the females alive to talk to the Anthracites, and that only left Mandetta. She knew the language, was strong with the calling bell, and no one else had learned the powerful language of the rock beasts.

She wondered for a moment if King Hawker would let her live to keep her for himself, but the thought was fleeting and she recognized it for what it was, a twisted version of hope where she might be spared. She was lying to herself though, and she didn't allow the moment to play out any further in her mind.

Mandetta held the sack out, and her mother approached and put the bag on the ground. Her mother looked at her, holding her hands firmly on her shoulders, and then pulling her in tight. There were no more words to say. They'd talked about all manner of escape, but their only conclusion was the safety of obedience to the next Monarch.

They had talked about paying the servants to sneak the family out, but they were safer here than out among the Runners. Mandetta was part Runner, and still the giant tattooed men scared her. They had been tamed into their packs, following the commands of the Monarch and counselors, but there was still something dangerous within each one, waiting to fight, to torture, and to let their animalistic tendencies take over.

Mandetta had been raised in the castle under the protection of her Monarch father, and now she was a prisoner, and the Runners were brutes. If she had the castle crushed and the power-hungry counselors with it, there was no telling what the Runners would do to her.

Her stomach churned at the thought, and as though they had heard her stomach's call, the castle rumbled and she knew that the Anthracites had completely unfolded. Mandetta felt the panic of tears welling up and she went to her mother.

"Mama," was all Mandetta said, but her mother read a thousand questions in the concerned look on the teenager's face. They would be called on very soon. King Hawker would want them to bring the Anthracites back, and Mandetta daydreamed that she could smash the bell into pieces so that the Anthracites could never be called again, but these tools and her control of the Anthracites were her only hope.

The ground rumbled again and dust fell from the rock ceiling. The three boys moved to the door. They knew it would be unlocked soon as the counselors came for the Queen, and they were ready to try to push their way out and fight.

"No," their mother told them. "Wait until I come back." She took the bell and bow and moved to the door and met eyes with her eldest son. She could see that he had already taken the same account of their predicament, and she would not deny him his fight, but first she would see this King Hawker for herself.

The bolt opened and she stepped to the door. The guard was a beast of a Runner with bulky muscles on his bare chest. She looked in his eyes and tried not to notice the patchwork of tattoos that ran over his bare skin and one side of his face. She held her head up as she always did as the wife of a Monarch, but deep down she was afraid of the Runners.

They were part of her heritage, but centuries had divided her people into the uneducated brutes like the one who stood in front of her, and the counselors and Monarchs who controlled Cormicks. She preferred the Runners that were her usual guard, but none of those men had returned from the raid on Fontanasia.

She had heard about the night at the field of grass where the enemy outsmarted her husband. The enemy had lit fire to the Anthracites and killed many Runners just before his prisoner, Hawker, ran her husband through with his own sword. It was this prisoner, Hawker, who now called himself King of Cormicks.

The Runner looked over her and pointed at Mandetta.

"I have the bell here," she said, her voice unable to hide a quiver of fear.

"She comes, too," the Runner grunted.

Mandetta touched her mother's arm and the light touch made her wince. She would no longer be able to protect her daughter from the world outside their door.

They were escorted up to the parapet where the King waited. All eyes were beyond the wall where a third black figure was tearing from the ground. It stood slowly, two rock legs connected by a stump, and turned to follow the others. After all of these years, Mandetta hadn't overcome her innate fear of the Anthracite beasts, and she typically couldn't look away, but now she watched the new King instead. He was a tall, thin man with long, black hair, and even without words she could tell that he was pleased with himself.

The bald weasel of a counselor next to the King barked at Mandetta to call the Anthracites back. Mandetta stepped forward to grab the bell, but her mother pressed her elbow lightly into Mandetta's side to stop her.

"Don't move," her mother whispered under the rumbling sound that the Anthracites made even though they were almost out of sight.

Mandetta's mother stepped forward and bent her arm to hold the bell out in front of her chest. She pulled her other arm straight back and ran the metal bow along the rough edge of the bell. She was practiced at the instrument, and the metal started to vibrate right away. As she pulled the bow slowly back and forth, the bell vibrated louder and louder, sending a high pitch across Cormicks. It was a great sound to come from such a small bell, and Mandetta saw the new King watching closely. Her mother continued to move the bow, but the Anthracites did not hear the sound. The ground had stopped rumbling, and they were gone.

"Command them," the White Robe counselor said to Mandetta's mother. She put the bell and bow down at her sides and let the vibration stop.

"If they cannot hear the bell at this distance, they will not hear my voice."

"It has worked from this distance before," he barked.

"It works much better when they are not already in motion. They cannot hear the bell from this distance over the sound of their own steps." She was used to holding her head up, to standing beside her husband the Monarch and calling the Anthracites, but now she looked at the ground. She had noticed a mask of fury cross the new King's face and then disappear, and it sent terrified goose bumps up her spine.

"Can anyone else call them?" King Hawker asked the White Robe who pointed at Mandetta.

"Give it to me," the King said holding out his long arms to the kasic bell.

Mandetta was going to step forward, but one look from her mother stopped her in her tracks. "The Anthracites must have sensed fire. They will be back."

King Hawker's eyes rolled up and then flashed back to normal as though he was trying to cover up his disdain. Then the edges of his lips curled up in a sadistic smile and he sauntered toward Mandetta's mother, his long black hair and floor length black cape swaying with his steps. She felt terror in the pit of her stomach as her mother lifted the bell and the bow to try again. In a lightning quick move, Hawker grabbed her wrists tightly and she almost dropped the bell.

"Perhaps she should try," King Hawker said looking down at Mandetta.

"She knows how to ring the bell, but she has not perfected the call." It was a lie, but she was terrified that Hawker's attention would turn toward Mandetta. She could see that he was a calculating man, smart enough to outwit her husband and become ruler of a land that he'd been in for mere weeks.

He looked back at Mandetta for only a moment and then his eyes returned to her mother. She relaxed in his grip and tried to smile.

"Maybe you're not that good of a teacher," Hawker sneered and let go of her wrists. Before she could lower the bell and bow though, he ripped them from her hands and laughed.

"King Hawker, it takes months to even..." He slapped her face with the metal bow, and she stepped back, feeling the blood that ran from the slice he had made. Then he slapped her across the other cheek.

"There, now you have proper marks on your face like everyone else here in Cormicks." He laughed as tears welled in her eyes. He wiped the bloody bow clean on his own pants, and then to her horror, he lifted the bell and the bow as she had, and tried to play it. It took months to learn how to coax a good vibration from the bell. He would not be able to play it, and in that she knew there was no hope for her. She'd been around brutal men all her life, and she could feel his underlying brutality bubbling to the surface. She kept her eyes on the bell and the bow to hide her tears from Mandetta.

Hawker's long fingers pushed the bow out and then back along the rough edge of the bell, but nothing happened. He tried once more and then dropped them on the rock floor. The bell clanged to a stop as everyone watched and waited to see what the new King would do next. He did not hesitate. The King took one long step to Mandetta's mother and grabbed her arms. Her bloody hands pulled away from her face and warm blood dripped onto her shoulders. In a moment of strength that she didn't know he possessed, Hawker lifted Mandetta's mother off the ground and threw her from the parapet.

Kings were not supposed to sneak out of the castle in the dead of night to keep secrets from the people, but that's what King Avalon Hall was doing on this pitch-dark night with only three trusted soldiers alongside. One could argue that these were necessary secrets because the truth would cause a panic in Fontanasia, but King Avalon felt a shadow growing. In their own way, these secrets could be added to the mounting lies told in the past fifteen years and topple the two-century Hall reign.

These were small lies compared to the one that Avalon had been harboring since her father made the decision to tell the people his daughter was a son and heir to the throne. That had been his lie when Avalon was first born. It was a lie that she had inherited and grown into, and it was her lie now.

Her father had been murdered a year ago, and even that was a secret. She loved the people of Fontanasia, and yet Avalon had not spoken the truth to them, nor would she ever. Some secrets were too big to tell, and now more than ever, she needed to remain King Avalon Hall.

Kensington, the head of her King's Guard and her new brother-in-law, had approached King Avalon three nights ago. It was the night of his wedding to her sister, Princess Zaria, and yet he'd said that he needed to visit the homes of the soldiers who had not returned from the Window. It wasn't really a window, but that's what the King had called it. It was a small pond that one could see their reflection in, and it served as passage to another world. It was a way to the enemy, and the enemy's way to Fontanasia.

The King's Guard received wages each month, and the families of the soldiers who were away had not been paid. As the head of the King's Guard, it was Kensington's duty to make sure that his soldiers were taken care of, and in this instance, that meant their families, too.

Avalon had not thought of that detail, but she didn't beat herself up about it. She had other details to worry about. Still, she wanted to visit the homes of the soldiers to let the families know face to face how important their work was. She had tried to convince Kensington that they could do this without him, and that he needed to take time off to be with his new bride. Kensington had blushed and then smiled, insisting that he could sneak out for a few hours for a couple of nights and not be missed. When they had started this process two nights earlier, Avalon could see the pride that Kensington took in his men, and she was glad to have his confidence.

It was almost midnight in Fontanasia when Avalon rode on horseback down through the Fingers to the borough called the Reaches. She and Kensington followed Avalon's sword trainer, the trusted guard Gamon, with Taggerty close behind. The day's work was done and the shops were closed, and the Fingers were quiet but for the crackle of small fires lighting the street and a few men heading home late in the night. She was going late on purpose so that there would be few witnesses on the street to see where the King had gone.

Avalon looked back but couldn't see the castle this close to the wall. She knew it was there, but this late at night it was impossible to see her home that had been built into the mountainside. She had looked down on this city from the castle for fifteen years and finally knew what the streets looked like this late into the night.

Avalon tried to contain a smile while glancing back at the King's Guard who followed. Taggerty was there, ever vigilant. Taggerty had become the King's most trusted guard because without being asked, he had kept the King's secret. Taggerty knew that King Avalon Hall of Fontanasia was a girl, and Avalon knew that within the week, he would kiss her.

When Avalon turned around and looked back at Taggerty, he didn't look at her, but he hadn't looked at her in the last two nights. She could tell he was uncomfortable with her attention, and as much as she didn't want to understand it, she knew why he wouldn't look at her. Taggerty was protecting his King, but Avalon cared less and less what others might think. It was a danger that she was willing to ignore if it meant getting Taggerty's attention. She needed him to see her. She needed him to smile at her.

"Here," Gamon said, stopping his horse and dismounting before pulling a sack from his saddle. Avalon and Kensington dismounted, and Taggerty took their reins to tie the horses. Avalon straightened her jacket and cleared her throat as Kensington stepped up onto the wooden porch and knocked on the door. They were greeted with the immediate barking of a dog, and Taggerty looked up and down the street to make sure no one came out to check on the noise. There was a bustle inside and the dog stopped barking, and then Avalon could hear the click of the bolt lock being opened.

The door swung open quickly, and the lady inside looked around at the men on her porch. She immediately recognized the uniforms of the King's Guard, and after another moment of looking into the dark street, she recognized King Avalon. "Your Highness," she said as she knelt low, her worn nightdress billowing out around her legs.

"May we come in?" Kensington asked urgently.

"Of course," she said. She moved aside, and Avalon swept into the small house. There was a fire on the grate in the sparse but clean front room, and Avalon could see four children peaking in from another room. The oldest boy recognized her and his mouth hung open. "This is the

King," the woman of the house said. She closed the front door and bowed again. The oldest boy stepped in and bowed and the three smaller children followed his example. They stayed in that crouched position for ten seconds before Avalon realized they would not rise without her word.

"Rise," she said, and the oldest boy stood followed by his two brothers and one sister. The little ones left the room, but the boy stayed, and Avalon did not ask him to leave knowing that he was now the man of the house.

"Can I offer you anything?" the woman asked politely.

"No, thank you, Mother Newton," Avalon replied.

"Then please, sit here," she said, offering the hard sofa. Gamon checked the other rooms and then he stood by the door. Avalon sat on the sofa and offered the chair to the lady of the house. The woman was at least twice Avalon's age, and she flattened her hair with her palms before slowly taking a seat opposite the King. Avalon tried to sit comfortably on the old sofa so that she could make the lady of the house more comfortable in her own home, but the woman sat on the edge of the chair, and Avalon knew that she should finish up as quickly as she could.

"I came to ask you a favor," Avalon said slowly.

"Me?" Mother Newton said surprised, holding her hand up to her chest. "Anything, Your Highness."

Avalon nodded, but she kept a straight face. "It will not be easy, but you should consider it part of your duty as the wife of one of the King's Guard." Avalon looked at the boy so that he would know that this message was for all of them.

"It is my honor to serve the King," Mother Newton said sincerely. The dog scampered out from the back of the house and Taggerty sprang forward, grabbing him before he could sniff at the King. The oldest boy came forward and took the dog's collar, ushering him back to the other room and locking him away. "Sorry," the boy said in a choked whisper.

Avalon nodded, glad that tonight she hadn't brought her tiny jakkow lizard, Jackie. She had no doubt that the dog would have been frantic sensing another animal in the room. "I understand that it is a hardship without your husband here. Newton is a good man," Avalon said. Avalon had learned the guard's name from Gamon when they were leaving the castle. She did not know him personally, but if Taggerty had chosen him to stay at the Window to protect Fontanasia from Cormicks, Avalon was certain that he was one of the best.

"It's no hardship," she said, looking down and wringing her hands in her lap.

"Still, with four children, it can't be easy," Avalon said.

She looked at Taggerty and saw his salty green eyes reflecting the dancing firelight. Avalon was in love with Taggerty, and they had not even kissed. She could not imagine what this woman could be feeling after years of building a life with her husband. Avalon wished for a moment that she would get that same chance, but Taggerty looked away at that thought, and she wondered if he had read her mind.

Avalon looked up at the oldest boy who she placed around nine years old. "You are the man of the house while your father is away?" The boy stood tall and nodded his head, proud to have the King address him. "What is your name?" Avalon asked.

The boy looked at his mother for permission to answer the King. She smiled and nodded. "I am Newton like my father, but everyone calls me Newt."

"Well then, Newt, I'm asking you a favor. Help your mother with any chores she puts to you, without complaint. Your father is off doing very important work for me, and although it is a hardship for you, I still need him to do this important work. Do you understand?" Avalon asked the boy, indirectly talking to the mother.

Avalon was in the process of visiting the homes of any soldier who was still away, to make sure the families were all right, and to make sure they kept quiet. Noticing the long removed soldiers, she was sure that the people talked, but if the families didn't feed the flame of gossip, Avalon knew she would have more time to figure out a long term plan to keeping the city safe. There were enemies that the Newtons could not believe existed, and Avalon wasn't ready to tell that secret.

"I understand, King Avalon, and I help already. I will do even more if I can."

"Good," Avalon said. She looked at Newton's wife who was smiling at her son. "I have visited a couple of other families, the ones of the guard who are still out on assignment. I have a small package for you, and I apologize for the delay. I was not fully aware how the guards were paid, and I am sorry for that. Gamon will make sure you receive Newton's pay until he returns."

Avalon smiled and stood quickly, and Newton's wife hopped to her feet and bowed, her son bowing in turn, and the small children who were still half-hidden around the corner following suit.

"Thank you, my King," she said without looking up at Avalon.

"Good evening," Avalon said, and she turned and left the house with Taggerty. Kensington and Gamon remained inside to hand over a ham along with the small purse containing Newton's collected pay.

Taggerty was already at Avalon's steed and he held the reigns as Avalon approached. She could see his head moving in the dim moonlight as he scanned the street and the houses for anyone who might be watching. Avalon did the same, but there was no one awake at this hour. She put her hands on the saddle to mount, but Taggerty laid his hand on her shoulder.

"You shouldn't look at me," he whispered.

Avalon almost laughed. "Then you shouldn't stand in front of me and talk to me," she answered, but before she was through speaking the words, she knew what he meant. She had looked at him when talking to Mother Newton, and her face might have given away her feelings for Taggerty.

"I know," Avalon said as she looked straight into his eyes and wished this moment could last for hours, but Kensington stepped out of the house and cleared his throat, and Avalon slid her foot into the stirrup and pulled herself onto the horse. They had three more houses to visit this night, and as they turned down the street, Avalon knew she shouldn't chance to look at Taggerty, but the simple thought turned her head in his direction.

Although she should have been exhausted, Avalon woke refreshed. She had been out half the night visiting the families of the soldiers who were still gone, but each morning she woke with urgency, knowing that this could be the day that Taggerty would come to find her in the King's suite. One day this week, he would kiss her. When Avalon dreamed, the dream always came true. It was a rare genetic gift passed down through generations of Hall Kings, a gift that she had inherited. Three nights ago, Avalon had dreamt that Taggerty would kiss her.

The dream had calmed her in a way because she was certain that Taggerty had feelings for her too. Avalon closed her eyes for another minute to pull her dream of three nights ago back into her mind so she could savor the details. Lately, she could think of nothing else. She was in love with him, and she knew now that she had chosen him the day she first saw him smile. She had first noticed him at the Festival of Fontanasia on the tournament field wearing long sleeves under the hot sun. She had been angry with him that day and for a long time afterward, but she recognized it now as her first crush.

Avalon found herself constantly daydreaming about running away with Taggerty. They were both resourceful and they could live on their own, but she knew it could not become reality. She would be leaving behind everything she knew and a life with Taggerty was all she wanted anymore, but she couldn't abandon Fontanasia knowing the danger that Cormicks presented. She couldn't leave the people defenseless against Hawker, and so she knew her daydream could never come to be.

Avalon crossed to the basin and splashed cold water on her face and then turned to focus on her attire. She let out a huff as she pulled the bulging undershirt over her head. She wrestled into this costume every day, and it became more difficult as her body changed from that of a girl to a young lady. Her sister Zaria had shown off her figure when this had happened, but Avalon had to hide hers away. She was grateful for Myra George who had sewn several of these garments herself. They pulled tight across the chest, and added some stuffing to Avalon's tight stomach to even out the midriff.

The clothes were designed to make Avalon look like a bulky figure with the stout stature of her father, and Avalon could pass as a boy as long as she needed to, but it was not going to be easy. She didn't relish the day that Myra George was no longer there to help her conceal her secret. Avalon could wash the garments on her own if she had to, but she didn't know how to sew, and she was sure these would not last her entire life. Of course, if her Uncle Hawker had his way, she wouldn't have to worry about her clothes because her life would not last much longer.

There was a soft knock on the thick wood door to her chamber and her sister, Princess Zaria, pushed the door open. Avalon waited for the door to close and then sighed.

She had just put on her dress shirt, and she was annoyed that Zaria would open the door when she wasn't yet fully clothed.

"How are you?" Zaria asked softly.

Avalon looked at her sister and tried to read her thoughts by the expression on her face. "Why?" she asked.

"Nothing," Zaria said, walking further into the room and sitting on the foot of the bed. "You just look tired, that's all." Avalon would be restless until Taggerty kissed her, but she would not admit to it, so there was no reason to even have that conversation. Avalon hadn't told Zaria about her dream, and she realized her sister was referring to the late nights Avalon had spent outside the castle walls with Kensington. Avalon crossed the room and splashed water on her face again, trying to clear her mind.

"I thought we could walk down together to see father's statue," Zaria said. "There is still a lot of work to be done, but the bust is complete and to see his face again..." Zaria trailed off and Avalon knew what her sister meant. Avalon nodded, not willing to try to speak through the lump in her throat. "Kensington will meet us outside when you are ready to go. Are you ready?" Zaria asked.

"Yes, I am," Avalon said, trying to smile at her sister. Zaria wasn't asking if Avalon was dressed and ready to go downstairs. She was asking if her little sister was mentally prepared for what she was to see. Zaria had come to Avalon two weeks earlier and had told her that she should go down and see the likeness of their father. It would be moved to the Hall of Kings in a few months when it was complete, but neither of them wanted to wait for the finished product.

When Avalon was ready, Kensington and two of the King's Guard escorted them down to the craftsman's area in the basement of the castle. The artist had met them at the door, his smock and pants covered in the marble's white powder. Avalon had assumed that Zaria had already seen the statue, but although the artist was polite, she could see that he was irritated with their request.

"It is not tradition," the sculptor said, bowing his head but standing firm. He was a great artist so Avalon let it pass.

"I am the King and I will say what is tradition," Avalon commanded. "We will see the statue now."

"At least allow me to clean up the area. It is very dirty in here, and I am afraid it will not be easy to clean out of Princess Zaria's lovely dress." He was sincere, wiping his hands on the inside of his smock and then on his shirt.

Avalon nodded, and they didn't wait long to enter the workshop. The sculptor bowed his head as he skirted by the King's Guard into the hallway and turned to watch the King enter his workshop.

Avalon held her arm out for Zaria to enter, but Zaria shook her head. "We will wait here for a moment. You should see it first." Avalon shrugged but hesitated. She was in Cormicks when her father had died, and she had never really said goodbye. She had the overwhelming feeling that she was stepping into his tomb, and a chill ran through her bones.

The workshop was well maintained but dirty because of the nature of work. Tools were on the walls and tables, with several scattered in the area of the sculpture. It was tall, a few feet taller than her father was partly because the statue was on a pedestal, and partly because it was carved at a slightly larger scale than the man had been. Avalon knew the statues in the Hall of Kings. They had always seemed larger than life, and she could see now that they were carved intentionally that way. In this way, her father looked like he was as big as the great warrior Walthan had been.

Her step displaced the powder and several chunks of rock, and Avalon looked at the floor as she made her way around to the front of the sculpture. She took a deep breath and then turned to look at the stone replica. At the top of a huge block of white marble, Avalon gazed at her father's face. She thought she might cry at this moment, and she was certain that was why Zaria had sent her in on her own, but what Avalon saw was a stone tribute to her father's greatness, and instead of sadness, she felt pride. He was a legacy now, a king for the ages.

She gazed upon the statue half-expecting the figure of her father to break through the white stone and to walk into the room. The thought reminded Avalon of the black rock Anthracite beasts she had seen in Cormicks. She tucked the thought away for later. She had been thinking of the Anthracites every day and there was something about the Anthracites that was bothering her, but she couldn't figure out just what that was.

Avalon heard a knock and then Zaria and Kensington came into the workshop. "It's awful in here," Zaria said as she tried picking up her dress so that it wouldn't come close to brushing the white marble chalk from the floor into the fabric.

"I told you that this is no place for a woman," Kensington said playfully. They shared a smile and Avalon could see the love on their faces, and she was happy for her sister. It was funny, because a year earlier Avalon would have rolled her eyes at the intimate interaction, but now she understood.

"It's wonderful," Avalon said still looking at the statue. Zaria came around the front and Kensington stood beside her.

"It does look like father, and it isn't even polished yet," Zaria said, forgetting about the dirty floor and removing her hands from her dress. She placed one hand over her mouth and linked the other through Kensington's arm.

"Thank you for bringing me here," Avalon told her sister. "I wasn't sure how I would react, but I am amazed." Avalon could see that Zaria was crying and she waited a moment before continuing. "We'd better let Myra see it before the unveiling because she is going to blubber like a baby." They all laughed which broke the spell that the statue had cast. "I owe you another thanks," Avalon said, facing her sister.

"You are my brother, and no thanks is necessary," Zaria said.

"Still, you invited the counselors to your wedding ceremony instead of just the reception, and they all felt honored. They have each sent me a note of thanks, and I can use all of the good will I can get from the Council. You seem to understand more than I have given you credit for."

Zaria smiled. "I pay much more attention since father died and Kensington came into my life." Zaria squeezed Kensington's hand. "With your blessing, Kensington and I are going to dine in each of the counselor's homes over the next two months so we can get to know them and their families better."

"Is that true?" Avalon asked, surprised. Their father had invited the counselors to dine in the castle over the years, but he had never gone to their homes.

Kensington's face turned red. "If it pleases the King," he stuttered, assuming Avalon wasn't happy with the idea.

"It's fine with me," Avalon said. Kensington cleared his throat and looked at the floor, and the sisters shared a smile. Avalon longed to talk to Zaria about her dream and Taggerty. Zaria would have loved to gossip about possibilities, but Avalon didn't want to bother her so soon after her wedding. "See you tonight?" Avalon asked Kensington, referring to their overnight visits to the soldier's families.

"Not tonight," Kensington said. "Taggerty has something you should see."

"You're not coming?" Avalon asked.

"We just got married," Zaria protested, although mildly, knowing her husband would do whatever the King asked, and also knowing she would allow it.

Avalon sighed. "As you wish, Zaria." She noticed her sister's sly smile and turned her head to the ground to hide her blush, wondering what Taggerty had in store.

"We will meet you outside, Kensington," Zaria said, and Kensington squeezed her hand and nodded, turning to exit the small workshop. Avalon didn't know why Zaria had dismissed her husband, and she assumed it had to do with the statue of their father. Avalon looked up at the statue again, glad to have seen it. They both gazed upon the stone features for a moment, and Zaria took Avalon's arm.

"I like marriage, Avalon. I am happy," Zaria said sincerely.

"I'm glad," Avalon answered, unsure where her sister was headed.

"You are young still, but I think you would like marriage too."

"We'll see," Avalon said non-committedly. Again Avalon thought of telling Zaria about her dream, but she didn't want to ruin the thrill of what she knew was to happen. Zaria would just turn it into an impossible future, and that would bring a sadness Avalon already felt tugging at the edges of her consciousness.

Zaria let go of Avalon's arm and looked at her sister. "Avalon," she said.

Avalon's face tightened. She was not going to have this conversation. "Zaria, don't," Avalon pleaded. Fontanasia needed a strong leader, and Avalon had been born a Prince and trained to become King all her life. It was best if she remained a boy. It was all she knew, and Zaria didn't seem to understand that Avalon's commitment to her city outweighed any deep need to become the girl that she was underneath the king's clothes.

Avalon rubbed her eyes and exhaled deeply, holding tight to her vision of Taggerty in her dream and the love she knew she saw in his eyes. She didn't want to question the future because she knew the future. She knew how she felt this week. She knew what would happen this week, and that was all she could hold onto.

"I have come to realize that what is best for me and what is best for Fontanasia isn't necessarily the same thing." Avalon placed her hand on the base of the statue and turned to leave.

Chapter 2
Setting Sail

Avalon was looking over the map of Cormicks when there was a knock at her study door. The door opened and Taggerty stepped in and bowed his head without looking at the floor. "I hope you don't mind. I saw you were here," he said. Taggerty knew where the guards were posted, and there were always at least two additional King's Guard stationed wherever Avalon went, so he could always deduce where to find her.

"I wanted to see the map," he said, stepping to the high table next to where Avalon stood.

"You can see it any time you want," Avalon replied, offering Taggerty the position at the center of the table.

She had shown Taggerty and Kensington the hole in the wall hidden behind a picture of a field of tall, blue grass. Avalon had been looking at the picture her whole life, only finding out its secret a year earlier. Her father had shown her the hole in the wall and the map hidden within as his father had shown him. The intention was that King Avalon would show her son the map someday. It was too soon for her to have a family, and questionable whether that would ever happen.

"I need to go back to the Window," Taggerty said as he stared at the drawing.

"You will do no such thing," Avalon said loudly. She was angry for a moment, and she wanted Taggerty to know that she was serious, but he didn't look at her. "The Guides are handling the Window, Taggerty. There is no reason for you to go there."

This time Avalon saw his jaw move as he clenched his teeth and tried to hide his sigh. He looked up at her and his expression softened from impatience to understanding. "Avalon, I need to go. There is nothing that I can do here," he said softly with frustration in his voice.

Avalon wasn't sure if he was talking about the enemy or if he meant their situation. He would kiss her, that was a fact. There was no reason for her to question their future. She shook off the feeling of dread that was trying to work its way to the surface.

"Kensington tells me that there's something you want to show me tonight," Avalon said, walking to the opposite side of the table.

"Yes," he replied, looking back at the map and offering nothing more.

Avalon felt relaxed enough not to ask him where he was taking her. She tried not to feel the pressure of Zaria's words and remained untroubled in the knowledge that she and Taggerty would have some kind of future together.

"We need to control the Anthracites," Avalon said tapping her knuckle on the map. Every day she remembered the epic terror that they had smashed into her memory.

"I think the Guides might be able to shed some light on that," Taggerty admitted. Avalon looked to him for further explanation, but he shrugged, meeting her eyes and not looking away.

They were both leaning in on opposite sides of the map looking into eyes that were filled with question and possibility. Taggerty smiled, the dimple in his strong squared chin becoming more prominent. For the first time, Avalon stared back and allowed herself to take in his features. His earthy, green eyes were striking under his black, curly hair, and she saw a faint scar on his right cheek that she hadn't noticed before.

Taggerty never lost his smile, but it softened as he gazed at Avalon. She suddenly felt hot, and her rising pulse made her start to sweat. She tugged at her sleeves but they were tapered and tight, and they only rose a couple of inches above her wrists.

"Your skin is so pale," Taggerty said.

Avalon looked down at her exposed skin. "My arms haven't seen sunlight since I was ten years old," she said barely above a whisper. She knew this wasn't the moment from her dream. It was daylight and they were in the wrong room in the castle, but Avalon felt her body move forward, placing her face closer to his over the map table. Taggerty's face grew serious and he inhaled deeply also leaning in closer. Avalon gulped back the expectation that had formed a lump in her throat.

Just then there were two sharp taps at the door and it opened. Taggerty pushed back from the table and cleared his throat, a little more obvious than Avalon who had simply looked down at the map that she hovered over and pointed to something. She didn't pay attention to where her finger landed, only noticing her white forearms and pulling the sleeves back over her wrists.

"Am I interrupting?" the aged voice of Counselor Julius Creighton asked as his hunched body shuffled into the room, his magenta robes barely swaying with his small steps. "I thought this was our meeting time, but I can come back." He kept shuffling forward and closed the door behind himself indicating that his words were only out of politeness. Of course, he would leave if the King asked him, but he knew that Avalon would not.

"Join us," Avalon said, and Creighton shuffled to the table to look over the map. He'd seen it before, and Avalon was certain he had memorized its contents. Still, he looked it over thoughtfully before turning his gaze to Taggerty and then to Avalon.

"You were discussing the Anthracites," he said to Avalon. She had recovered from her moment with Taggerty and was trying to collect her thoughts.

"Why would you say that?" Avalon asked.

"Because you are pointing to them on the map," his honey-deep voice answered with a gentle smile. Avalon looked down and noticed her finger had landed on the five peaked lines that noted hills on the map. She knew too well that those were not simply small mountain ranges. They were the Anthracites, black charcoal rock beasts that could rip from the ground and trample anything in the way.

"We were," Avalon admitted and hoped he couldn't tell that she was lying.

Creighton was something of an enigma. He was a hunched old man wearing robes on the outside, but he was actually just thirty-two years old. He had been a prodigy librarian that her father had hired, and he pretended to be old so that people would take him at his word without second-guessing his ideas. Avalon had found him extremely smart and also cunning. He seemed to be two steps ahead of everyone else at all times, and Avalon pushed back from the table and hoped he hadn't discerned what he'd walked in on.

"I was just telling King Avalon that the Guides might be able to help with the Anthracites," Taggerty said. He was standing halfway between the table and the door as though deciding if he should stay or leave.

"Is that true?" Creighton asked. "What would make you think that, young Taggerty?"

"I just think they might," Taggerty stuttered. Taggerty had been born a Guide but raised in the city to become one of the King's Guard. At birth, the Guides had prophesied him to be "the King's future", and he had proved that when he had saved Avalon's life. Taggerty secretly met with the Guides and knew many of their secrets and traditions. Creighton knew none of this, and neither Taggerty nor Avalon was willing to share the secret.

Creighton nodded his head slowly. "We should ask them then," he said, accepting Taggerty at his word. "If Taggerty is right, perhaps the book that I gave you can help, too. You still have it, of course." His statement was a question about the ancient Anthracite book Avalon still had in her chambers. "You are certain that you aren't missing something in those pages?"

"I will look again," Avalon told the counselor, trying to ignore his question. She could never tell if he was asking a question from curiosity, or if he already knew the answer and he was just trying to catch her up. His shoulders seemed to hunch lower as the minutes passed. "Let us sit," she told Creighton. She walked to her desk and Creighton followed, but Taggerty moved to the door.

"I will take my leave," he said with a bow, and Avalon dismissed him with regret.

"Do you really think the Guides know something about the Anthracites?" Creighton asked Avalon after the door clicked shut.

"Sometimes they seem to know more than anyone," Avalon said, vowing to review the book and then to talk to the Guides. "I just hope Hawker doesn't know anything about the Anthracites. If he were to gain control of them..." Avalon's words trailed off as she remembered her uncle's sick penchant for playing with fire, and the way the Anthracite dust had crackled alive in the air around her. Hawker's thirst for fire and the Anthracite rock would be a horrible combination.

"My King, assuming Prince Hawker has taken control of Cormicks as Taggerty saw when he crossed over, we have to assume that whoever controlled the Anthracites for the Monarch will now do so for the Prince."

Hawker Hall's first instinct was to wait for the next full moon, and as soon as the elbagrass turned blue, he wanted to rush his soldiers back through the Window to slaughter the men on the other side. He hesitated though because he wasn't certain that the Runners would accept him as their King. He had killed their Monarch right in front of the white-robed counselors, and although he knew that he had the loyalty of the White Robes, he could not be certain that the soldiers would kneel to their new King so easily.

He spent months thinking about his nephew, Avalon. He wouldn't allow himself to admit it, but he'd spent his entire adult life obsessed with Avalon in a way. Hawker despised hating his nephew. It somehow brought them closer, and the only person Hawker had any affection for was his late mother. That too had been a relationship tinged with hate.

Hawker had taken the Monarch's travel carriage and reveled in his new autocracy until he had been taken back to the castle at Cormicks. He was the King, and he expected to be treated as such, but these mongrels had no idea how to pamper a King. The Monarch had been a warrior and a slob, and even he hadn't known how to command the proper comforts of monarchy.

On the second day, surrounded by the half-dressed and tattooed beasts that made up the King's Guard, Hawker called the White Robes in and made his demands. If he was going to bring Cormicks back to its greatness, he needed to be treated like a King. He demanded that the White Robes give to him their best servants.

"Not the dogs that protect you, the servants who comfort you!" he had yelled when two of the soldiers had stepped forward at their owner's command. Each of the small, bald men did send servants to Hawker, and he could tell by the shapes tattooed on their wrists who had donated them. The Triangle White Robe who had backed him at the clearing sent a tall, beautiful girl who knelt and pledged her servitude. Hawker saw the triangle on her forearm, and he was glad to see that he had a confidant in the Triangle White Robe.

The rest of the servants sent were good at their jobs, and his suite had quickly been cleaned up and decorated. He was impressed at the size of the rooms and reveled at the grandeur he would soon bring to them. He was already making changes to the great hall and the throne that he planned to sit on. He would not sit on an old throne, he would have one made for himself, one worthy of his stature and of the legend that he was carving out of nothing.

There was one more item on Hawker's agenda, and he relished it. The White Robes wanted to know what to do with the Monarch's family. Hawker didn't want a large crowd around when he decided on their fate, but he did invite Triangle and one other who had smiled when Hawker killed the Monarch. Hawker called him Square-Dot because he had four dots on his forehead.

Hawker had the Monarch's family brought before him in the hall. He'd already killed their mother in a fit of rage, but she'd been incompetent at calling the Anthracites back, so there was really no reason to keep her around.

When they first entered, the Monarch's three sons had refused to kneel, and Hawker had cut their heads off then and there. Hawker made the daughter put her head to the ground while he paced in front of her. She was crying loudly as blood dripped from his sword. Guards had been called quickly for the bodies to be taken outside and burned while Hawker was considering burning the girl alive with her dead brothers. He relished this thought.

He had only killed one person by fire before, but that was an accident. When he was young, a stable hand had been caught in the fire that Hawker had started. Hawker had only burned animals since then, and he savored the idea of making the girl a lesson to the White Robes. He couldn't though. He'd been told that she was the last person alive who could communicate with the Anthracites, so he would spare her, for now.

He heard weeping again.

"Stop your blubbering!" he yelled. His voice echoed off the stones, and the small voice sputtered into silence.

"They are ready to start the fire," Triangle said. "I would like you to see something first, King Hawker," he added with deference.

"Yes?" Hawker asked, intrigued.

"Can you come to the low battlement outside? I think you will find it interesting." The short man's shaved forehead crept up in interest, and Hawker liked the gleam in his eye.

Triangle gave some orders to one of his guards, and then they went outside. Hawker watched as one of the boys' bloody bodies was pulled off the cart and it rolled down the pile of kindling onto the dirt. The men ran back to the safety of the cart and turned to watch.

Hawker squinted, wondering why they would be staring at the dead boy. He leaned forward, wondering what they were seeing that he wasn't, and then he jumped back when he saw the dead boy's arm move. He laughed out loud at his reaction and then leaned his head over the brick battlement and watched carefully. Hawker thought that the arm was red with blood, but then he saw a wave of bright red move over it. The dirt around the body started to fall in on itself, and then a cloud of dust was kicked up in the air, and he couldn't see the body anymore. When the wave of red had gone, all that was left was a black stain in the ground. He stared at the stain for a full minute, his heart racing at what he had just seen.

"I have heard of this, but I cannot place it." Hawker's mind raced through the volumes of books he had read about this place, and his eyes rolled back and forth in his head trying to name the phenomenon he had just witnessed.

"It is the everred spiders, my lord. They smell the blood," Triangle said. "That is why we had the hall cleaned so quickly. They can't move through stone, but we don't like to take the chance."

"It's wonderful," Hawker answered. His excitement built up, and he laughed uncontrollably, the two White Robes watching in amusement. When he was done laughing, he turned and looked down at two bald counselors.

"Understand me, I want to attack Fontanasia as soon as we have the army ready, but I find that there are some tools I need to learn about before I hatch my plan. We need to rebuild the forces that were lost by my predecessor. We will take some time together to prepare."

Both men nodded and then bowed their heads, and lightning ran through Hawker's veins. They were deferring to Hawker as their King, and he loved it. The people in the castle at Fontanasia had deferred to him because he was a prince, but mostly because he was King Birch's brother and they wanted to manipulate him to bend the King's ear to their will.

Hawker was his own man here. He was the ruler and no one would tell him what to do ever again.

These two men would be good servants to him, and he would have asked what their names were, but he didn't care. He would not waste his time with trivial things.

"Let's have a fire, and then you can tell me how I can control the Anthracites."

Taggerty arrived just after dinner. They had both been up several nights visiting with the families of the soldiers at the Window, and Avalon was tired, but seeing Taggerty recharged her. As they left the castle, she wondered if this would be the night that he would finally kiss her. She was pleasantly surprised to see a carriage waiting, and her heart turned to butterflies thinking about being in the close space alone with Taggerty. She was disappointed though, because after she climbed in, he closed the door and took to horseback with the other King's Guard.

Avalon was forced to wonder what the evening would bring as they made their way slowly down the Fingers. Through the small carriage window, she could only see the shops that ran along the long brick wall of the Fingers. There were five such walls running down the side of the mountain and separating the boroughs. They had been nicknamed the Fingers because from the valley below, it looked as though a hand might scoop Fontanasia out of the mountainside.

They turned left and went below one of the openings in the wall before descending to the hillside near the Helon Sea.

"Welcome to the Reaches," Taggerty said quietly as Avalon climbed down from the carriage.

"I know the Reaches," Avalon retorted. It was the borough that had spilled outside the walls of the city and settled closest to the Helon Sea. She had been here as a child and she could remember splashing around with Connor in the water, but she had put a stop to that when she found out that she was a girl. Avalon hadn't missed playing in the water. She had taken to her sword at that age, focusing on self-defense and archery and tasks more befitting the Prince of Fontanasia.

"Tab has been very accommodating," Taggerty said with a sly smile, referring to Counselor Jennings by his first name. Avalon was certain that Taggerty was toying with her feelings because he had certainly noticed the jealousy Avalon had shown toward Jennings' daughter at her last birthday celebration.

"I have come to like Counselor Jennings. He has been most forthcoming and trustworthy," Avalon said. Avalon had in fact been jealous, but she was confident of Taggerty's feelings now, and she shrugged off his demeanor and didn't take the bait.

Taggerty nodded. "You will continue to be impressed by him once you see what I wanted to show you."

Avalon rounded the carriage to where Counselor Jennings stood. His piercing eyes caught hers in the setting sunlight. Jennings bowed and then stood with a smile on his face.

"Thank you for taking the time, King Avalon. I hope you will be impressed."

Avalon expected to be let into Counselor Jennings' large home, but they had stopped at the back of the house near a path that led to a small ramp and a pier.

"Thank you for allowing us to intrude," Taggerty said as he moved around Counselor Jennings.

Avalon smiled up at Taggerty but a movement behind him caught her eye, and her jaw fell open. On the water of the Helon Sea, there were several flat rafts like the ones Avalon had seen before tied to the small dock, and next to them was an immense wood structure that was the size of a small house. It rocked a little in the swells, and Avalon realized that somehow it was actually floating.

She could see two of the King's Guard standing in front of the structure. She had never laid her eyes on the craft that was tied to the end of the dock and yet she knew by the added guard that was where Taggerty was taking her.

"Have you been on a boat before?" Counselor Jennings asked, knowing the answer.

"Not yet," Avalon replied just above a whisper. Taggerty held his hand out to the path and Avalon left Jennings behind and made her way down to the water. The boards of the pier creaked beneath their feet, and Avalon could hear the boat rubbing against the end of the dock. Avalon looked back at Taggerty with an eager smile.

"You need no permission to go aboard, King Avalon. They are ready when you are." Taggerty stood confidently, and Avalon could tell that he was proud of his decision to bring her here.

Avalon noticed six flat staffs protruding out of the side of the structure as she climbed aboard. The sensation of her body swaying on top of the water was amazing but also scary. She had thrown sticks in the sea as a child and watched them float out into the waves, but this craft was much heavier than a few sticks, and she wondered if it would sink.

Avalon heard someone yelling commands, and soon the rope was thrown off and the boat floated free of the dock. She followed Taggerty up a ladder to a small platform and they held onto the railing as the boat slowly floated away from dry land. It was exhilarating.

"I have been talking to some of the boaters in the Reaches, and Counselor Jennings thinks that they can construct more crafts this size." Taggerty took a step closer to Avalon and their arms almost touched. "My thinking is that we could evacuate some of the people via the lake. They could use the oars to pull the craft to safety somewhere else along the bank." He pointed down and Avalon noticed the flat staffs undulating in and out of the water.

"They row us away until the proper wind takes us. It's quite ingenious."

Not missing his meaning, Avalon clenched her teeth. Taggerty meant that if the Runners invaded Fontanasia, this might be another way out. "Is this your idea or Counselor Jennings?"

"Mine, of course," Taggerty said. "Jennings thinks that you are interested in the Reaches harvesting more food source from the waters." Avalon made a face and Taggerty chuckled.

"I tasted the gift he brought to Council and I'd rather eat bugs," Avalon said quietly. She didn't want any of the others on board to hear her distaste of their so-called delicacy.

The sun was moving lower in the sky beyond the sea, and Avalon was in awe of the multitude of colors. She had watched the sunset countless times from her window, but being right on the water allowed her to see shards of sunlight reflecting off the wave crests, and it was beautiful. The sensation allowed her mind to relax, and she didn't want to talk strategy with Taggerty right now. She wanted to soak in this unusual moment. Taggerty was right to plan, but part of Avalon hoped that he had brought her here as an excuse to spend time together.

Taggerty looked at Avalon and put his hand on the railing just inches from hers. He looked at the sunset that Avalon had been enjoying. "It's remarkable, really."

"Yes," Avalon agreed, keeping her eyes on the water.

"Your eyes are wonderful in this light," he said above a whisper, and Avalon blushed. She felt the breeze on her face and closed her eyes relishing everything about this moment. They were quiet for a long time, and then Avalon heard someone behind them and she willed herself not to jump away from Taggerty like they had been doing something wrong. Taggerty was not as calm when he turned around.

"What is it?" he growled.

"We are turning back so we can make shore before dark," a man said.

"Thank you," Taggerty pushed through his lips. He was trying to calm his temper, and Avalon could hear him sigh as he turned back toward the sunset. Someone below began calling orders, and the boat started to turn. Avalon looked back toward land and was surprised how far they had floated from shore.

She wanted the moment with Taggerty back, but the sounds of men working the oars below completely removed her from their silent reverie. Avalon turned her back to the railing so she could keep her eyes on the setting sun as they headed back to shore, and Taggerty moved to the railing opposite her.

He was looking at the floor, and Avalon couldn't read his mood. He'd sounded angry, and she wondered if he was as upset as she was at the loss of their perfect moment. They were quiet for a long time listening to the rhythmic sound of the oars cutting through the water. Avalon tapped her foot for a moment, but Taggerty still wouldn't look at her.

"I'm reading a book you might want to look at," she told him.

"What book is that?" Taggerty asked.

"Counselor Creighton gave me a book from the archives about the Anthracites," Avalon said, and he finally looked up at her.

"He did?"

"He said that I needed to study the book, and I've been looking through it. Can I ask you a question?"

"Sure," Taggerty replied, taking a step closer so their voices wouldn't carry.

"Do the Guides know how to control the Anthracites?" she asked.

Taggerty shook his head. "I don't know if anyone could correctly make those sounds. What makes you ask?"

"Well, the Guides are just so mysterious, and they seem to know more than anyone else. I figured if anyone knew, it would be them."

"Hmm," Taggerty grunted.

"What?" Avalon asked.

"Maybe they feel that Fontanasia is a better place to live and they don't dwell on history. I have heard Chylyn say that the old world is in the past, and we should leave it there."

Avalon chuckled. "Are we talking about the same people? I've never met anyone more steeped in tradition." Then Avalon stepped closer to Taggerty because she didn't want anyone to overhear what she was about to say. "I know you don't believe that we should leave it in the past. You said yourself that we need to retake Cormicks for our own safety. Hawker will never give up."

"So let him rule. We will defend Fontanasia forever. He will never get through, and we will burn the elbagrass again if we need to."

Avalon felt the blood rising to her face. "Yesterday you were so sure that we should attack, and now you are sure we should not?"

Taggerty stepped closer to Avalon. "I am older than you, and wiser." He smiled, his green eyes carving a hole in Avalon's heart.

"Try again."

He looked over his shoulder at the myriad of colors that took the sky as the sun set. "I have seen many things in the past year, and not all bad." He smiled at her. "I have discovered some of the finer things, and I have learned that in time, anything can happen." Taggerty held Avalon's gaze until she cleared her throat and looked away. She knew that he would kiss her within days, and she was certain now that he was talking about them being together.

"The finer things in life?"

She saw Taggerty smile his arrogant smile, looking into the graying sky where the sun had disappeared. "Yes, like boating."

It was late and she should have been asleep, but Avalon was in the King's suite looking out over the city. It was dark, and she had only one candle burning in the large room so that there was little reflection in the window and she could see everything outside. She looked down over the boroughs of sleeping Fontanasians and saw some torches moving in the streets.

This was the same quiet city she had been watching over for all of her fifteen years, but tonight was different because she was different. This was the first time that Avalon wished she wasn't King.

Avalon shook her head and apologized to her father in her mind. He had claimed she was a boy when she was born so that he would have an heir to the throne, and when she was old enough to understand, Avalon had willingly participated in the deception. It was everything she had wanted, but her resolve was faltering. The way Taggerty had looked at her on the boat had kept her awake.

He had ridden in her carriage back to the castle and they had not spoken a word. He walked up to the King's suite one step behind her, and she was certain at that moment that he would kiss her on this night, but he hadn't. He'd entered the suite and lingered for a moment, indecision in his typically assured mannerisms. She tried to strike up a conversation, but he said he was tired and he turned and left.

Avalon had been pacing since then, occasionally trading her walk around the room for staring out the window.

"Not now, Jackie," she complained to her pet. The tiny, red jakkow lizard scrambled over the furniture as Avalon sat and then stood and paced. He raced from her coat pocket to her shoulder, but Avalon was in no mood to play.

Avalon relived each moment of her evening with Taggerty. She remembered his frustration, but any time her mind tried to take her down a dark path, she remembered her dream of their kiss. She brought herself back from the point of desperation each time and realized just how much of her hope rested on that one dream. It was a memory for her, a memory of a moment that hadn't taken place in time yet.

Avalon heard a small click behind her and the door to the suite opened and closed. She saw a gray figure in the black of the room and wished she'd lit more candles.

"It's just Taggerty," he whispered. "I sent Thomas for a break. It's very late, King Avalon. I wasn't sure you'd be awake."

"I guess neither of us could sleep," she said. It had been four days since her dream that he would kiss her. She recognized the jacket he now wore and knew that this was the moment and she unconsciously moved her hand to her lips. Avalon wished that she hadn't seen the future because she felt more foolish in anticipation of what Taggerty would do next. She tried to act natural, but she had no idea what that might mean in this situation.

Taggerty walked to the window and stood next to Avalon. He looked out over Fontanasia. "It looks so different now, the city. I mean, it hasn't changed at all, not really, but with the men starting their drills to protect the city, it does look different."

"It's the same for me," Avalon replied. She was giddy only half-listening to his words, and she chuckled knowing that everything would change for her in this moment. "I used to see my father standing here looking out over the Fingers and I thought he was just getting old and reflective about life. I wonder if he was thinking about the Runners."

"Probably," Taggerty added, and Avalon was glad that he didn't remind her that it was she who woke the enemy. It was because she wanted to go see Cormicks that they were in this position. If she had not gone, her father would probably still be alive and her Uncle Hawker would still be pretending that he was a loving brother to the king.

Avalon shook her head. She couldn't live in the past any more. Questions of what could have been had drowned her spirit for months. If she thought too long about what was to happen in the future or what could have been done in the past, she would curl up into a ball and be useless. She had to accept where she was now and do whatever she could to keep Fontanasia safe, and she needed to savor the present moment with Taggerty.

"I'm leaving at first light with the soldiers," Taggerty said.

Avalon had not expected this and she turned to face him. "But you've been back less than a week," she said. "You can't leave again already. We have plans to make." Avalon knew that she sounded desperate, and she hated the weakness that she felt, so she backtracked. "We need to discuss the safety of the city."

"I have spoken to Kensington. He and Gamon are making plans and you can speak with them and the Council, if you choose. The Guides would also like to be included in any preparations you deem necessary."

"Have the Guides bring the soldiers to the Window. You can stay here." Avalon's voice was pleading, but Taggerty simply shook his head, and Avalon could feel her hands start to shake so she balled them into fists. "It's too dangerous there," she told him.

"It's too dangerous here," Taggerty countered, turning toward Avalon and taking her elbows in his hands. "I'm glad that I know your secret because of the way that I feel about you, but tonight on the boat I wanted to hold your hand. I wanted to put my arms around you, and I allowed myself to get too close. Sooner or later someone will start noticing the way we look at each other, if they haven't already, Avalon."

"No one will notice," she countered, but he shook his head.

"I have known that you are a girl for a year," Taggerty said.

"Zaria told you," Avalon was certain, although Zaria had denied it.

"Not on purpose," Taggerty admitted. "It was a slip of the tongue the first time we returned from Cormicks. She referred to you as "she" when we found her locked in her room with Myra George, and I almost missed it." He shook his head. "Sometimes I wish I did because then things would be different and I wouldn't have to feel this way." He let go of Avalon and turned again to look out the window, holding his hands behind his back.

"Don't say that," Avalon whispered, but she understood the sentiment. She had spent months wishing she didn't feel this way for Taggerty so that things could go back to being black and white. Still, she loved the intimacy of this gray area that they were finally sharing.

"I can't undo what has been done, Avalon. I can't un-know what I know. And I can't make myself not feel this way about you. But if I'm going to truly be the King's future, that means the King must have a future, and I can do that. I can do whatever that means, even if it means leaving." Taggerty gripped Avalon's arm and pulled her toward him and she saw the glint of tears in his eyes. For all of her waiting, she was startled when he pulled her in and kissed her lips. It was her first kiss, and she was very conscious of herself. She held her hands away from him unsure of what to do next.

Taggerty pulled back and looked into Avalon's eyes, and she saw regret there before he pulled her in and kissed her again. Their lips met softly at first and then they both pulled in closer. Avalon's arms instinctively moved around Taggerty's neck, and they remained locked in an embrace. Finally, Taggerty pulled away and looked at Avalon in the dim candlelight. Avalon was smiling, and she found it wonderful that she didn't feel embarrassed at all. The only thing that brought her back to the moment was the look of concern on Taggerty's face.

"How do you feel?" Avalon asked, longing to hear that he thought about her every waking moment as she thought of him and wanting to know that he was anxious to see her around every turn.

"I," Taggerty started, but he shook his head as though he wouldn't allow himself to believe his heart. "Because of my feelings for you, I must leave. My duty is to protect you, and I will not jeopardize anyone's confidence in you. I will go to the Window and ensure that the Runners never get here."

Avalon took Taggerty's arm, but he had turned away already. She saw his faint reflection in the window, and she knew that she had to get him to change his mind before he left this room because if he left, it might sever the truth of this moment forever. "But you are the future of the King," she begged. "You can't leave me."

"Don't you see?" he asked. "You will have no future as King if I stay. The guards are loyal to you, but in time our secret would get out. What good would that do for anyone? You have seen Cormicks, and you must protect Fontanasia. I will not be the downfall of the Hall reign or responsible for the destruction of Fontanasia."

"Just stay here so I know you are safe. We don't have to see each other. We can make sure that we don't spend any time alone." Avalon was pulling at Taggerty's sleeve but he still wouldn't look at her.

"Avalon," he said, and she liked the way his face softened when he said her name, "how long will we be able to keep away from each other? Others will notice just how I feel when I look at you, and if we spend any more time together, neither of us will be able to hide our feelings."

"I can do it," she said. "I have liked you for a whole year without so much as a word, Taggerty. I can keep this secret."

"You are already keeping too many secrets," he answered, his voice already sounding far away. Avalon squeezed his arm to let him know that she wouldn't accept letting him go. She had to keep him in this room forever. She had thought of him for an entire year, and she had finally gotten her wish. This was supposed to be their beginning, but now he was leaving.

She watched his eyes opening and closing in slow blinks, and she could tell he was trying to control himself. Taggerty looked up and pointed to the brightest star in the sky. It was easy to spot on any clear night. "Do you know what that is?"

Avalon smirked. "Of course. I was named for that star." Avalon's childhood was filled with stories of how she had been named for the brightest star in the sky.

"I will be looking at that star while I'm gone."

She squeezed his arm with both of her hands to get his attention, but Taggerty cleared his throat. He reached up with one hand and pulled hers away, turning to leave. She was glad that he couldn't see the tears that were streaming down her face, but they were apparent in her voice. "I command you to stay," she said as he started to walk away.

Taggerty stopped, but he didn't turn back to look at her. He looked down at his feet as though he wasn't certain what they might do in that moment. "Please don't do that," he said just above a whisper.

"But I do," Avalon said as she stepped toward him. "I command you to stay in Fontanasia at least. I need to know you are safe."

Taggerty took a deep breath. "We have seen the same things, Avalon. If they never come, we are both safe. And if they do come, neither one of us is safe no matter where we are." Taggerty looked over his shoulder at Avalon who took another step closer and held out her hand. She smiled through her tears but Taggerty shook his head. "I will go to the Window, Avalon. It has to be this way." He stepped toward the door, and Avalon knew he was lost.

"Will you take Jackie with you?" she asked in a wavering voice, hoping that if she talked business he would remain in her presence a little longer.

Taggerty didn't look back. His voice was strained, and she thought he might be crying, but his figure was grayed out by the shadows near the door in the dim candlelight and she couldn't be sure. "Not this time," he said. "We will not cross over to Cormicks until my King commands."

Taggerty cleared his throat and left the room leaving Avalon alone in the dark. She would think about tonight and the kiss that they had shared every day for the next six months, and she knew that the tender intimacy she felt for Taggerty would live with her for the rest of her life.

Chapter 3
Wise Council

When she woke from crying herself to sleep, Avalon spent many hours trying to figure out how she could live her life together with Taggerty. She played her options out in her mind but there were only two. They could run away, or they could tell the truth and she could live life as the girl she was. She knew that it was impossible because Taggerty would allow her to do neither.

In her despair, Avalon became angrier than she could ever remember. She screamed and threw the porcelain basin of water across the room and let it shatter. Thomas had opened the door seconds later, and when he saw that Avalon was fine, he closed the door behind him without a word.

Avalon hated what she had done. It was irrational to take emotions out on objects. She'd seen men do that before, and it never made sense to her. She was embarrassed by her rage and crouched over the pieces of the basin slowly moving them into a contained pile. She crossed to the bed and flopped down face first and screamed into the bedding until she felt her tiny jakkow lizard scramble up onto the back of her head.

"Jackie," she said as she turned her head to knock him off. His sticky pads gripped at her short hair. "Ouch! Jackie, get off me," she complained, reaching up and pulling her pet out of her hair. She looked at him for a while as he scrambled from arm to arm, and he reminded her of a dog trying to play with its owner, but Jackie was tiny and she couldn't exactly play fetch with him. He was a good distraction for a while, but as Avalon watched him scurry around her bed, she felt anger and despair rising in her heart.

She changed her clothes and cleaned up as well as she could without her water basin and grabbed the book of Anthracites from its hiding place in her cabinet. There was only one course of action to take, and when Avalon left her suite, she was determined to take action against Hawker and the Runners. It seemed to be the only way to move her life forward.

Avalon walked down one level and stopped outside an ornately carved door. She took a deep breath to calm her fiery mind, and Thomas stepped around his King and pulled the library door open to look inside.

"Enough," Avalon snapped, and Thomas pulled the door all the way open and stepped inside. Avalon knew he was only doing his job, but she didn't have time for it. She saw Counselor Creighton at his desk already beginning to rise in preparation for the King.

"Go ahead," Avalon said to Thomas, and he quickly moved among the stacks to make sure the room was clear, but it was very early and there was no one else present.

"My King, we can meet in the chancery," Creighton offered, his hand moving at a snail's pace to the far corner where there was an office. Avalon didn't have time to watch him pretend to be old right now. She had a purpose, and she wanted answers.

"We can meet here," she said, dropping the large book on the desk in front of him. She knew it was an old volume and she had been very careful with it up until now, but she wanted Creighton to know that she meant business. "I have questions for you," she told Creighton as Thomas stepped out into the hall and closed the door.

Avalon pulled a chair over and sat opposite her counselor, pulling in a deep breath and trying to ignore her anger. It wasn't his fault that she couldn't be with Taggerty, but he would help her find the answers so that she could have a future.

"I have been looking through this book, and I don't know what I'm missing. You have to tell me, Counselor, what am I not seeing here?" Her voice was low and controlled, and Creighton pulled the book to his side of the desk and opened it slowly.

"This is only one of a handful of books that made it over from Hawkerness when our people were decimated by the Runners. There were two decades after that before any substantial writing began. I can only assume that finding the way to a safe location and building a suitable place to live, food concerns, and water concerns kept the people busy," he said. Avalon knew that she shouldn't have dropped the book, but she wouldn't be scolded either.

"Julius, you need to tell me what you aren't telling me," she said exasperated. He was the one counselor that Avalon had confided in, and he knew of her entire trip to Cormicks. From his years of studying in the library and the archives, he knew more than anyone on the topic.

"Of course, I will tell you anything I can that will help." Avalon's eyebrows rose as he turned to a page in the book and slid it towards her. Avalon saw the same drawing that she had stared at countless times. It was a picture of five hills with the figure of a person standing on top of the largest hill.

"Look at that very closely, and then turn the page," he said, sitting back in his chair. Avalon turned to see the other two drawings that she had also stared at countless times. There was the Anthracite, unfolded from its dormant position and moving on two legs toward the man on the ground. On the next page the Anthracite was stepping on the man next to a fire. It had been almost a year since she had seen the Anthracites in person and she'd almost been crushed to death, and even the crude hand drawing brought the encounter back, and she suddenly felt sick to her stomach.

"Okay," Avalon said, sliding the book toward Creighton. "What am I supposed to see here? The Anthracites tore out of the ground and killed the man for lighting a fire."

"It's not a man," Creighton said.

"Who is not a man?" she asked holding her breath.

"Look here," Creighton said, turning back to the first picture. "I know it is a little archaic, but you should know that most of the people didn't write back then. Even now the children in the Fingers who learn a trade don't continue their education. Whoever wrote this book was definitely educated later in life and had used drawing, although not very well, to tell stories. Do you see this small triangle that is drawn over the midsection of the figure? That represents a woman."

"And how do you know that?" she asked.

"You can tell because of..." Creighton began seriously, and then he chuckled. "Of course, I thought you would see it, but you didn't read all of these other books that might have pointed that out to you," Creighton indicated the hundreds of volumes around him. "Pardon me, King Avalon. I recognized the significance from other works I've studied, but now I see that it's not something you would know."

Avalon's temper boiled, and he must have noticed her face turning shades of pink because he jolted forward in his chair. "You see the woman in a couple of other places." Creighton began flipping through the book to small drawings and pointed out the small triangle to Avalon. He then returned to the three drawings he had noted and pointed again. "Here, she is on top of the Anthracite. That tells me that while she may not in truth step onto them in fact, the artist is trying to show a peaceful correlation. See in the next picture where the Anthracite is following her?"

Avalon nodded her head, trying to comprehend what she was seeing. "Yes, he's chasing her and then he smashes her," Avalon said sarcastically.

"Look again," Creighton said. "There is no triangle in that picture."

Avalon leaned in and studied the crude drawing of the man smashed under the Anthracite's foot. There was no triangle, but Avalon still wasn't convinced.

"These two pictures are conclusive in my mind, King Avalon. We know that something can control the Anthracites. There is some way that they have remained under control of Kings in the past, and now Monarchs. I believe these pictures are evidence of that."

Avalon's forehead pressed together in doubt.

"Why not a woman? They control so many men, as it were." Creighton chuckled at his own joke, but it was lost on Avalon.

"Well, yes, you are too young for that sort of thing, aren't you?" he said. Avalon didn't like the way Creighton was looking at her, so she moved on.

"Those things don't talk," Avalon said. "They are massive and they make the most awful grinding noises when they move. There is no way a woman could just go and talk to them."

"Wait here, Your Highness," Creighton said. Although they were alone, he stood slowly and tried to straighten his back as an old man would, and Avalon let him be. He crossed the room to the chancery and returned a couple of minutes later with a smaller book in hand.

"This is an old journal, I'm not certain whose," he said as he placed the small leather-bound book in front of her. Creighton leaned over her shoulder and opened the pages slowly. Avalon felt uncomfortable with him this close, but she grit her teeth and didn't move a muscle.

"It says here that men will always be the king, and women can never rule because that is too much power for one voice to command. So you see, it's right there."

Avalon tried to control her temper, but she was getting angry again. Taggerty was leaving and she was getting nowhere.

Creighton sensed Avalon's mood darkening so he continued to prove his point. "This book shows the woman on the Anthracite and then leading it, as though she had commanded it to rise up and follow her. I believe that women can control the Anthracites, and this book proves it, although perhaps in riddle. It says 'too much power for one voice to command'. A woman who commands the people and the Anthracites is all-powerful in a way. If anyone says anything against her, she would have control of the ultimate intimidating force."

Avalon wasn't sure that she understood all that he was saying, but his point was taken that there might be a way for a woman to control the Anthracites, and she knew where to look further. Avalon rubbed her eyes and stood. "Thank you for your time, Counselor Creighton." She didn't like grasping at straws, but he was a very intelligent man, and although she didn't want to take stock in two old books that may or may not have been showing her the way, she had to move forward and this was the only direction she could find.

Avalon returned to her room to change into her formal uniform. She was going to see the Guides to talk to them about the Anthracites, and she wanted them to see her for the King that she was. She knew that they respected her, but their answers never seemed to fully disclose the information they held. Today she would let them know that she expected direct answers. She hoped to find out if there was any credence to Creighton's theory, and she needed the Guides' help because they were the only place she had left to go for answers.

As Avalon pulled her sword belt on, there was a quick knock at the door. "Enter," she called, and she was surprised to see Kensington. He had always waited in the front room of the suite, and he looked nervous as he pushed the door open and stepped in.

"Kensington, I'm busy right now. Can it wait?" Avalon asked, not wanting to be deterred.

"No, King Avalon. I need to tell you right away that Taggerty is gone. He left with a handful of soldiers this morning to man the Window."

His words stung, and Avalon closed her eyes. She expected Taggerty to leave, but not this soon. She nodded and looked down to work the belt buckle so Kensington couldn't see her frown. It was Taggerty's way. He couldn't stay at her request, and so he would leave as fast as possible. "Thank you for telling me, Kensington."

She took Jackie from her pillow and tucked him in her pocket. Kensington shifted his weight from one foot to another, and Avalon knew he was working himself up into another assertion.

"Is there something else?" she asked coldly. Avalon's heart was breaking and she didn't mean to take it out on Kensington. She tried to mute her thoughts. She had a goal right now, a purpose. She had to end this conflict with Hawker and the Runners as soon as she could. She needed to fix everything so that Fontanasia would be safe for centuries to come. A small voice was telling her that once that was done, her life might have options.

"Taggerty left?" Kensington asked. This time it was a question, and Kensington had folded his hands over his stomach and waited for an explanation. "He left me a note that he would be at the Window and to send correspondence with the Guide only. I didn't know he was going to leave. He never told me he was leaving."

Kensington was clearly hurt. She knew that they were best friends, and Taggerty's behavior baffled him.

"Did you send him away, King Avalon? If there is a difficulty, I would like to serve my King by rectifying the situation," he said, assuming that could be the only answer.

Avalon cleared her throat and steadied her nerves. She stepped toward the door and Kensington moved aside to let the King pass, but he kept his gaze on Avalon in search of an answer. "That was Taggerty's decision," she told Kensington.

"So he said goodbye to you?" he asked.

"In his own way," Avalon said, a frown pulling at the corners of her mouth. She cleared her throat, needing to change the conversation.

Avalon was exasperated. She was tired of all of the secrets, and she wrung her hands together. "I have been wrong to hide the truth, Kensington. Tell your men to let the people know that there is an enemy. We don't know if the enemy will come here, but we need to be ready. We can't keep this secret anymore. We have to share the burden with the people. Their lives are in the balance too, and it is right that they should know."

She walked out of the chambers and saw Zaria was waiting on the sofa in the outer room, and Avalon could see that her sister was agitated because her always prim and proper sister was picking at her nails.

Zaria stood, concern playing on her face. She looked at Kensington who had followed Avalon out, but his shrug told her that Avalon had said nothing to clear things up. "Taggerty left, Avalon." Zaria said this with sorrow in her voice, but all Avalon heard was, "Taggerty left Avalon," and it hurt.

Avalon cleared her throat. "He did. He's gone," she said, brushing off her emotions. She was devastated, but she would not address her emotions in front of others. Kensington left the suite and Avalon tried to follow. She patted Zaria on the arm and stepped around her, but Zaria took Avalon's hand.

"You're not going to tell me what happened between you and Taggerty?" Zaria asked. Avalon could see in Zaria's eyes all of the hope and disappointment that she too felt. Zaria had expected Avalon and Taggerty to somehow find what she and Kensington had found. And if Avalon would allow herself a moment, she would admit to Zaria that she had expected the same thing. Avalon sighed and again swallowed her emotions.

"Nothing happened between me and Taggerty." Avalon would not talk about their kiss, even to Zaria. It was hers and Taggerty's alone, and she would not spoil it. Avalon turned to leave but Zaria didn't let go of her arm. Avalon looked into her sister's eyes and let Zaria see the hurt on her face. Zaria must know that this was infinitely worse than any outcome Avalon could have predicted. He was gone, and he was not coming back.

"Please, Zaria," Avalon whispered. "I can't do this, and Kensington's waiting." Her sister released Avalon's arm and used her now free hand to wipe the tears from her own eyes.

Avalon ducked below the small gate that led through the wall of Fontanasia out to the Guides' small village. She turned back and looked at Kensington, and he had the men close the gate with the King on the outside. He grit his teeth and nodded, and Avalon nodded back, glad that he would not ask her again to take some of the King's Guard with her to the village.

Avalon walked down the dirt path and focused on the questions that she planned to ask the Guides. Children saw her first and they gathered around Avalon with smiles. Avalon pulled Jackie from her pocket and tried to hold the tiny lizard out to be seen by the children, but he scrambled up Avalon's arm and around her neck before she could catch him. The children laughed as Avalon tried to gain control of her small red pet. He was too fast for her and he scrambled around her jacket only stopping when one of the children held out a nut for him to eat. Jackie raced down Avalon's arm and sprang into the child's hand, chomping on the nut as the other children moved in to watch.

"King Avalon," Chylyn called over the children's noise. Avalon nodded at Taggerty's uncle.

"Hello, Chylyn," Avalon said with apparent pleasure. They had been through a lot together, and although she wasn't close with any of the Guides, she felt a connection with Chylyn. Avalon clucked her tongue twice and Jackie grabbed the rest of the nut in his small jaw and hopped into Avalon's hand. Chylyn smiled and Avalon held her pale hand up to his olive toned skin. "Jackie likes you," she said as the lizard touched his nose to Chylyn.

"I'm not sure the feeling is mutual," Chylyn said dryly. He was remembering when the tiny lizard ballooned to a size larger than a horse on the other side of the Window. Avalon chuckled and couldn't help but stare at the black mark on Chylyn's wrist. It was very similar to Taggerty's, but this time she noticed small differences.

Avalon looked down the row of stone houses. "I have business to discuss with your chief," Avalon told him, and Chylyn shooed the children away.

"Does your business have anything to do with why Taggerty left?" he asked.

So, Taggerty had taken time out to say goodbye to Chylyn. Avalon shrugged. A part of her had hoped to see Taggerty in the village, but he was truly gone.

"Will you not take time out to meet with our council first?" Chylyn asked. Avalon had intended to go to the chief only, but she reconsidered. If there were things that Creighton and the other counselors knew that the King of Fontanasia didn't know, perhaps the same was true here.

"Very well," Avalon nodded, and Chylyn led her to the largest stone building. Avalon thought she would have to wait for the Guides to assemble, but they were already seated inside and they looked up as though they were expecting her.

Chylyn held his hand out to the mound of cushions and Avalon squatted and sat down at the low table within the circle of counselors. She looked at the aged faces around her but the chief wasn't present.

"King Avalon, we are honored by your presence."

"Thank you for allowing me to interrupt," Avalon said graciously. As hurried as she felt, she knew there was no rushing the Guides. She knew that they loved to see a rare jakkow, so she clucked her tongue and Jackie scampered out of her pocket and onto her shoulder. They all smiled and stared at the tiny reptile.

"What is it you would like to discuss?"

Avalon had been forming a plan in her mind, and she took a deep breath. "I intend to go to Cormicks and to draw the Anthracites away from the city to work with them. If I can control them, I can take back Cormicks."

It was strange to hear her plan out loud, and when Avalon said it, she realized that parts of this plan had been forming in the back of her mind for several months. She was surprised that there was no outburst, but the Guides stayed true to form as they looked at Avalon thoughtfully. Their silence caused Avalon to press on.

"Do what you have always done and assist the King. You don't want to fight. You don't want a war, and neither do I. I believe that I can stop the enemy ever coming to our side of the Window, and I believe that you can help me."

They were all silent and still, her words lingering among the sounds of children playing outside. The oldest Guide next to her smiled then which angered Avalon because she thought he was mocking her. She clenched her teeth, but he reached his hand out and put his hand on her hand, his aged skin soft and warm on her skin.

"I do not mock you with my smile, King Avalon. I smile because you are so young, and yet you make this decision like a much older man." Avalon didn't know what to say, so she waited as he withdrew his hand. A woman appeared and served a strong tea, and they all sipped in silence. Avalon knew these were smart men, and she tried to be patient as they each deliberated in silence. It was a long time before someone spoke.

It was the elder with short hair on her other side who spoke next. "Your great-grandfather's grandfather, the first King Hall, found the Window to Fontanasia. He walked in the woods often and camped, too. He heard a story from a man about a little girl who was lost in the woods and when she was found spoke of a blue valley. Hall went looking for it, and he eventually found what she was talking about."

Avalon had read the journal of the first King of Fontanasia, and she was aware of his journey, but she didn't interrupt because she knew these men could help her, and she knew that their stories typically led to the answer.

"He took stock of the area where the blue grass glowed. He didn't dare walk into the field because he had never seen anything like it and he sensed its danger. He noticed there were no animals around or above the grass, and he believed in listening to the animals."

Avalon remembered the story. "His journals show that he camped next to the field for six months until he saw a small animal eating the alleya leaf to survive the poison. Only then did he travel out into the grass."

The Guide nodded and continued. "That is what the legend tells. He went missing for a few months, and then returned to Hawkerness with a beard down to his chest and a story of being lost in the woods of another world."

Avalon pursed her lips trying to decode some message he was trying to impart to her, but she'd read the story before and had no idea where he was going.

"Do you believe in destiny, King Avalon?" he asked.

"I don't know," she said half-heartedly. She wanted to, but Taggerty leaving had killed her belief in any prophecy.

"Well, I do. I believe it was fate that your great-grandfather's grandfather found the door to this place and that in the slaughter that took Hawkerness, he was the next survivor in line to lead the people to safety. He brought the people to a place no one else would have been able to. They happened to be attacked on a full moon at a time when he could lead the people safely away from Hawkerness. He saved my people too, and still I don't believe in coincidence."

Avalon hadn't really appreciated how the futures of their people fit together. Now she understood better the Guide's reverence for the kings over the centuries.

"King Avalon, I believe that it is your destiny to become the greatest King of Fontanasia."

Avalon couldn't meet the Guide's eye right now, but she knew after hearing the story that all of her father's planning and all of her own preparations must have been for a reason. Avalon couldn't say that she believed in destiny, but she would accept coincidence if it would help her take Cormicks back.

"I don't know about that," Avalon said with a smile, "but I will take any assistance you can give me in learning more about how to control the Anthracites. I didn't see anything in the journal about that, and my father certainly didn't know. Will you help me?" Avalon asked.

The men each looked at one another and nodded, and Avalon relaxed a little. She would get their help.

"Our Khee will meet with you, King Avalon, to answer your questions," the shorthaired Guide said. "If there is any assistance to give to you, he will provide it."

"Thank you," Avalon said.

"Don't thank us yet," one elder replied. "You will not find what you are looking for because you will never control the Anthracites."

Chapter 4
Stranger's Pass

Avalon tried not to be angry with the Guide, but his comment that she would never control the Anthracites seemed harsh, and she clenched her teeth. "Thank you for your council," she said with a nod. She clucked her tongue and Jackie scampered back down her coat and into her pocket.

As if on cue, Chylyn stepped back in and held the heavy cloth door open. Avalon rose from the cushions and left with him.

She didn't know how he could have heard the quiet discussion, but Chylyn didn't lead Avalon out of the village. Instead he led Avalon to the same stone house she had come to when they'd returned from Cormicks, and she knew it was the chief's house.

"Khee is expecting you," he told Avalon, and she did not stop but walked straight through the low doorway and down a half flight of stairs. The building was larger on the inside than it looked on the outside. The gray stone was white washed and there were light tapestries hung along the walls. There were no windows, but windows anywhere were a luxury because glass was very difficult to make and maintain.

Avalon recognized Khee. His hair was grayer than the counselors she had met with, but his face was less wrinkled than most. She instinctively expected the chief to be older and smiled at the thought because she was a King and her own face was still that of a teenager.

Khee smiled back at her, but he did not rise from his position near the small fire. He tipped his head forward and reached out his hand, offering Avalon the pillow opposite his. She looked around the room, taking her time to remember the decor, but also to make sure there was no one else present. She wanted to be honest with this man about her intent, and she didn't want anyone who wasn't privy to hear about the Anthracites.

"Thank you for taking this meeting," Avalon said. She straightened her jacket and then knelt on the pillow. He smiled gently and Avalon felt the morning's tension roll off of her. He was a calming presence and Avalon was grateful.

"It is my purpose to serve," Khee said, and she could tell that he meant it with every fiber of his body. She had come unannounced and he wasn't agitated or put off at all. Like his counselors, he seemed as though he had been waiting for her, and his calming presence caused Avalon to take a deep breath and relax.

"You have a lot of responsibility. How are you able to fulfill your purpose and also feel happy?" Avalon asked.

He nodded his head slowly with a faraway look in his eyes as though he had just remembered everything he had ever known. "Well, I never knew I would lead my people. That is not how we do things. Unlike you, I am not the king because my father was king before me. I am Khee because my steps in life and my people made it so. I am not trying to fill any expectations. Being me is what got me here. That is the only expectation I have, to be true to myself first. I suppose that would make anyone happy."

As the soft tone of his words enveloped Avalon, Jackie climbed out of her pocket to her arm. Avalon held out her hand palm down, prompting Jackie to run to her fingertips and jump across the short expanse landing on Khee's arm. He laughed and watched Jackie investigate the black tattoo on his wrist.

"But when you were read as a baby, they knew, right?" she asked, thinking of Taggerty's prophecy.

As soon as she thought his name she regretted it, and Avalon's face turned red. She was angry again, mad that Taggerty left, mad that she was the King. Her chest tightened and sensing her discomfort, Jackie bristled and jumped back to Avalon's arm.

Khee's head tilted and then he smiled at Avalon. "Not everyone here is so clearly read as young Taggerty, but yes, my reading put me in a position to become Khee." He watched Avalon for a few moments and in her discomfort she watched Jackie run back and forth.

"How do you know what your true destiny is if you are not at the end of your life?" he asked Avalon.

Avalon's brow furrowed and she stared at the wise old man. She had never considered another path. Her destiny was to be King of Fontanasia, and she understood that with every bone in her body. She shook her head. "My future was planned the day I was born," she answered confidently, and thankfully he didn't disagree with her. Avalon was on shaky ground today as it was, and she couldn't afford to entertain questions about her future.

"Thank you for meeting with me. I have come to talk to you about the Anthracites," Avalon told him, watching his face closely for a reaction. He looked down at Jackie and his long, gray hair fell to the sides of his face.

"Aah," was all he said.

"I will start by telling you what I know, and you can then share with me any details I might have missed," Avalon said graciously. She wasn't certain about anything Counselor Creighton had told her, but she had to make a move and she had nowhere else to turn. Avalon told Khee about the book she had seen and the triangle over the person in the images. He listened intently, slowly nodding his head.

"I don't really know if any of this is fact, but there is some way that the Runners control the Anthracites. What is their secret?" Avalon asked.

"There is a song that they listen to," Khee replied.

Avalon was stunned because she hadn't really expected an answer to her question. "There is a song?" she asked incredulously. She could hardly believe that the rock beasts could communicate at all.

"They listen to the song," he repeated. "The book that you found is correct, they will only listen to a female voice. That is why a woman will never rule Fontanasia."

"What?" Avalon barked. The comment had rocked her back in her seat and Jackie scampered up onto her shoulder.

"It was known from when we lived in Hawkerness," Khee said gently. "The Anthracites only respond to the tone of a female's voice. They only respond to the song. It was many generations before Hawkerness was lost that it was decided man would rule men, and woman would rule Anthracites. It is simply a division of power."

"Tell me," Avalon said, leaning forward on the cushions.

Khee nodded and pursed his lips. A look of concern crossed his face, but he would tell his King what he knew. "The sounds of the song were passed down from one queen to the next. The Anthracites were rarely called upon, and they were mostly left in peace by those of Hawkerness. They were a very big weapon though, and no one questioned the authority of the King." Khee looked up at Avalon who was listening attentively.

"Go on," Avalon said.

"One of the servants of the Queen fell in love with the son of one of the more dignified factions of the Runners. They had been invited to eat with the king in the castle many times and that is how the son met the servant girl.

No one knew how they felt about each other. This servant girl was always with the Queen, and she too learned the Anthracite's song. Then over time, the Runner's son used her to gain control of the Anthracites. He was cunning, and he killed his own father to take control of the Runners. We don't know what happened to the servant girl because that was the end of our time in Hawkerness, but the Runners still control the Anthracites, so we can only assume that she became the new Queen."

Avalon found the story incredible, but today she understood what someone would do to follow her heart. She had been driven to Creighton in a desperate act to take some sort of action, and she would do whatever it took to find a resolution. "How can I learn this song?" Avalon asked.

"We know the song," Khee said.

Avalon looked at him incredulous. "You know the song?" she accused. All of this time the Guides could have taken control of the Anthracites and put an end to the Runners.

"Of course we know the song. We created it. We gave it to the good people of Hawkerness to protect them against the bad Runners. We thought we were helping, but it was no help in the end." He said this with regret as though he'd been in Hawkerness during the slaughter of his people.

"Why was I not told about this before now?" Avalon accused.

"You didn't ask before now," he told her calmly. Avalon could tell by the way that his lips were pulled tightly together that if she hadn't come here today, the Guides would have kept this secret forever.

"We lived out beyond Crescent Moon Hill and we met your great-grandfather's grandfather there by the elbagrass. He was a scientist of sorts. He studied the elbagrass and the Anthracites and the moon and stars. He was a wise man. When he showed us that there was a way out of the land of Hawkerness and away from the danger of the Runners, we took the chance for a peaceful life."

"I want to hear the song," Avalon said. "I want to learn it." Avalon felt the future coming to her. She could learn the song and cross over and take control of the Anthracites and smash the Runners. She could once and for all rid Fontanasia of the threat that Hawker presented. She could return to a life where she didn't live in fear every day.

Avalon felt the utter power of hope course through her veins. In one month, she would put the future back on course to where it was before she'd ever heard of Cormicks.

"The Anthracites will not respond to a man's voice," Khee reminded her.

"I don't care," she said. "I will learn the song." Avalon tried not to show any emotion, but she was now more conscious than ever that she was a girl. "I must make this right. Some of the Runners already came across once, but we were able to stop them by burning the field of elbagrass. Now that Hawker is in control of Cormicks, it's only a matter of time."

"Is that certain?" Khee asked, but Avalon held his gaze with a look of pure determination on her face. He sighed heavily, an unusual show of emotion for one of the Guides, but he nodded at the same time. "Chylyn will take you."

Avalon left the small stone building and squinted as she waited for her eyes to acclimate to the brightness of the day. Chylyn nodded as he walked by her and entered the house. Avalon waited only a moment before he returned.

"You should eat some lunch before we go," he suggested. It was already noon, but Avalon wasn't hungry and she shook her head.

Chylyn appraised Avalon's attire. "Are you certain that you want to wear something so formal?" he asked. Avalon shrugged, not knowing what her attire had to do with meeting the women of the village who knew the Anthracite's song.

Chylyn spoke to a woman who was waiting, and she ducked inside the next hut. Avalon thought they might follow her, but Chylyn didn't move. A minute passed and the woman returned with a leather bag that Chylyn threw over his shoulder. "We can eat when we get there," he said and turned to leave.

"I'm not hungry," Avalon said as she set out after him. It didn't take her long to discern why he had questioned her attire. Avalon had assumed that the women would be in the village, but Chylyn led her up a small path on the side of the mountain. Soon she was sweating and her dress boots made the trek slippery. Chylyn didn't slow down and he didn't look back either, and Avalon rushed to keep up with him. Some of the path was very steep and there were no handholds, and Avalon cursed her boots that were now covered in dust. She had to lean forward and use her hands and feet to pull herself up in some sections.

"It's just up ahead," Chylyn said. Avalon felt the ground level out, but all she saw was grass, rock and trees with no sign of anyone from the village. Avalon looked down the mountainside and saw the back of the castle below them. The stone wall that kept the city safe had been built up all around the part of the castle that grew out of the side of the mountain. Avalon wondered why she had never climbed up this high before.

They went around a bend in the mountain and now faced seaward. A cool breeze blew off the Helon Sea, and Avalon was grateful to catch her breath. She looked over the sparkling wave crests and remembered her time on the water with Taggerty. It was just yesterday, but Avalon felt so removed from him now that it could have been months ago.

She shook her head in regret and watched the water for another moment before turning down the path to continue, but Chylyn was gone. Avalon jogged a few steps and looked around the next bend in the path, but he was nowhere to be seen.

"Hello?" Avalon called out.

"Hello," Chylyn's deep voice said behind her, and Avalon spun around, but he was not there. Avalon tried to listen over the sound of the sea, and she thought she could hear some sort of animal screeching in the wind. It was a horrible sound, and Avalon assumed it must be the lingering sounds of prey in the throes of death.

"Chylyn," Avalon said again. Fear crept over Avalon, but her tone was low and commanding to convey that she was not up for games.

The bed of green moss that covered the steep rock next to her moved, and Avalon realized that she had walked by Chylyn without even knowing it. She stepped closer and pulled the curtain of moss aside slowly. The pungent odor of dirt and mold was strong as she stepped through, and then the curtain fell back and Avalon blinked in the dark.

"I'm here," Chylyn said, and Avalon pulled her hand up to her chest. He was standing within inches of where she was and she hadn't even seen him in the dark. "Just give it a minute," he said, and she could hear the smile in his tone. He seemed to be enjoying her discomfort.

Avalon felt Jackie scamper up to her shoulder as she blinked and tried to see anything in the dark, but she couldn't even see her hand in front of her face. After a minute, she could see a slight green glow where she was standing, and there was light off in the distance. She was in a cave, and she could see Chylyn's gray outline next to her.

"We call this Stranger's Pass. I think it is because you would pass right by if you didn't know it was here." She could hear the smile in his tone again, and Avalon would have felt annoyed if she wasn't glad. Chylyn's chiding meant he saw her as a friend.

She blinked several more times and then heard a blood-curdling echo. It sounded like an animal was being mauled and chills ran up her back. Jackie ran down into the safety of Avalon's pocket, and Chylyn walked swiftly into the dim green light as Avalon followed. She could hear her steps crunching on small gravel as they came to a fork in the cave and followed where the light was coming through. The horrible sounds came louder and echoed off the walls of the cave. Chylyn turned into a large cavern, and Avalon could see the sunlight piercing through small holes in the rock. The cavern echoed the hideous screeching sound that tapered off and stopped.

They moved into the open space and Avalon expected to see some kind of animals fighting in the cave, but all she saw were three girls who looked like they were dancing on the larger rocks in the space. The smallest girl leapt into the air and flipped before landing in front of Chylyn, the staff in her hand stopping inches from his neck. She was shorter than Avalon with a tiny frame, but she was nimble and she smiled up at Chylyn whose hair had rippled in the breeze caused when the staff came to a stop next to his face. Avalon's mouth hung open. She hadn't even reached for her sword.

"You are losing your touch," Chylyn told the girl. Her thin lips curled up in a devilish smile and she touched the staff to Chylyn's shoulder before springing back into action, somersaulting, flipping, spinning, and somehow landing on the boulder above them.

"That is Nugget," Chylyn said to Avalon while still looking up. "She was born Kaelan of the Winds, but she was so tiny that they called her Nugget. Don't let her size fool you, King Avalon. She is powerful."

They watched for a minute as Nugget attacked unseen enemies with her staff, her legs kicking in all directions, and her body flipping and twisting in the air between movements. Avalon's mouth fell open. She had never seen anything like this style of fighting.

"She is showing off for the King today," Chylyn said loud enough for the girl to hear.

Avalon was extremely impressed. The small girl had more acrobatic skill than anyone she'd seen before, and the staff moved like an extra appendage and weapon at the same time.

"Sonrah, the King would like to hear from you," Chylyn said and the young lady moved forward in slow, graceful steps. She was tall and elegant, with flowing red hair and a green dress that was made out of thin fabric that hugged her perfect figure. She looked older than Zaria, and she walked with the same confidence. Even in the dim light, Avalon could tell that she was beautiful.

Sonrah turned to face the wall instead of the King and cleared her throat. She inhaled deeply, and holding her arms out in front of her, she flipped her palms up. As her arms slowly opened, she bellowed a screeching sound that ricocheted around the cavern.

"Rook-jaaaaaaaa. Aaaaa-kaaaaaaa!" she belted.

It was all Avalon could do not to cover her ears. The girl finished with a mixture of vowel sounds in a range of high-pitched notes. She then turned toward Avalon with a smile on her face and bowed.

Avalon realized that she was squinting in discomfort. The howling of dying animals that she'd heard was actually this beautiful girl belting out otherworldly guttural screeching noises.

"What do you think?" Chylyn asked, and Avalon realized that Sonrah had made the sounds that somehow communicated with the Anthracites. There was no way Avalon could have replicated the noise if she tried, and she almost felt embarrassed at the thought. She felt hot with frustration knowing that she had to move forward with the plan she had been forming all day. It wasn't only for Taggerty. Peace meant the safety of her people and a future for Fontanasia.

"I must learn these songs," Avalon said.

"Two of these girls were chosen at birth to carry on the tradition of the past. Their voices have been trained since they learned how to speak so that they can clearly make these unique sounds. It takes a long time," Chylyn told her apologetically, but Khee had given his approval and she had been shown this secret. It was the only way forward that Avalon could see right now, so she pushed on.

"Chylyn, I must learn these sounds. Please, help me."

"Hmmm," Nugget grunted reproachfully from the rock above Avalon. Avalon had just requested instead of commanding, and the fierce girl on the rock had taken note. Avalon looked back at Chylyn who watched Avalon for a long moment, but she did not look away under his uncomfortable stare.

"King Avalon, you go to your death. Do you understand what I am saying?" Chylyn asked.

"Do you see the future?" Avalon asked with sarcasm.

He shook his head. "No. Have you seen the future?"

"Not today," she answered, trying to smile.

Chylyn had been with Avalon the night she had dreamt of Counselor Glenn's treason. She awoke knowing her father was dead and without question Chylyn had believed she could dream the future. He had always helped Avalon, and she knew he would do all he could to help her now whether or not he agreed with her.

He reached over and touched Avalon, his soft skin warming her cold hand, and Avalon's building frustration melted away.

"I understand what I'm asking," she said, her eyes piercing his with the truth. "I can't wait any longer. If I can do anything to bring peace again, I must act now." Avalon didn't mention Hawker, but Chylyn nodded.

"You are not responsible for the sins of your uncle," he said.

"I am responsible for my people," Avalon answered, unwilling to enter into a conversation about Hawker. "Please," she asked again. "Help me with my plan. Teach me these songs."

He sighed. "Will you take an army to Cormicks?"

"I won't need an army if I have the Anthracites. If you allow me to learn their speech, I will only need to risk myself."

"We must send someone with you, King Avalon. A man may not speak to the Anthracites. It takes a certain tone that only a female can produce," he told her. Avalon held her tongue. Khee had told Avalon the same thing, and she had been expecting this argument. She was prepared to give her secret up to Chylyn, but when she looked up at him he held his hand up.

"Nugget," he said loudly, and this time the girl slid off the boulder and walked to Chylyn. She stood respectfully with her head down and her hands folded in front of her. "She will go with you," he said, pointing at the girl. She had been an intense acrobat, but standing here in front of Avalon was a small figure, younger than Avalon.

Avalon shook her head. "I will go alone," she said in a commanding tone. "You told me that I go to my death, and I will not endanger this girl."

"This girl has trained as Taggerty did, from birth. She can help you, King Avalon."

But Avalon shook her head.

"Nugget, can you demonstrate more of your physical training?" Chylyn asked. The girl nodded, and Avalon saw a smile cross her face. What happened next was a surprising flurry of action on the girl's part, and it was over before Avalon had even moved a muscle.

The girl somersaulted to the side of a low rock and flipped over it. The other two girls came at her with their staffs swinging, and she used her staff to stop them. She trapped one of the staffs with her foot and kicked it, the finished wood splintering with her strike. She spun and kicked and dropped the other two girls to the ground and then jumped to the vines that crept through the light holes and scaled one to the top of the cavern. Her staff was tucked in her legs and she used her hands to scale over Avalon's head and across to the rock wall, sliding down from a height Avalon found unimaginable.

She then cartwheeled between Avalon and Chylyn, unsheathing Avalon's sword with such a light touch that Avalon didn't even have time to react. The small girl was on her feet and across the cavern with Avalon's sword in the blink of an eye. Nugget's shoulders rose and fell slowly, and Avalon could see that she was barely out of breath.

"Thank you, Nugget," Chylyn said with pride in his voice. Nugget stepped forward and knelt with her face turned to the ground, Avalon's sword held flat across her hands above her head. She remained still and Avalon crossed to her and retrieved her sword.

Avalon sheathed her sword and bit the inside of her lip. She had two choices, and since she was unwilling to leave for Cormicks without the key to controlling the Anthracites, she relented. "We leave in five days," she said.

"So soon?" Chylyn asked.

"I can learn on the move. Have Nugget come to the castle each morning." Nugget stood and she and the other two girls moved away from Avalon and Chylyn to give them privacy in their conversation.

"It took these girls years to become proficient in making the song. You cannot learn it in five days, King Avalon, but that is no matter since the Anthracites do not understand a man's voice. Nugget can go with you and she will control the Anthracites with your commands."

Avalon cleared her throat and wondered if she would ever be able to make the sounds that she'd heard. Nugget did seem to be able to take care of herself, but Avalon didn't want to take her with. Still, Avalon needed to learn the song and control the charcoal beasts with her own commands. It was a matter of trust, and Avalon knew she could not trust this task to anyone else. She would delay her trip if it meant being able to control the Anthracites with her own voice.

"We will practice together as long as it takes for me to be proficient," Avalon told Chylyn. For the next six months, she came to regret that decision.

Chapter 5
A New Song

Avalon had left the Guide's village with a plan to crush Hawker and the Runners at the next turn of the moon, but six months had gone by, and she was still in Fontanasia. She had been to the cave at Stranger's Pass at least four days a week to train with Nugget, Sonrah, and Cincin to learn the song of the Anthracites. The voice training was more grueling than the physical training, and one month in, Avalon had felt defeated.

Sonrah was leading the others in the voice commands, and although guttural and hard on the vocal chords, the graceful red-haired Guide made it look easy. Nugget was able to keep up, and her projection wasn't as strong, but she had the correct pronunciation. After the first few weeks Avalon and Cincin still struggled, and Nugget's continuous prodding of Cincin angered Avalon because she knew that Cincin was doing better than she was.

"Roooook-jaaaaaa!" Sonrah belted and then held out her hand for the others to try. Avalon took a deep breath and tried to push the air through the back of her throat so that her voice could vibrate the same words in two different vocal ranges. It was impossible, and when she stopped her throat was raw, and Nugget had that ever-knowing grin on her face again that pressed at Avalon's last nerve.

There was an enemy being led by her uncle and they could appear at any moment. Taggerty was at the Window and it felt like he would be gone forever, and Avalon was losing patience with the whole exercise. She yelled in frustration and then turned and walked through the dark tunnel and out onto Stranger's Pass.

The castle and all of Fontanasia was below her and Avalon shook her head and pushed her lips together in irritation. She picked up small rocks and threw them downhill, wondering how she would ever make this work. Maybe it was best to just go without learning how to control the Anthracites, but they were the key to her plan and Avalon didn't want to place that burden on anyone else. Still, she couldn't make the sounds and she had been trying her hardest, but it had been weeks and the tone of her voice wouldn't do what the Guide's voices could.

Cincin had come out of the cave and stood near the entrance. Cincin had been quiet the entire first month that Avalon had spent with them. Where Nugget talked incessantly and flashed her training around the cave, Cincin was slow and methodical, and aside from the Anthracite words, she never spoke. She was round in the middle and her motions were slower, but she was powerful, and Avalon respected her.

"We can see so far from up here, and yet nothing on the horizon matters," Cincin said. Her words were typical of a Guide, Avalon thought. They were poignant, yet didn't seem to mean anything. Cincin was young, but her demeanor was that of an old soothsayer, and Avalon didn't have time for riddles.

"Chylyn told you that a man cannot make the sounds," Cincin said.

Avalon looked over at Cincin, but she did not respond. It was dirty in the cave, but Cincin was in a white robe because she was a traditionalist and she did everything by the book. The future given to her as a baby was to learn the traditions and history of the Guides, and she was more at home studying scrolls than practicing hand to hand combat and learning the Anthracite language.

"I was not born for this. I have spent my time learning our culture in the village and in books, and they only brought me here after King Birch died. It took me three months to make the sounds."

Now Avalon was interested, and she studied Cincin for the first time. "So you have just learned the language?" Avalon asked.

Cincin nodded. "I have known our tradition of defense since I was young, just like Nugget, but I have not practiced much before now." They looked at each other, both thinking of Nugget swinging her staff, somersaulting, and striking the air, and Cincin smiled. "Well not quite just like Nugget, but I know the moves and I am an effective caller too."

"You are all about tradition. You wear a clean white robe to train in a dirty cave each day, and yet you go against history by training with a man. If men don't call the Anthracites, what makes you think that a King could make the sounds?"

Cincin smiled at Avalon. "I believe you will make the sounds. Whether the Anthracites respond is the question. It is said in tradition that they only hear a Queen's call."

"They will respond," Avalon said, and Cincin nodded.

Cincin took a deep breath and looked out at the horizon. "I wear white because even though Sonrah and Nugget don't, that is the tradition for a caller, and I do things by the book because I honor our past. Tradition honors our forefathers and protects our culture, but I would be a fool to think that tradition is law in a land that is not our own." Cincin turned and made for the cave opening, but she looked back at Avalon and shrugged before going inside. "One can study the past, but no one can study the future."

Cincin was right that afternoon, and over the next five months, Avalon had learned. The resonances still sounded like a horrible screeching noise to Avalon, but she had come to learn the basic commands, and she understood now why they called it a song. The words needed to be released at a certain tempo and they now represented words to Avalon.

She could understand now why mastering the tones could take years. Chylyn admitted that no Guide had tried to speak to an Anthracite in over two hundred years, but he assured Avalon that each generation had trained a handful of girls to the task, and the sounds remained authentic.

Avalon returned to the castle at sundown and retreated to the suite. The King's Guard had gotten used to letting the King out through the locked gate, and none of them had shared the knowledge that the King left the city four days each week. When she returned, Avalon locked herself in Zaria's old room and enjoyed a warm bath with scented salts.

Myra George didn't like the fact that Avalon would disappear most days and return exhausted and with a sore throat. There were occasional scratches and cuts and the always-bruised thighs and ankles, and Myra had come to drawing Avalon a bath at the end of each day. Avalon liked Zaria's old room because no one would come looking for her there. She also liked it because Zaria had a large mirror to admire herself in, and Avalon studied her own figure when she was done with her bath.

She was sixteen years old, and Avalon had flowered. She took in the curve of her hip and the exposed flesh of her chest. Zaria and other girls dressed in a way that accentuated their figure, but Avalon's chest had pink marks where the bandage she used to flatten her chest chafed during her training. Avalon stood in the reflection of the candlelight and considered the possibility of an alternate future. Her body had changed into that of a young lady, and if she admitted it, she had changed emotionally too.

Avalon moved her hand over her stomach. Her sister was pregnant and due with her first child soon. Avalon wondered what that would be like. She often laid her hand on Zaria's belly and felt the baby kicking. It was a wonder, and Avalon sometimes imagined herself pregnant.

She allowed herself these moments in the mirror, but she had little hope of any truth to her thoughts. Her future as King was the truth, but imagining other futures allowed her heart to pump again outside the monotonous business of the day to day that had become her life.

She dressed in fresh clothes and sat on the edge of Zaria's old bed and relaxed her sore muscles, and she allowed herself to think about Taggerty in these minutes. Avalon would never forget their kiss, and she would never forget him. As she drifted off to sleep, she was sure she would be in love with him for the rest of her life.

Avalon woke at the foot of the bed curled into a ball. She could see the gray light of dawn filtering in, and she padded out into the front room in bare feet. She had liked living alone these months since Zaria had been married. There were very few visitors anymore to the suite, and Avalon felt more relaxed when she didn't feel like she had to always be on guard.

She moved to the windows and looked out over "Heaven's Bed" which was the nickname that Fontanasia had been given as the clouds hung low in the mist over the mountain. She watched for a long time as the haze disappeared and the sky became a yellow-gray causing her to squint. She saw low clouds moving over and she realized that the sky looked as hazy and gray as she felt.

There had been three changes of the guard at the Window, but Taggerty did not return. He had sent letters to her but they were battle action points and fortification suggestions for the King. Avalon tried to read some emotion into the letters, but she knew that Taggerty would not take the chance of someone else reading a personal message meant for her.

She savored the scratch of his writing style wondering what her name would look like if he drew it next to his. He had drawn a tiny sketch of Jackie in the bottom corner, and at first she'd thought it was a clue to battle strategy, but then she realized it was a note for her, something that no one would know about. Avalon had drawn it on her letters to him, too, and it had turned into a small token of a private message and Avalon knew that he was still thinking of her.

Avalon sighed and felt a wave of regret travel through her body. Taggerty had taken her in his arms in this very spot and kissed her soul. Avalon had grown to like the hazy gray of the mornings like today. It was her time to reflect, to want, and to forget the future that she planned in her mind in the dark of each night.

She felt Jackie climb up her leg and scamper over her shoulder waking her from her wants. She held out her arm and he ran down into her hand. He wiggled around in excitement for the new day. She'd been leaving him in the Guide's village during the day for the last six months while she trained and Jackie had become something of a celebrity. His belly had grown round with all of the nuts that the children liked to feed him. She was worried that he would outgrow her pocket, and Avalon had stopped feeding him when they were in the castle.

Avalon went into her room to change into her clothes. She wrapped her chest in a flexible cloth to hide her budding chest and pulled on her padded undershirt. Most of the men wore fitted pants, but Avalon still wore two layers a bit baggy to hide the curve of her hips. Jackie hopped from the bed onto Avalon's hip and climbed up until he found his home in her pocket. Finally, she pulled on her boots and inhaled deeply, ready to face another day.

Before breakfast, Avalon ate a sweet biscuit with tea in her suite. She was expecting Kensington who had been meeting with Avalon each morning for a few minutes to discuss the day's business, and he always met her with a half-smile. It was a tense time in Fontanasia.

Soldiers left to do their duty and were gone for months at a time, and this had never happened before. In the past it would have meant a hunting trip with the King lasting a week or two. Now the mood was grim. There was an enemy out there somewhere, and everyone felt the danger as they watched the men of the city work alongside the soldiers under Gamon's direction. Their forefathers had felt this danger after Hawkerness was sacked, and through the generations it had been forgotten because each new generation hadn't lived in danger for themselves. The fear was real again, and the mood had shifted immensely.

Zaria wanted Avalon to talk to the people, to give a speech and make public decrees, but she wouldn't agree to that. They were ramping up their defenses, and the men who were manning the walls of the Fingers and working alongside the soldiers heard the stories first-hand. There was a faraway enemy of craven beast-like men ready to attack Fontanasia. This was the same enemy that encouraged King Birch and Walthan to build the walls of the Fingers. The stories moved from man to woman to child, and they would protect themselves if the day came.

The whisperings and stories were more than Avalon could do to put fear in her people, enough fear to work diligently. Groups of angry citizens came to the castle every day, and Avalon wasn't sure what Kensington said to them to make them turn away in peace.

Avalon took another bite of her biscuit and shoed Jackie back into her pocket when he came out to find some food. Avalon thought of Taggerty again. Kensington's morning updates were helpful, but they always made her think of Taggerty because she knew that Kensington missed him too, although neither would bring him up in conversation. It was as though he was a ghost that they could both see in the room, but neither would claim.

There was a knock at the door and Kensington entered. "Your Highness," he said with a bow before he turned and closed the door behind him. Avalon could see the grimace on his face.

They met privately to discuss the upcoming day. Zaria thought that they did this all three together at breakfast, but she heard the shortened version. Avalon knew Zaria deserved to hear about everything that was said, but she still wanted to spare her sister from the full truth of the danger. Zaria's baby would come soon, and there was no need to spoil her excitement with the reality of the situation.

"Would you like some tea, brother?" Avalon asked. He shook his head as he always did. They were both ready to get on with the business of the city as early as possible. Non-training days were long for Avalon, but she knew the work was important.

"I'm hearing more rumors," Kensington said, sitting down on the sofa opposite Avalon. "The soldiers are only saying the truth as far as you have instructed, and they aren't talking about Cormicks or the elbagrass, but the city is a small place when it comes to gossip. The men are leaving for two months and then returning, and that is not going unnoticed. The people have made up all sorts of fairy tales."

Avalon nodded. Myra George had approached her a month ago with whispers about an old city and an old enemy. Myra deserved the truth, but Avalon had sidestepped the inquiry. She knew that Myra was smart and could figure things out pretty well on her own, and her trusted servant did not push. She would not want to force Avalon to lie, and whatever fairy tales were being told, the truth was much worse.

"There are more stories, some pretty far-fetched, but some not so far off the mark. It's the old legends coming alive as the older folk try to remember the tales told to them as children." Avalon cleared her throat. "Kensington, I'm going to leave soon," Avalon said, and Kensington's face reddened.

She had told him her plans of crossing over, and he knew the training she was undergoing. He was concerned for her, but also angry that she would not let him go with her to Cormicks. He was about to have a baby with her sister, and there was nothing in the world that could convince Avalon to have Kensington come on this expedition.

"King Avalon, I must again humbly protest," he said, bowing his head and not meeting her eye. "It has been almost a full year since they came. I don't think they will return."

Avalon was not angry with Kensington, but he didn't know Hawker. She knew that he might wait years building his army back up and entrenching himself as the Monarch of Cormicks. He might wait, or he might not, but either way, if she didn't go there and stop him, he would be in Fontanasia someday with his army. There was no way she could live her life waiting for that day. If she could control the Anthracites, she was certain she could win a decisive battle, and she wanted that battle to take place on the other side of the Window.

"I have heard your protest, Kensington, and don't ask to accompany me either." He looked at her then with regret.

"I am the head of the King's Guard," he said shaking his head. Avalon didn't realize before now the position he was in, torn between his wife and their forthcoming child, and the duty he had sworn to uphold.

"Does Gamon have the people ready in case they are needed?" Avalon asked, trying to change the subject.

"They are ready, Your Highness. It's ironic though. It's been months of training with the civilians, and it seems the more the rumors move around the city, the more bored the people grow of the training. They talk and speculate, but they aren't soldiers and they are getting tired of the daily regimen. They talk about an enemy, but for all of their fear I don't think they really believe. They want their weekends back to spend with their families."

Avalon smiled because Kensington was right, it was ironic. She fully intended to bring the fight to Cormicks and to keep it on the other side of the Window, and she realized that the civilians were probably as prepared as they were ever going to be. If the Runners came to Fontanasia, the techniques her people had learned in the last six months would mix with fear and adrenaline and they would defend their home to the best of their abilities.

"Give them their weekends back, Kensington. They are as trained as they will need to be if the fight comes here." Kensington looked up surprised at Avalon, but he didn't speak. "The Runners are a horrible enemy, Kensington. I know. And the destructive power of the Anthracites, you wouldn't believe it unless you saw it." Even after months of training to speak their language, the words caught in her throat. "But the people haven't seen this, and even digging up old fairy tales full of half-truths will never bring it home for them. These people did not live through the invasion of Hawkerness, and their minds won't be changed unless they have to live through something horrible like that. I don't think I truly believed it until I saw it."

Kensington bowed his head and Avalon knew that he was remembering the brutal bloodthirsty Runners coming out of the elbagrass. "I understand that, King Avalon," he whispered.

"The moon is full in one week. I'm going to leave in two days, and it's time for me to tell Zaria."

Kensington flinched. "She's going to hate me, King Avalon," he said. "I've been keeping a lot of secrets from my wife."

Avalon liked to sit and stare up at the white stone sentinel that her father had become. The statue calmed her nerves, and lately she had needed to look upon the stone edifice more and more.

Over the six months she had been training, Avalon's life had become all business. Counselor Nelson had earned Avalon's trust and respect when he had saved her life and was wounded for it. He now walked with a permanent limp for his troubles. She had put him in charge of reporting to the other counselors any duties they could perform in their boroughs, and she met with him once a day for a few moments after she met with Kensington.

There had been small changes taking place quietly and slowly over the months to limit suspicion. Avalon had commissioned the creation of two more large boats. It took decades for the men in the Reaches to make the first big boat, and even after proving its sturdiness, few wanted to go out on it.

The men of the Reaches liked their small crafts, and anyone not already on the water was afraid of what they couldn't see under the water. Avalon hadn't even thought of worrying about that when she was on the boat. Of course, she had been concentrating more on Taggerty and the sunset than anything else. She hoped it was a waste of time building these ships, but she agreed with Counselor Jennings that it might be necessary for the safety of the people if they needed to evacuate Fontanasia.

Avalon's meetings with the Guides were completely different. She stopped in the village on the way to Stranger's Pass four days a week where she trained with Nugget and the other Guides. In the village the children would spoil Jackie for a few moments while Avalon talked to Chylyn or another of the Guide council. These meetings often consisted of cryptic questions from the Guides and nonspecific answers from Avalon.

Avalon had shared her plans with them, and she had offered to bring them inside the walls of the Fingers for safety, but they had opted not to. They asked Avalon about the moon and about her jakkow and of everything she could think of from her meeting with the Monarch. They interviewed her over and over about her uncle Hawker, and still she could not figure out which puzzle they were trying to put together with the pieces of questions they were asking. She assumed they knew more about most of these topics than she did, and still they asked.

Zaria found her sister in the Hall of Kings staring at their father's newly unveiled statue. She walked as gracefully as her rounded figure would allow.

"Kensington said you would be here." Zaria looked as though she would deliver the baby any day now, although Myra said it would be more than a month yet. She was not a doctor, but neither of them questioned Myra's prediction, which was of course spot on with the opinion of the doctor.

Avalon looked at her sister and then back at the figure of their father. "I will be a statue one day, frozen in time."

"They will make a statue of a very old King Avalon Hall because you will live to be a hundred at least," Zaria said. Avalon knew the conversation would be very difficult, but she had to tell her sister everything because although she hoped she would return, she realized the certain danger that this trip implied.

"It's not too late for me to change that though," Avalon said softly. "I don't have to be a statue." When she said it, Avalon realized that she was becoming one already, stone in a way, pushing down all of her feelings to play her part. She could feel her chest wrapped tightly in cloth, her sensibilities buried deep beneath an ever-growing gruff exterior that had been built to hide a secret.

"There is no way to avoid it," Zaria told her. "They make statues of all the kings. It has always been so." Avalon knew her sister had heard what she'd said, but Zaria was avoiding stress and serious conversation. Avalon would try to make this as easy as possible, but she knew Zaria would take it hard.

"I don't feel much like a King," Avalon said, and she was surprised to see Zaria nod. "You agree?"

"Losing father was very difficult," Zaria said, subconsciously moving her hands over the rounded shape of her stomach. "It was almost impossible to see any future when that happened, and yet look at me now." Zaria smiled and Avalon noted the glow that her sister had about her. She was a natural princess, but her beauty while pregnant was undeniable.

Zaria smiled at Avalon. "I don't feel like a mother, but I will be one soon no matter. Life moves ahead without our permission, and time keeps the best secrets."

"Well now, you sound like Myra George," Avalon chuckled.

"Let me spell it out for you then, Avalon. You are the King, no matter how you feel."

"Sit with me," Avalon said, patting the bench that she was sitting on along the outer wall of the King's Hall.

"It's worse than I thought," Zaria said as she moved to take a seat.

"What do you mean?" Avalon asked.

"I know Kensington is keeping something from me." Zaria smiled at Avalon's expression. "He's my husband, Avalon, and I can usually read him pretty easily. Poor Kensington leaves his heart on his sleeve, and he makes it much too easy for me." Zaria giggled and Avalon let her have the moment because the rest of their conversation would not be pleasant.

Zaria's eyebrows rose and she shifted uncomfortably on the bench. Her hands moved to her stomach and then she reached out for Avalon's hand and put it over her belly. Avalon froze as she felt the small and incomprehensible movement that came from under Zaria's gown.

"He or she is a fighter," Zaria said proudly.

Avalon let her hand rest for a while, feeling the small kicks and waiting for more, but they settled down and she eventually pulled her hand away. "I'm so happy for you and Kensington," Avalon said.

Zaria nodded. "Well, out with it."

Avalon took Zaria's hand and looked at the statue of their father one more time. "Zaria, I'm leaving again. I will be gone for at least two months."

"At least two months?" Zaria repeated. "Where are you going?" she asked, but she knew there was only one answer. She knew that her sister trained most days of the week and returned to the castle filthy and drained.

"Things are different now," Avalon said cryptically.

"So both my husband and my own brother keep secrets from me?" Zaria asked.

"It's not Kensington's fault. It was my secret to keep," Avalon said deflecting the question because she did not want to lie to her sister.

"You should know that I often lunch with the wives of the counselors, one on one. They are delighted to invite me to their boroughs and I am delighted to get to know them. We do not gossip, and I would never divulge anything I have overheard, not that I have heard anything because both you and Kensington insist on keeping secrets from me; but Avalon, you can't keep this secret forever.

"Soldiers are gone, you have had men practicing drills for months, and you have told everyone in Fontanasia that there is an enemy on the horizon. You have told everyone but me, that is, and so I get my information from the wives of counselors who ask me questions that I cannot answer. Please, tell me what is happening." Zaria's face showed concern and she squeezed Avalon's hand, but all Avalon could notice was the bulge of Zaria's stomach.

Avalon wanted to tell Zaria about the Anthracites and the Runners and about their Uncle Hawker, but at the same time she wished she never knew about the threat from Cormicks. Whatever Zaria and the ladies in the boroughs were thinking, it was harmless when compared to Hawker leading an army of Runners to slaughter all who would stand in his way. Their imaginations could not come close to knowing what it was like to be trampled by Anthracites or to be eaten alive by everred spiders. Avalon wanted to confide, but she wouldn't change Zaria's entire outlook on life today.

"I have to go, Zaria," Avalon said, pulling her hand away. "It's true, there is an enemy, and I have some unfinished business to make it right so this little Hall prince or princess can live safely." Avalon touched Zaria's stomach lightly and sighed. She was expecting Zaria to get angry with her or to beg her to stay and tell her the whole truth, but when Avalon stood, her sister didn't try to stop her.

"You are going where you were when father died, aren't you?"

"Yes, I am."

"You were gone for weeks. I thought that father's death changed you, but it was that trip, wasn't it?"

Avalon didn't answer, mostly because she didn't want to go backwards anymore.

"So is fate really fate, or is it inevitability?" Zaria asked, and Avalon looked at her introspective sister as an adult for the first time.

"You've been spending too much time with Myra," Avalon said, and they shared a smile.

"Do you have to go?" Zaria asked.

"I have to try," Avalon said. She knew that she had to bring war to Cormicks to keep war from coming to Fontanasia.

"Well, since you won't tell me what you are doing or where you are going, just know that I will be here for the counselors if they need me," Zaria said. "Are you going to at least tell them your plans, Avalon? They won't sit by for months without the King here. Not that I think any of them mean any ill will toward you, but they want you to need them, and you do need them."

Avalon looked at Zaria quizzically, continuing to see her sister with new eyes. "You know, I always thought you were just into your hair and your outfits and your suitors. I never really gave you any credit, but it sounds as though you have thought a lot about this."

"Well, I was into my hair and my dresses," Zaria said with a smile. "But I too have been around father all my life on the sidelines listening. So, when I met Kensington we would discuss Fontanasia, and it really gave me a better understanding. And last time you left, it felt good to have something to focus on, although the counselors don't really need help and I can't say they look to me, but they are polite and they do include me."

"I need someone to keep an eye on them, Zaria. I need you to work with the counselors. Keep Fontanasia on track while I'm gone. Kensington can help."

With those words, Zaria looked down at her clasped hands and cleared her throat, and Avalon could see that her sister had been worried that her husband was leaving too.

"I can't take him from you, Zaria, especially not right now." Avalon pointed at Zaria's stomach. "Kensington isn't happy with me, but he'll get over it."

Zaria nodded and pressed her lips together. Avalon noticed a tear making its way down Zaria's cheek and she was surprised. "You need everyone who you trust with you, Avalon, and that includes Kensington."

"No," Avalon said definitively. "It's just myself and a couple others going this time. Kensington must stay here and help run the city. You won't be able to do this on your own while you wait on the baby, and I need someone I can trust here with you."

"And will you see Taggerty where you are going?" Zaria asked. She watched Avalon for a reaction and her little sister tried to control her expression, but her face flushed red.

Avalon shook her head. "I will see him on my way, but he will not go with me."

"Good luck with that," Zaria chuckled. "He will be harder to tell than Myra."

Avalon cringed. She longed to see Taggerty again, but she was not looking forward to telling him that she would cross over without him. She relished talking to Myra even less.

Chapter 6
King's Councils

Hawker loved being the King of Cormicks. The best part was seeing abject fear in men's eyes. They were all dogs to him, and he treated them as such. He had spent the past few months burning objects and small animals on a whim just to scare the White Robes. Fire was not a toy especially here in Cormicks. The Runners had respect for, or more likely trepidation for, the Anthracites, but Hawker feared nothing.

He had called for the Anthracites several times over the months, and his one frustration was that he could not control them on his own. There was a girl locked up in the castle whose job was to translate the King's bidding to the giant black creatures. She knew how to talk to the Anthracites, but it wasn't really a conversation. When he heard the screeching words, it sounded like a melody of dying animals to Hawker.

Hawker revered the Anthracites and their massive power. He had them come in close to the wall that surrounded the castle and stop, and he would watch in awe as their figures crumbled and reshaped in front of his eyes.

The Runners always scurried away when they heard the Anthracites approaching, and Hawker would laugh at their cowardice.

He reveled in his time as King. His boyhood fantasies played out daily as he barked tasks and men hurried to please their King. The power he commanded over the soldiers and the Anthracites was like a drug, and he bathed in the energy that coursed through his veins when he gave commands.

It was this pleasure that had slowed down his plans to invade Fontanasia. He had guards posted at the elbagrass to make sure no one came through alive, and he wasn't worried that his nephew, Avalon, would bother with an offensive.

Hawker knew there were Guides at the elbagrass in Fontanasia, and by now there must be soldiers to guard the area, but Avalon couldn't even run him through with a sword. His nephew was a coward, and that too made him laugh. Hawker had time to do what he pleased, and in the past months it was ruling on whimsy and dining on power. There was really no rush because Hawker knew that Avalon would never make the first move.

Hawker had only one problem with being King. He was getting bored. There were no books in the castle to be read, and really no intellectual conversation to be had. The White Robes were smart, but they were nothing compared to Julius Creighton or even old man Lincoln in the archives. Hawker considered invading Fontanasia soon if for no other reason than the intellectual property stored there.

On that thought, one of the White Robes entered the throne room. "King Hall," he said, hunching his figure low as he approached.

"Yes, Triangle?" Hawker had taken to calling them by the symbol that was tattooed on their foreheads. He chuckled to himself when he did this because he knew that they hated it, but they would never speak up against him.

"The army is lined up and ready to be inspected, Your Highness."

Triangle bowed and Hawker waited a moment before rising to see his troops. He liked to linger when anyone bowed in front of him. It brought joy to the part of his chest where his heart should have been. Hawker liked to think that his heart was a black rock as dark as the Anthracites.

Some evenings Avalon would meet with Counselor Creighton, but today she had called him to her study just after breakfast. She had planned and practiced long enough, and it was time to get underway.

He still walked slowly and a little hunched over, but Avalon could see that he had changed. When they talked, Avalon couldn't decide if he revered or was afraid of Hawker. She had learned to trust the people closest to her and she was not looking for traitors especially not in Creighton, but sometimes he would get a faraway look in his eyes when they discussed Hawker, and Avalon couldn't help but wonder what the look on his face displayed.

"I'm leaving the morning after next," Avalon said when Creighton took a seat across from her desk. "The Anthracites will not be our enemy much longer." She had tried to sound confident, but Avalon was certain her fear had come through in her tone.

"Is that so?" Creighton asked.

"Everyone believes that Hawker is dead, and I need to make sure that doesn't change," Avalon told him. She felt a pang of regret at the statement. She was starting to hate herself and the deceit that had brought her to this position, and for an instant, Avalon wished she was no longer the King.

Creighton pursed his lips and nodded slowly. "I see regret on your face, King Avalon." Creighton leaned forward and stared at Avalon, and she cleared her throat and looked down at the papers on her desk, not really seeing them. Then she glanced at Creighton who was still studying her.

"I don't like that I have to protect my lie by going to Cormicks. And I don't like telling lies either, but I can't tell the Council the whole truth." Avalon was not just talking about Hawker, and she sighed heavily. "I called you here while the rest of the Council gathers. I am going to leave Zaria in charge again to work with the counselors, and I expect you to lead by example."

"Of course, I like to work with Princess Zaria." Creighton paused, knowing more was coming.

"When Zaria has her baby, you will go to Kensington with any matters." Avalon waited, wondering what kind of reaction this would bring. Creighton smiled wide.

"So, King Avalon, it seems that you now trust four people in Fontanasia. I hope this means you also trust me." Creighton was trying to lighten the mood.

"We'll see," Avalon said with a smile of her own. Then she turned serious.

"I need you to remain quiet in Council today. I don't know what will be asked of me, but I need you to keep your knowledge to yourself. I haven't spoken freely about Cormicks with the other counselors, and I expect they will be shocked to hear what I have to say."

"Of course, King Avalon. A counselor who cannot council, that is what I have always aspired to." He was being sarcastic, and Avalon stood and walked out the door toward the council chamber, not waiting for Creighton's snail's pace to catch up to her.

Avalon strode into the council chamber and as she walked up to the dais, the counselors bowed their heads. Kensington and Gamon remained standing by the door and she nodded at each of them. She had asked them both here because she wanted them to hear her plan. Kensington knew most of it, but Gamon knew none of it. Avalon had small conversations with the counselors over the preceding months, and they each knew about Hawkerness, but only Creighton had an inkling of the full picture.

Avalon sat and immediately put her thumb in the groove on the arm of the chair, rubbing the wood where her forefathers had. This had soothed Avalon before, knowing she was not the first to sit here, and she hoped she was not the last.

Counselor Creighton shuffled into the room and bowed to Avalon, moving slowly to his seat. "I beg your pardon, King Avalon. I'm sorry for the delay."

Avalon pulled her lips into a smile, but there was no happiness behind her eyes.

"Please, be seated. I have called you here to share my plans with you. Each of you know the tasks that I have put to you and your boroughs, and I thank you for your diligence." Avalon met each of the counselor's eyes. They were quiet now, but she expected comments with her coming announcement.

"You have heard of Hawkerness, the city where our people came from. There is an enemy there that I have recently become aware of. You all know this and the steps we have taken to ready our defenses. What I have not told you is that this enemy is very aware of our presence, and they know how to get to Fontanasia."

The chatter started, the counselors not speaking with anyone directly, but airing their surprise that the enemy knew the way here. No one had used the word enemy before now, and Avalon noticed Gamon nodding his head slowly as though he'd just been given the last piece in a puzzle.

"I am going to meet this enemy, to conquer them before they have the ability to conquer us. I leave in two days time."

"This is not possible," Avalon heard in the commotion of counselor's voices, but she sat patiently. Creighton feigned incredulity, and Avalon appreciated his performance. Only Counselor Nelson sat silently, no doubt ready to believe anything after killing the old librarian in Avalon's defense.

"I will take eighty soldiers with me, and there are others waiting for us," Avalon said. She was not going to be too specific because she didn't want to give up information she didn't have to. There was no way to explain the training she had undertaken with the Guides to face the Anthracites, or even how to describe what the charcoal beasts were.

She also didn't want the entire truth revealed to the Council. If the Runners made it here, the truth would be apparent. Avalon realized she was still trying to protect her people's way of life. It was honest, joyful, and without the terrors of war.

"King Avalon, if I may," Counselor Nelson spoke up. Avalon nodded, and he stood, leaning on the stone table. He had never fully recovered from when she had stabbed him, and Avalon felt regret as she watched his knuckles curl up white as his weight pushed forward onto the table. "Eighty men are not enough. You should take two hundred or two thousand if that is what it takes to keep Fontanasia safe."

Avalon nodded. "Thank you, Counselor Nelson. None of us, especially me, want war to come to this city. Our people live peaceful lives. Kensington and Gamon trained them for months to defend this city, and without an apparent enemy, even they have grown bored of the drills."

"Your Highness, they would practice every day if they knew that there was imminent danger," Gamon called out from behind the counselors. Avalon read the concern on his face, and she understood.

"Gamon, you have done a great job with the people of this city. Your efforts are to be commended. If the time comes, I have no doubt they will close off the city quickly and defend our people to the last." Gamon nodded, though Avalon could see the strain in his wiry shoulders, and she knew that he was worried.

Avalon breathed out slowly and evenly, trying to pull the power of kings before her to this moment. "This enemy is real, and they are dangerous, but I don't want our people to lose their peace of mind. Our forefathers have kept us safe, and I expect to continue that tradition."

She took a moment to keep her breath steady as she leaned forward in her chair. "The Guides have helped, and they are willing to continue with that help. It is my hope that this enemy we knew nothing of just a short year ago remains hidden." Although he was on the forefront of her thoughts, Avalon had no intention of mentioning Hawker.

"Perhaps you should take more men with you," Counselor Robert said.

Avalon nodded and sighed. She'd been over this in her mind a thousand times, and she expected the Anthracites to do a bulk of the work. There was no way to explain her plan though. "Can I trust you?" she asked Counselor Robert.

"Of course," he said appalled, and she could hear the offense in his tone.

"I expect this enemy to be defeated in short order," she said confidently. "You have been preparing in your boroughs. Remain vigilant, but do not share my plan with your people. If the time comes, Kensington will rally the city with Gamon. I am trusting each of you to do your part. And while I am gone, you can discuss any business with Princess Zaria," she added quickly.

A couple of the counselors turned their heads to look at Kensington. They had already come to lean on Kensington because Avalon had been mostly unavailable in the last six months while training with the Guides, and she was glad that they were looking to him as a leader in his own right. Avalon did not feel threatened in the least by Kensington, and soon Zaria would be unavailable herself once she gave birth to their baby.

"There must be more we can do," Counselor Jennings said.

All Avalon cared about now was getting to Cormicks to stop Hawker. The Runners were not civil, and she needed to either control them or destroy them. Her blood flared hot as she sat in this room talking to the Council. She was ready for action, and she had no time for politics.

As though he could read her mind, Counselor Robert stood and nodded at Avalon before addressing the Council. "Gentlemen, we can best serve the King by keeping Fontanasia safe as he leads his men into battle." Counselor Robert turned to Avalon and tipped his balding head forward pulling his robe back in a deep bow. "King Avalon, you have any support that you need. Please, don't let us take any more of your time."

"Thank you, you may take your leave," Avalon said. She wished she could let Counselor Robert know just how grateful she was for his interruption.

Counselor Creighton stood next and bowed to Avalon, turning slowly to leave. Counselor Nelson approached Avalon, and she stepped off the dais to meet him.

"King Avalon," Counselor Nelson said. She could see that his already aging face had taken on another decade worth of wrinkles.

Avalon reached out her hand and he took it, turning it to kiss the King's ring, but Avalon put her other hand over his, cradling his hands in a warm grip.

"Counselor Nelson," Avalon said in just over a whisper so no one else could hear, "I owe you my life, and I want to thank you for your support today."

Counselor Nelson tried to smile, but he had become a serious man and only half of his mouth turned up. "King Avalon, you can repay me for your life by saving my life, and the life of everyone in Fontanasia."

Avalon nodded and released his hand. "I intend to."

Counselor Nelson bowed his head forward and Avalon thought she could see tears forming in his eyes as he turned to leave.

Counselor Jennings approached with a tight smile. "King Avalon, I wish you well," he stammered, and she could tell that he was nervous. Avalon nodded curtly although she understood. This was unprecedented in Fontanasia.

Jennings cleared his throat. "My daughter came with me to the castle today, and she is waiting for me, but I wonder if you would like to spend some time with her. You need some distraction before you leave, my King. Perhaps you should take a walk with my daughter." Jennings nodded, but Avalon shook her head.

He was pushing now, but Avalon knew she had encouraged Jennings in the past, and it wasn't his fault. Still, she didn't have the time or patience to deal with this right now. She said the only thing she could think of that would end this conversation.

"I go to war, Counselor Jennings. We can have this conversation when I return. I truly enjoyed sailing on your ship." It wasn't a lie, Avalon had enjoyed the evening, but she inferred to him that she would enjoy sailing with his daughter upon her return from Cormicks so as to give him what he wanted.

Jennings bowed deeply and Avalon noticed him smile before he turned and left the chamber.

Avalon had sat in the King's study for uncountable hours over the last six months trying to find a way around what she was about to do, but she could find no alternative. If she was going to face the Runners, she had to take the offensive. She would have to storm Cormicks quickly and fight fast.

Once through the Window, there would be two full weeks before the elbagrass would allow anyone back through, which meant there could be no retreat. This was an all or nothing plan and there would be no negotiating with the enemy. She knew that the Runners were not civil, and she knew even better that there was no compromising with Hawker. It was kill or be killed.

She felt a chill but she wasn't sure if it was the change in the weather or the thought of Hawker. At least it would be warm enough in Cormicks this time of year that she wouldn't have to worry about freezing overnight like she had on the last trip there.

Avalon folded the thick paper and pulled the ring from her finger. She pulled wax from her desk drawer and held it over the candle letting the hot, red wax drip from the stick. When it dropped on the crease, she pressed her ring into the melted wax. She then wet her pen in ink and wrote Myra George's name on the front.

It had been difficult to write a letter to Zaria, and Avalon was surprised at how much harder it was to say goodbye to Myra. She had been a nanny to Zaria and Avalon, and also the most faithful servant to Avalon's father and mother. They were not of blood relation, and yet Avalon felt a deep tearing in her heart when she thought she might never see Myra again.

As though she had summoned her with her thoughts, there was a knock on the door and Avalon heard Myra's voice calling to her from the other side. She pulled the letters together and dropped them in the desk drawer. The words that she had written on the page were still in her heart, and Avalon had to swallow back her sentiment.

"Please, come in," Avalon called. She stood and tried to smile. Myra opened the door and took two steps inside.

"King Avalon, I didn't mean to disturb your work," she said. Avalon waved her forward, and Myra's usual confident demeanor was subdued.

Myra looked around the room and then sighed. "Do you know I've never been in this room? I imagined it as a lot of different things over the years, and look, it is but an office."

"I didn't know that," Avalon said. She had summoned Myra here because she thought she could control her emotions easier if she was in a space where she thought about the business of Fontanasia.

"Please sit down, Myra," Avalon said, holding her hand out to the chair across from her desk. Myra sat, and Avalon felt wrong with the desk dividing them. She stepped around the desk and took the chair next to Myra.

"I want to tell you something that very few people know, but I owe you the truth." Myra tried to keep her expression neutral, but her mouth turned down in a frown.

"Are Jakon and Davev all right?" she asked hesitantly. Her nephews had both been gone for months.

Avalon allowed a smile. "Yes, your nephews are fine. I'm so sorry, Myra that you were worried. I've been so preoccupied." Myra let out a sigh.

Avalon reached out and took Myra's hand, and Myra's wide eyes flashed a smile. It wasn't the touch from her young charge that had caused Myra's reaction, but the fact that Avalon was reaching out at all. She had cut herself off from everyone since Birch had died and she had become King. Avalon's touch after all this time raised the hair on her skin, and Myra knew that there was something very wrong. She took Avalon's hand in both of hers and found the power within her strong soul to smile at Avalon even though she wanted to cry.

"I'm going away," Avalon muttered. "I expect to return, but it's dangerous. I wanted you to know that..." She had practiced a short speech, but now that the moment had come, Avalon didn't know what to say anymore. "You have been a mother to me," Avalon choked out.

"I am not your mother," Myra told her out of respect for the Queen that she had served.

"But you are the only mother I have ever known," Avalon said. She looked at their hands folded together like a braided loaf of bread. They were family, and Avalon felt the tears leap into her throat at the thought of goodbye. She tried to speak again, but she knew she couldn't without sobbing, so she sat silent.

Myra watched Avalon's mouth open and close a few times before letting go of Avalon's hand. She reached up and ran the back of her finger across Avalon's cheek as she did when Avalon was a baby.

"Babies should never see war. No one should. I'm sorry this is happening." She put her large hand on Avalon's shoulder and they sat in silence for a moment.

"Well, that's that," Myra said in the most positive tone that she could muster. "You will take Jakon and Davev with you, do you understand?"

Avalon nodded.

"Promise me," Myra said. She stood and Avalon stood, too.

"I promise that I will take Jakon and Davev with me," Avalon said in mock defeat. They would not cross over together, but Avalon planned to have them in Cormicks, so it wasn't completely a lie.

Myra pulled Avalon in and hugged her tight, and Avalon took a deep breath and held onto the warmth of the moment. Then she pulled back from Myra and smiled.

"I will see you in a couple of months, Myra."

Myra pulled her hand up to cover her mouth and Avalon could see that tears were not far behind. Myra bowed and croaked, "Your Highness," before backing out of the room. Avalon watched her go and fell apart when the door was closed.

Chapter 7
Steal the Night

As Avalon approached in the gray light of dawn and saw who it was holding the reigns of her horse, she looked away so as to not meet his eye. Avalon knew what Kensington would ask of her, and there was no way Avalon could take Kensington away from Zaria.

"Whatever you are planning, you can't do this alone," Kensington told Avalon. He knew her plans, but he also knew Avalon well enough to realize that she hadn't quite shared everything with him. She had been spending time with the Guides for six months to train, and she would never tell him more than that. He'd tried to follow her a few times, but she'd always found a way to go through the Guide's village and up to the mountain above, disappearing into thin air each time.

"Stand down, Kensington. I have two Guides and eighty more soldiers that I take with me," she said, exasperated with his persistence.

"It's not enough, King Avalon."

"I wanted to take less, and so you see I have conceded to your wishes. And Taggerty has more men at the Window," Avalon said as she pulled herself up and sat in the saddle. "I can't leave the city completely defenseless, and you are the father of my future niece or nephew. You are too important here, Kensington. I order you to stay here and not to endanger yourself so that Zaria will have you in her life."

They stared at each other, the wind blowing over the men as they all mounted their horses. Avalon lowered her voice. "I won't take chances with your life, Kensington. I have a plan. I can do this." Avalon saw the same pained expression on his face that he'd had last night when they'd had the same discussion, although then she had been louder and more heated in her reply.

In her heart, Avalon understood what he wanted, but it was impossible. "I am your King, and you will obey my orders." She sounded stronger than she felt, and she was glad when Kensington finally bowed and backed away from her horse.

Avalon rubbed her pocket to feel for Jackie, and when she was satisfied that he was safely tucked inside, she led the soldiers down the Fingers. It was quiet this early in the morning, and even though the men had spent the night in the dorms at the castle, there were some families lining the streets.

Avalon looked at the people as the horse's steps echoed off the brick walls. Some waved to a loved one before bowing to Avalon. She recognized some of the families from when she had visited when their husbands and fathers hadn't returned at first. Avalon was going to see some of those men now, the ones who had been rotated back to the Window on duty, and she wished she could tell these people that everything would be all right, but she couldn't guarantee the words, so she would not utter them.

The faces of the people were both proud and somber. There was an untold danger these men were marching toward. Eighty men were a lot to be leaving at the same time, and with some of the guard already at the Window, Avalon was leaving the city with little protection, but it could not be helped.

The soldiers were wide-eyed and silent as their horses carried them to the open field. This group of men had not left Fontanasia for more than a few days before, and they were curious and alert. The men who had returned spoke of nothing, as though they had never left, but it wasn't like their minds had erased the time. Their faces betrayed their secret by admitting a far-off look in their eyes, or an almost imperceptible clenching of the jaw when they shared knowing looks with each other. These soldiers had returned more serious than ever about protecting the King and Fontanasia, and the men who left today wondered what had prompted their determination.

When they closed on the outer wall, Chylyn was waiting there with Nugget, Sonrah and Cincin. These were the girls Avalon had been training with for the last six months, and although Chylyn hadn't discussed bringing them with Avalon, she wasn't surprised to see them.

Nugget sat as tall on horseback as her little body would allow, and she appraised the soldiers with one eyebrow raised, as though the need of their skills on this trip was questionable. Out of habit, Nugget slid her hand back to her waist and touched the short staffs that she used as weapons.

Avalon looked back and saw the surprised faces of the soldiers who were mostly focused on the beautiful Sonrah. She was tall with flowing red hair and silky tan skin, and her face was striking upon first sight, her yellow green eyes vibrant even from a distance. Sonrah sat in the saddle behind Cincin, her grace and beauty apparent even in stillness, and Avalon felt bad for Cincin at that moment.

Cincin was short and heftier like Avalon looked in her layers of clothing, and although she was pretty in her own right, even Zaria's beauty might seem lesser next to Sonrah. Avalon smiled, wondering what the soldiers would think if they could hear the deep barking sounds that emanated from Sonrah when she was producing Anthracite commands.

Avalon nodded at Chylyn who turned to lead the group through the hidden passage in the wall. She noticed the large pack that Chylyn had strapped to his horse and wondered what weapons the Guide might have inside. It wasn't like him to carry a large pack on these treks, and Avalon was curious.

Avalon looked for the opening in the wall as Nugget turned her horse to fall in just behind Chylyn. Avalon had been here once with Kensington a few months ago so he could show her how to find the opening, but Avalon hadn't returned since that day and she was out of practice. She looked off into the distance to find the clump of trees that would show where to rest her eyes on the wall, but she couldn't find it. She wondered if Nugget knew where the break was, but as hard as Avalon looked, she still didn't see it until they were upon the ten-foot gap that led through to the plains outside.

They rode at a slow trot and reached the edge of the forest in two hours time. Avalon had no speech prepared for the men this time. They simply rested for a bit and then the soldiers followed Avalon into the woods. Some of the soldiers thought the place was haunted, but there were no whispers between them as the darkness of the tree cover overtook them.

This was Avalon's third trip to the elbagrass and it was much more familiar to her, but she didn't spend her time looking for each hidden marker that showed the way. She simply followed Chylyn and Nugget while practicing the Anthracite song over and over in her head. Avalon was still trying to visualize her meeting with the Anthracites. The guttural sounds were very hard to make much less remember under pressure.

She had come far with her practice in the last six months with both the commands and her fighting. Nugget and Cincin had shown Avalon a style of fighting that she had never seen before. She was used to the sword fighting and hand-to-hand combat that she had learned from Gamon, but the Guides were light on their feet and they dodged attacks like a dance, striking back easily. It had infuriated Avalon for the first month because she had been training over half of her life, and they bested her almost every spar, but she had learned to adapt her typical fighting style to be able to strike Cincin back at least a few times a day. Nugget was a little harder to catch with her guard down, but Avalon did land the occasional blow.

Avalon knew that she had one advantage over Nugget. She had seen the Anthracites with her own eyes and felt the ground shake with each step. She knew what she was getting herself into and wondered if Nugget or the others would choke when the black rock beasts ripped from the ground and stomped toward them.

When they stopped to take a break, Avalon was again afforded the privacy that a King deserved, and she wondered how Nugget and the others were getting along, but she didn't befriend the female Guides on this trip. They had grown into a sort of team, but Avalon was King, and she needed to project her image as their leader more than ever. Avalon could see that Chylyn was prepping Nugget, and he would make sure the girls had the privacy they needed among the young soldiers.

At each marker, Avalon could hear Chylyn telling the girls what to look for, and when she was paying attention, Avalon found some of the markers herself this trip. She had been studying the way and was amazed at the small telltale signs that they were on a path. The boulder and ravine were the obvious markers, but the tree in the shape of a long bird and the smaller white rock shaped like the moon were much harder to spot. She walked through the wood letting her mind wander, and playing out the past and future in her head. It took a level of concentration that Avalon didn't have to spot the smaller signs. She didn't have the discipline that the Guides seemed to have to keep their minds in the very present. She thought that might be how they spotted things sooner than anyone else.

The walk was tiring but adrenaline kept everyone pushing on. They camped one night in the forest and reached the ravine late the next day. Myra's nephew, Davev, had been stationed here at the ravine, and as soon as the King arrived, he requested that Avalon take him with her to the Window. She agreed since she already intended to take him with her to Cormicks. He had asked the question with his head bowed to King Avalon, but his eyes were glued on Sonrah, and Avalon wondered if the magnificent beauty of this young woman could entrance the Runners and tip the battle in their favor.

Avalon was impressed with the changes Davev had made at the ravine. There was a small camp inside the tree line and a lookout platform above it to better see the other side of the ravine. There was also a small obstacle course Davev had designed to keep his men sharp and at the ready.

The soldiers would spend the night near the giant nets that Taggerty had built. The ropes were still in place to get the men across the expanse easily. There was an axe stationed at each column that held the rope webbing for easy destruction in case the enemy made it to the other side.

Avalon told Davev that he was a leader of men and that Walthan would have been as impressed as she was at the preparations he had taken upon himself to make. She told him to choose his replacement from the men she had brought with and told him to leave one man in charge of the ravine who was worthy of the station. Davev bowed and left Avalon to make his preparations.

At sunset, Avalon approached Nugget and Cincin who were standing at the edge of the ravine under the rope netting. They had been standing there for a long time, Nugget occasionally jumping up and swinging from the rope.

Avalon gazed back to where the ropes were tied off to the tall trees, and she thought of Taggerty. She had tried to keep him from her thoughts these last months, but every time she looked at the moon or the star she was named after, she wondered if he was looking too. And here under his rope structure, she wondered which ropes he had tied himself. She would have reached out to touch the rope if Nugget and Cincin weren't watching her.

"It is a great structure, is it not?" Avalon asked.

"It is a paltry structure compared to the castle at Fontanasia," Nugget replied, dropping from the rope.

"I think it is," Cincin said in a whisper. She was the most quiet of the three girls, but when it came time to calling for Anthracites, Avalon knew that she would be loud enough.

"It is Taggerty's doing," Avalon said, her eyes trained on Nugget. Avalon hadn't been able to find out the connection between Taggerty and the small girl, but she could see that in the times that Chylyn had mentioned Taggerty, Nugget always changed her demeanor and became more attentive, showing a level of deference.

Here Nugget looked over the rope structure again and then said, "Upon further inspection, I agree with Cincin. It is a great structure."

Avalon smiled at Nugget's change of heart. "Well, now that we are all in agreement, you should get some rest. Tomorrow won't be any easier." Nugget took the comment as a challenge, and she jumped up, swung onto the rope netting like a monkey, and jumped sideways like a soaring bird. She looked as though she would go face first off the edge, but Avalon and Cincin didn't move to help her. They both knew Nugget's grace of movement, and just when it looked too late, Nugget grabbed the bottom of the rope and somersaulted to her feet.

Avalon turned to move back to the camp before the dark of night set fully upon them. "Will you camp with us tonight?" Avalon asked Cincin. The girls and Chylyn had moved away from the group of soldiers and into the woods, and Avalon assumed it was to keep their privacy.

"No," Cincin said.

"It is stupid to sit by a fire in the dark. When the enemy comes, all you will see is the light in your eyes as they slaughter you," Nugget said to Avalon. She could hear the challenge in Nugget's voice. The small Guide had something to prove and Avalon ignored anything that sounded like a challenge from Nugget because Avalon was the King and she didn't compete with anyone.

Avalon had told herself that many times in the last six months as she cleaned her wounds and stretched her muscles after their training together, and each day Avalon would return with competition on her mind.

Avalon did return to the campfire for a moment just to prove to Nugget that she did as she preferred. Avalon listened to the soldiers talking about the red dirt on the ground. She had seen the change from black to red three times, and she had come to expect it. She hadn't thought of preparing the men for the changes, and she would make sure in the morning that Davev would warn them about the sand eels before the men crossed the bottom of the ravine.

Avalon thought that the soldiers might be a bit out of sorts with the King relaxing among them, so she took to her small tent as soon as Cincin and Nugget were out of sight. Her body was tired and her mind was already exhausted, and they hadn't even reached the elbagrass yet, but she would see it tomorrow night. She put Jackie on the small table so he could eat a grape and then she climbed onto her cot and fell asleep, wondering if she would dream.

At daybreak, Avalon watched Davev and ten soldiers climb to the bottom of the ravine and begin their run across. Next, Chylyn instructed the three girls in their language, and after he sent his bulky pack down the rope line, they followed him down the net.

Sonrah wasn't a fighter but she was graceful, and she handled herself on the netting with the soldiers watching and ready to assist. Avalon smiled as Sonrah pulled on a pair of gloves to protect her soft hands from the rough rope. She swung herself onto the net gracefully in her light gown, and began to climb down after Chylyn. Cincin followed suit, but Nugget waited at the top until they were almost all the way at the bottom. Avalon thought that she was waiting to make sure there wasn't too much weight on the net at one time, but she should have known better of the little show-off.

When the rest were down the net and Chylyn had directed them to begin their run across the bottom of the ravine, Nugget swung lightly onto the net and began to somersault down face first. Some of the soldiers looked concerned, and anyone else might have broken their neck, but Nugget rolled on her back and bounced to her feet over and over all the way to the bottom, catching the last rope with her hand and flipping gracefully to the ground. She turned to Avalon and gave a salute before starting her trek across the ravine.

As she followed Nugget down the rope, Avalon wondered what hidden strength the small girl possessed. Nugget was either daring or insane. When Avalon was at the bottom, she turned her attention to the soft sand ground and took to the rocks, making sure to avoid stepping in the dirt. She'd made that mistake before and had paid for it when the sand eels had paralyzed and tried to devour her.

Davev had been waiting at the bottom and he walked just behind Avalon. She got used to his, short steps following in sync with hers. The sound allowed her to meditate, and although she should have been on the lookout for the sand eels, her attention kept turning to the Anthracites and Taggerty. She wasn't sure which scared her more. She could face the Anthracites; they were heartless rocks that, while terrifying, were an object to be conquered. Taggerty affected Avalon on so many levels that she found herself shaking her head and mumbling her thoughts aloud.

They made the other side of the ravine and climbed the net, Avalon glad for her months of training with the Guides, which made the climb easier. At the top, Avalon was preoccupied with her own thoughts and it took her some time to realize that Davev's eyes were trained on the girls.

"You may go ahead. It would be good for one of my soldiers to learn the way. Walthan did."

"I will not leave my King's side," Davev replied.

"Nothing will happen to me here, Davev. Not with eighty soldiers at the ready."

He looked toward the edge of the ravine where the men were collecting and nodded his head.

"Do I have to order you?" Avalon asked.

"Thank you, King Avalon," Davev said, and he walked over to Sonrah who was sitting peacefully on her own.

A while later, as Chylyn moved out, Avalon ran the plan through her mind over and over. In some scenarios, the Anthracites understood her commands, and other times she and her party of Guides were smashed under the giants' black feet.

As they came to the section of the woods where the tree trunks grew larger in girth and crowded all around them,

Avalon knew that they were within reach of the elbagrass. Now there was only the anticipation of seeing Taggerty.

For six months, she had tried to forget, but she remembered his green eyes. She remembered the beautiful sunset they had shared on the boat, and she shook her head. She remembered touching the black mark of the Guides on his wrist and chills ran up her spine.

She remembered her jealousy over Zaria and all of her angst and love returned in a flush of red on her face, and she unconsciously touched her fingers to her lips. The last time she had seen Taggerty he had kissed her.

Chylyn stopped and looked to his left, staring for a long time. Avalon saw Nugget on her tippy-toes behind Chylyn trying to notice what the Guide was looking for, but it was still daylight and there was nothing to see. The blue glow of the elbagrass would not come for at least two more hours.

Avalon waited for Chylyn to look at her so she could command her men to take a break, but she was surprised when instead he lifted his arm in a forward wave and moved to his left. Avalon felt panic run through her, and Jackie squirmed in her pocket. They would reach the elbagrass today and everyone would know. In the light of day, it would be impossible for Avalon to hide the fact that she was in love with Taggerty.

Avalon slowed her pace as the trees thinned out. She didn't see the field of high grass yet, but she could hear the reeds rustling together in the wind and she knew they were close. Davev flirted with Sonrah at the ravine, but shortly after the group had started out, he'd become Avalon's shadow again, and she could hear Davev's steps behind her.

"Davev," Avalon said in a whisper.

"Yes, King Avalon," Davev answered, his hand on the hilt of his sword and his head swiveling to check the trees for danger.

"Go ahead with Chylyn," Avalon said. She was slowing her pace, aching to see Taggerty but dreading it now that the moment presented itself.

"Yes, Your Highness," Davev said, and in two quick steps he was ahead of her. Avalon slowed her pace even more and Sonrah and Cincin moved to her right and passed, but the rest of the men would not step in front of their King without an order, so there was nothing for Avalon to do but follow the Guides and Davev into the clearing.

Avalon looked at the field of tall, green reeds of grass that rose over her head. The last time she was here, she'd burned the field to black ash. It was a relief to see the poisonous stalks swaying in the breeze.

There was a loud whistle from the trees above her head, and Avalon assumed it was the all clear because some soldiers who had been tracking them came out of hiding and melted in with the group to say hello to their brothers-in-arms. Avalon watched the exchange, and it was easy to tell who had been here and who had just arrived. The clean-shaven men she had brought with her looked well-dressed next to the beard-laden longhaired men whose clothes were dusty and worn.

"No one touches the field of grass!" a voice boomed, and Jakon approached from the left. Avalon smiled when she saw the tall soldier scratch his sandy, blond beard. He had managed to keep his hair short, and Avalon could tell by the uneven cuts that he must have been cutting it himself with his knife.

Jakon bowed to Avalon from a distance and Avalon nodded. When the other men noticed their King was among them, the chatter ceased and they all bowed.

"Carry on," she ordered loud enough so they all could hear.

Davev approached Jakon and the two men looked each other over. Davev was a bit scruffy himself having been at the ravine all of these months, but Avalon realized then that his hair was still cut neatly and his clothes were as clean as hers. The shorter soldier looked as clean as the men from Fontanasia. He'd had access to more rainwater, Avalon surmised.

"So, I see that I'm still more handsome than you," Davev said with some bravado.

"And I see you are still doing less work than me," Jakon replied with a slap on his cousin's back. The giant hand would have knocked the wind from any other, but if Davev felt pain, he would never let on.

"Working smarter than you," Davev shot back, and the men clasped arms in greeting.

They were both strong but their physiques were different. Davev was much shorter but built like a rock and Jakon was massive like Walthan, and yet they were both of the George family. Avalon thought how different she was from her own sister, and her thoughts moved again to Taggerty.

Avalon realized that outwardly they might all look different, but inwardly they all longed for connection. Zaria had made her connection with Kensington, but it looked as though Avalon was hopeless in hers.

Jakon looked over Davev at the men who had come out of the forest with him. His eyes rested on Sonrah who hung back in the trees with Nugget and Cincin. Avalon half-expected him to comment on her presence, but to his credit Jakon's eyes lingered only for a moment. His face turned pink, and he cleared his throat.

"It's still three hours until dusk. Did you tell them what to expect?" he asked his cousin.

Davev shrugged and looked back toward Avalon because he didn't know the answer. Avalon realized that she had been so preoccupied that she hadn't prepared these men for even the sight of the elbagrass. She shook her head and held out her hand gesturing that Jakon and Davev could ready the men.

"Well, they saw the dirt turn red but they didn't see any sand eels," Davev said.

Jakon nodded with his lips pursed as he looked at Avalon, and she knew that they were both remembering the men who had been affected by the sand eels on the last trip. She wondered if he was remembering the way the keeley dust in her pouch had killed the creatures, but he looked away when he noticed the King looking at him.

"Men!" Davev called. "Gather here," he commanded as he pointed back toward the edge of the woods, no doubt wanting to keep the men away from the poisonous elbagrass until he could give them their orders. Jakon and Davev moved off with the men who all kept their eyes on the edge of the trees where the three girls stood. Avalon remained standing between the woods and the field of grass when a voice she longed to hear cut through the sounds of the forest.

"Well, you're a sight for sore eyes," Avalon heard Taggerty's voice, and she turned quickly. He was talking to his Uncle Chylyn as he appeared from the side of the field, and Avalon was relieved to see him.

Taggerty moved around the clearing and clasped arms with Chylyn, the men sharing a smile. At the sound of his voice, Jackie began to scramble around Avalon's pocket, and she covered the cloth with her hand so none of the soldiers would see.

Avalon didn't take her eyes off of Taggerty. She tried to think of what a king would do and tried to stop herself from reacting to his presence, but she couldn't control the blush that ran across her face and the sweat that collected on her forehead. The three girls came forward out of the trees and Avalon swallowed hard, but since everyone's attention was turned to the men, she had a moment to recover. She squared up her shoulders and prepared for Taggerty's bow.

Taggerty's dark, curly hair was a little longer now, and Avalon liked the way it contrasted with his green eyes. He looked stronger, probably from working non-stop, and Avalon thought about reaching out to touch the muscles that were tight under his shirt, but she restrained the impulse.

When Taggerty looked over Chylyn's shoulder at her, Avalon held her breath. She saw genuine surprise on Taggerty's face and then a moment of pleasure melted his features, and he smiled at her before the wrinkle of worry took to his forehead. She grinned like a fool, and when she felt the flush of red moving to her cheeks again, she turned her head toward the elbagrass. She worried that Nugget, Cincin, and Sonrah would be able to see on her face the love that she was feeling in her heart.

Taggerty cleared his throat and Avalon looked over to see him bowing low. After a moment he stood, but this time he kept his eyes on the ground. He always knew the thing to do so that she would not be embarrassed as King, and Avalon wondered if he would look into her eyes ever again.

"You look well," was all Avalon could say.

Taggerty's eyebrows rose at the compliment and he stood up straight in his worn uniform, impressed with himself. He still didn't look in her eyes, though.

"We have done a lot of work here. We have made more towers and connected some of them with small bridges." Taggerty raised his hands to the trees and Avalon's eyes followed, noticing small rope bridges connecting several trees around them. She couldn't see the platforms hidden in the branches and thick canopy of leaves, but she knew they were there.

"Very good," Avalon said.

Taggerty lowered his gaze and his face turned dark when he finally noticed the three Guides who had come with her. Anger flashed across his face, and he looked to Chylyn for an answer.

Avalon was grateful that they weren't alone right now. Her disagreement with Kensington was child's play compared to the coming conversation she would have with Taggerty. She had seen him frustrated in the past, but the heat rising to his face in this moment was palpable.

"Why are they here?" Taggerty asked Chylyn. The girls stepped in closer to stand by Chylyn.

"I believe you know Sonrah," Chylyn said, and Taggerty's curt smile toward the tall beauty made Avalon bristle with jealousy. Of course he knew the beautiful Guide temptress who could sing the song of the Anthracites. Sonrah had done nothing but cultivate her natural beauty, and Avalon knew that her jealousy wasn't really fair, but she didn't care.

"This is Cincin and Nugget," Chylyn continued. Cincin waved her hand shyly, but Nugget lowered herself in a grand bow to Taggerty and then stood back up as tall as her petite body would allow.

Avalon assumed that Taggerty knew all of the Guides personally, but they were a large village and he hadn't grown up there, so she had been wrong to assume. He had been born a Guide but hadn't lived among them. His skin was white at birth, so he was given to a family in Fontanasia and raised in the city to become one of the King's Guard. He was an ambassador of sorts between the King and the Guides, and Avalon had assumed that he knew all of their secrets. She wondered if he knew what these girls had practiced for years.

"Sonrah is old enough to understand her choice," Taggerty said to Chylyn, "but you should not have brought these young girls here." He was perturbed by their presence, and Avalon heard Nugget huff in protest. She had looked up to his position and she wanted to impress him, but he had shunned her at their first meeting. Avalon knew the feeling. Taggerty had done the same thing to her when they had first met.

"Is my tent still here?" Avalon snapped. She was nervous, but she would not allow Taggerty to distract her plans.

"This way," Taggerty said as he turned and led them to his tent. It had been Avalon's tent on her last trip to the elbagrass, and she was astonished to see the white fabric on the outside had turned yellow and brown. As they drew closer, she could see that the change had been intentional, no doubt dirt rubbed on to stain the fabric so it blended in better with the surroundings.

Taggerty pulled the flap aside so Avalon could enter first. Chylyn followed the three girls inside and then Taggerty entered the tent letting the flap close behind him.

The tent felt small with the six of them in a circle around the table. There was silence at first as they all took in the space. A cot was pushed up against the tent on one side, a table sat in the middle, and there was now a side table with a small map of Cormicks scratched into animal hide. Avalon was surprised to see the detail in the map, and she could see that Taggerty had spent his time fortifying his position and also planning a battle scenario.

"I apologize that we didn't get this space ready, Your Highness, but I wasn't aware of your visit. The men have been rotating nights on the cot so we will need time to clean it up." Avalon watched as Taggerty's eyes moved between her and Chylyn. He'd really had no idea that she was coming. Avalon had instructed Kensington to keep the secret, but the two were like brothers and she'd assumed that Kensington would have warned Taggerty of her plans. Her brother-in-law was apparently loyal to a fault, and Avalon felt a smile cross her face.

Jackie scrambled around in her pocket and she unsnapped the flap and clucked her tongue twice. Jackie's red head pushed the flap of the pocket up as he peered around the space, and then he croaked at Taggerty. His laugh broke the tension as the tiny lizard scrambled around

Avalon's coat. Avalon wanted nothing more than to touch Taggerty, but she could not allow herself to go there in this small space with the Guides present, so she held her hand out and touched the small table that separated them, and Jackie scrambled down her arm and across the table.

Taggerty reached out to pick Jackie up, but the lizard was too excited to wait and he jumped onto the back of Taggerty's sleeve and ran up his arm. The lizard ran two laps around Taggerty's shoulders before getting trapped in his mane of curly black hair. Everyone in the tent laughed as Taggerty grabbed at his head until the lizard squealed and was released from the tangle of hair, eventually settling on Taggerty's arm.

"May I?" Nugget asked Taggerty, stepping around Avalon. She held her hand out and Taggerty nodded, looking over the girl into Avalon's eyes. She could see that the jovial energy Jackie had brought to the tent was already gone, and Avalon needed to tell Taggerty her intentions.

"Here," Taggerty said as he let Jackie cross the distance between their hands. Nugget held her staff parallel to the ground, and Jackie ran a straight line up to the tip, and then circled the staff on the way back down. Taggerty was impressed that the lizard didn't fall off when he was upside-down on the staff.

"So, you two know each other well?" Taggerty asked.

"Yes," Nugget said, happy to have his attention. "Jackie and I are old friends now," the girl said. She bowed to Taggerty again and this time he could not dismiss the gesture. "I am Kaelan of the Winds," she said, embellishing her accent on the name that she had been given at birth.

"Everyone calls her Nugget," Chylyn said, shaking his head. Nugget turned to Chylyn with clenched teeth, and he smiled. "Don't let the nickname fool you though, Taggerty. She is a fierce warrior."

"And why has this fierce warrior come to the Window with Sonrah Stone Singer?" Taggerty asked, looking at

Sonrah. His eyebrows rose, and Avalon knew then that Taggerty might not have met Cincin and Nugget before, but he was well aware of Sonrah's gift. Avalon had not known that Sonrah's given name was Stone Singer, but it made sense, although the Anthracites were hardly made of mere stones.

"You will ready your men," Avalon said. "You will meet me in two dawns, and we will conquer the Runners at Cormicks." Avalon stood resolutely, staring at Taggerty with a hard heart so that she could remain on task. He was always professional in the presence of others, but Avalon almost expected an outburst.

Taggerty didn't answer Avalon directly. He bowed his head as if to concede, but then he turned to his uncle Chylyn and opened his palm toward the girls.

"King Avalon, would you allow these three to get something to eat?" Chylyn asked, gesturing to the girls.

Avalon nodded, her teeth still clenched. She and Taggerty stared at each other as the girls left the tent, and Avalon wasn't worried about falling to pieces in front of him anymore. When it came to strategy, they seemed to always butt heads, and she was dug in for the coming argument.

When the flap closed behind them, Chylyn turned back to Taggerty. "Do not worry. We have counseled the King, and he will be fine."

Taggerty clasped his fists but he kept his voice in check. "You counseled him?" He was furious, and Chylyn simply pointed toward the door and started to walk.

"Excuse me for a moment, Your Highness," Taggerty said with a quick bow as he followed his uncle out of the tent. They walked fifteen feet and were alone in the trees before Taggerty whispered through clenched teeth. "Did you just kill the King of Fontanasia?"

The Guide looked at Taggerty sternly, but Taggerty didn't look away.

"You are a man now, Taggerty, and I am proud of you. But this is not just about the King. King Avalon is one person, and we are many, and the city of Fontanasia is even more. When King Avalon came to us for help, he presented a strong argument, and we decided to do what we always do. We helped the King to the best of our ability."

"And what argument was so compelling that you are willing to send the King off to die alone?"

Chylyn tipped his head back, his long, black hair falling loosely off his shoulders. He answered with a question of his own. "You do not have faith in your King?"

Taggerty bit his lip and crossed his arms, letting out a long breath before leaning against a tree. There was no way to explain to his uncle what he felt for the King. This was the first time he had seen Avalon in over six months, and in all the time he spent trying to forget her, she had been in his every thought.

He could find no future with Avalon, and he had allowed himself to consider other potential opportunities. He could live in Fontanasia, married to another girl, or stay here forever in this forest next to the elbagrass with the few memories they shared. Taggerty had chosen the elbagrass. He was in love with Avalon the girl and that meant that he was in love with the King. There was no way to explain his resistance without giving up Avalon's secret, and he couldn't do that, even to a trustworthy uncle like Chylyn. It was not his secret to tell.

Taggerty breathed deep breaths and tried to focus on getting answers instead of arguing. "I have put all of my faith in the King."

His uncle took a step closer to Taggerty and waited for Taggerty to look straight at him before he continued. "We have been watching the King, and he has been watching us," he said cryptically. "He came to us and told us that we don't want a war, and he's right. We live in peace, and we will do what we can to maintain that peace."

"We all want peace," Taggerty said.

"Then we must take it," his uncle answered back. "We must fight the war in Cormicks to gain the peace in Fontanasia. That is what you have wanted this entire time, for us to go and conquer the Runners. Why do you argue against your own plan of action?"

"We should go fight, but the soldiers should go, not the King," Taggerty answered. He shook his head at the impossibility of losing Avalon forever. Taggerty could accept a life of solitude if he knew that Avalon was alive in the world somewhere.

"Ah, but it is the King's plan that gives us a good chance of winning."

Taggerty eyed his uncle who was smiling and waited for him to share the secret.

"King Avalon plans to steal the Anthracites."

Chapter 8
Blue Dusk

"Steal the Anthracites?" Taggerty asked his uncle.

"You saw Sonrah. What other purpose could she have here?" Chylyn answered Taggerty with a question of his own and gave Taggerty a moment to work it out. Taggerty could see that his uncle respected Avalon, but he still didn't like where this was headed.

"This King is brave, and I think this plan will work."

Taggerty scratched his forehead and looked around the woods for a moment. "And you have helped King Avalon form a plan where he takes Sonrah to Cormicks to steal the Anthracites? That's not daring. It's insanity," Taggerty said, but his tone was light because he actually liked the audacity of the idea. It was something he would do, and it would be so much better to raid Cormicks with the Anthracites on his side, or at the very least out of the way.

"Taggerty, we are here to guide our King. He made this plan, and it is the right decision for the people of Fontanasia, so we will help as we can." Chylyn put his hand on Taggerty's shoulder. "You have kept your King waiting long enough."

Taggerty nodded and they walked back to the tent. He took a deep breath. "King Avalon," Taggerty called from outside the tent.

"Enter," Avalon said.

Chylyn pulled the tent flap back and Taggerty entered first. Chylyn bowed his head to Avalon. "With your permission, Your Highness, I will make the preparations." Avalon nodded, and Chylyn ducked back out of the tent leaving Avalon and Taggerty alone. They stared at each other for a long time before Taggerty cleared his throat and broke the spell.

"Chylyn tells me that you intend to steal the Anthracites."

Avalon smiled at the expression. "That is my plan. We will lead them away first to make sure that we can work with them, and then you will meet us in two days to storm Cormicks and end this indecision forever." Avalon was talking about her Uncle Hawker and the Runners, but her words hung in the air. Taggerty took three steps toward Avalon and reached out his hand to take hers but then stopped, letting his hand fall back to his side again.

Avalon held her breath and bit the inside of her lip. She wanted Taggerty to take her hand in his, but she needed to stay focused on their mission and couldn't be distracted by her emotions.

"We can split the contingency of soldiers in half," Taggerty said, but Avalon shook her head.

"I will go with Sonrah, Nugget, Cincin, and Chylyn alone."

"You will endanger all of them at once?" he said and then regretted it.

"Believe me, I don't like it anymore than you do. We have trained together for six months, Taggerty. And Nugget is truly fierce. She will have my back."

"You will take some of the men with you," Taggerty said and then lowered his voice. "Please, Avalon."

She shook her head. "I've been working with the girls since you left, so there are four of us now who can speak to the Anthracites. Once we call them, we won't need soldiers to protect us."

"You don't know that. None of them, not even Sonrah, has ever been in front of an Anthracite. It may not be the language that they speak anymore, Avalon. What if you don't know the right words?"

Avalon found herself smiling, and she realized that she liked hearing her name on Taggerty's lips. It was informal and right, and she wanted to hear him say it again.

"That language has been passed down for generations," Avalon defended her position. "Have you ever known the Guides to not be utterly precise, Taggerty? It is the language, and we will win the Anthracites over." She reached out to touch his arm and felt the solid muscle ripple beneath his clothes. She wanted to trace her fingers up along his tattoo and through his long hair. She wanted his arms to wrap around her and pull her close as he had when they had kissed.

As though he could read her mind, Taggerty took one step closer and pulled her to him. Avalon shook her head and looked at the ground, and Taggerty slowly released her from his embrace. Taggerty lingered, drawing in Avalon's scent before pulling back.

"We could be caught," Avalon croaked.

She could have cried right then and there, but she shook off the impulse. All that mattered now was her people and the task at hand, and she couldn't have fresh sorrow clouding her judgment.

"Show me the work you have done in these months," Avalon said, turning away from Taggerty and scooping Jackie off the table. She rubbed her thumb over Jackie's head a few times to comfort herself before placing him in her pocket.

"Yes, Your Highness," Taggerty said formally. He moved to the tent flap and opened it, clicking his heels together and bowing at the waist before holding one hand out into the late afternoon.

They walked along the empty space between the elbagrass and the forest. Taggerty pointed out the lookouts on the tree platforms and some of the small bridges that linked the platforms together.

"It's your verticks idea come to fruition," Taggerty told her as he nodded to some of the soldiers who manned the platforms. They bowed their heads to Avalon for a moment before training their gaze over the field of tall grass again.

"It's tedious work," Taggerty said. "Your mind gets lost looking over that field of grass. Sometimes the wind makes it wave back and forth and it lulls you into a trance, but the men have not lost an ounce of intensity since they arrived. Some of these men are in their second rotation so they were here when the enemy came the night we burned the grass. The other men have heard the story, and they are all of one mind."

"To protect Fontanasia," Avalon said.

Taggerty nodded. "Will you hear my counsel?" Taggerty asked Avalon. He was walking a half step behind and on her left side, and his hands were behind his back, but he leaned his head forward a bit so that they were almost even. Avalon raised her eyebrows and looked at Taggerty, and they both had to suppress a smile.

"Don't take Nugget and Cincin with you. They are too young."

Avalon laughed at that comment, but not for the reason Taggerty might have thought. "Maybe you didn't notice, but young Nugget envies you, and she wants nothing more than to please you."

"Really?" Taggerty asked. "She told you that?"

"I saw it on her face when she saw you, Taggerty. I couldn't figure her out when we were training all of these months, but she looks at you the way most of Fontanasia looked at Walthan." Avalon nodded at Taggerty. "It's true. She's tiny but fierce, and we would be lucky to have her fight with us."

"I'll have to take your word for it," Taggerty said with new interest. "But I ask you again, please consider taking some of the soldiers with you for protection."

Avalon frowned this time, a sobering reaction to her future fears. "If we are going to poke at the Anthracites, it is best that I take less people with me."

"I hadn't thought of that," Taggerty admitted. They walked on and a few more lookouts waved to them and bowed when they saw the King. "Can you at least take Jakon with you, to watch your back?" Taggerty asked.

"He'll slow me down," Avalon protested.

"He is a warrior, Avalon. You will slow him down," Taggerty said wryly.

"He's not going to understand what he sees, and I don't have time to explain." Avalon wasn't completely against the idea, but she wanted to have as few people as possible standing next to her when she woke the rock giants.

"He can handle himself," Taggerty pressed.

Avalon remembered crossing the ravine with Jakon and the other men, and she realized that he had kept a cool head in light of what the sand eels were doing to two of the other soldiers.

"Fine," she conceded. "But please, spend five minutes preparing him for what he is going to see. Not that there is any way to really prepare your mind, but warn him for me."

"I will," Taggerty agreed. "We should turn back. There are some platforms further up, but they are more spread out in this direction and I want to make sure you stay protected."

Avalon nodded, but she didn't turn around right away. She liked the thought of being alone with Taggerty without any eyes upon them.

"We're alone?" Avalon asked, and her self-control faltered.

"We are," Taggerty answered, taking long looks in each direction and seeing no one.

Instead of turning around to head back, Avalon stepped into the cover of the woods and beckoned Taggerty to follow.

Avalon walked far enough into the woods to know they couldn't be seen from the clearing. She put Jackie down on the forest floor to let him investigate the leaves.

Taggerty's green eyes bore into hers. Avalon waited for him to speak, but he just stood in front of her, staring into her eyes.

"We should get back," she said, but she didn't turn to leave. When they were in the tent, anyone might have come upon them. Avalon felt a peaceful relief knowing they were truly alone here.

They stood there in the woods looking at each other, the breeze rustling the trees. Then Avalon's hand went to her mouth as Taggerty knelt down in front of her on one knee, the same way that Zaria had said Kensington did when he was asking for her hand in marriage.

Taggerty reached out to her. His hands were shaking, and Avalon couldn't believe that the hands of such a sure soldier could shake like that, and she knew now that he was as destroyed as she was in their parting again. There were so many questions about the future, but those questions were only valid if there was a future. They were only valid if she won this war. She and Taggerty were both dying here and now, and she gulped back the wave of emotion that was overtaking her.

Avalon tried to pull Taggerty to his feet, but he remained on his knees and pulled her hand toward him, kissing her ring. Every nerve in Avalon's body absorbed the warmth of his lips on her fingers and she felt as though she could both cry and laugh at the same time.

"Stand up, Taggerty," Avalon begged.

He stood, still holding her hand in his, but Avalon pulled away and shook her head. It was thrilling to know that Taggerty wanted the same things that she did, but she should not be thinking about anything but Cormicks.

Taggerty walked around Avalon and leaned against a tree, and she watched his exquisite form relax there for a moment. He was confidant again, and unshaken. He was the brash young man that she had first met, and he was utterly sure of himself in this moment.

He held out his hand to her, but instead of taking it, she bent over and scooped up Jackie, holding the jakkow out in her palm. Taggerty reached out with one hand and held Avalon's wrist, and with his other hand he took Jackie and gently placed the lizard on the bark of the tree that he was leaning against. Then Taggerty pulled Avalon in close and he kissed her full on the lips.

Avalon closed her eyes and allowed herself the moment. She enjoyed the darkness where she couldn't see the forest or the reality of their situation. She could feel the urgency in Taggerty's kiss, and she dreamt a future the way she wanted it to be with Taggerty.

Taggerty released the kiss and startled Avalon when he lifted her up, cradling her back and legs in his strong arms. She tightened her grip on his neck and they stayed embraced in their kiss for a long time. When Avalon opened her eyes, she automatically flushed and became self-conscious again. She was embarrassed because

Taggerty had slid down the tree and she was sitting on his lap cradled in his arms.

Taggerty chuckled at her embarrassment and Avalon pursed her lips and cocked her head sideways to admonish him, but she wasn't serious. She loved where she was at this moment, but when Jackie caught her attention on the tree, she looked around the tree trunk and her heart fell into sadness. The sun had fallen into dusk, and Avalon could see the rising blue glow of the elbagrass. Taggerty ran his hand through her short hair and kissed her forehead, but the spell had been broken.

Avalon pushed back and stood, straightening her clothes before tucking Jackie in her pocket, and Taggerty brushed the leaves and dirt off of his pants. His gaze followed hers and he too saw the blue glow in the dusk of the evening.

"Stay here," Taggerty lamented. He took her hand. "Live here. Be here," he begged.

Avalon knew that he was asking her to stay and live at the outpost they had made at the elbagrass. He wanted her with him forever. Taggerty looked at her with conviction.

"Truth be told, that's all I want anymore," she said with a half-smile. She wanted to explain to Taggerty what he meant to her, but she needed to know Hawker and the Runners were no longer a threat before she could consider a future. Taggerty looked hopeful at her words, but Avalon shook her head.

"I can't," was all Avalon could muster before she pulled her hand away and walked out of the woods.

"There's about an hour before dark." Taggerty said in monotone as they stepped from the woods. They had lost the magic of their moment.

Avalon turned back toward the main camp, and they started to walk back.

"You have eighty men?" Taggerty asked, already knowing the answer. Avalon wondered when he'd made time to count before realizing Davev or Chylyn must have told him. "And the Guide," Avalon said.

"I have twenty with me here. So we will need about three-hundred of the alleya leaf."

"Is that a problem?" Avalon asked. She hadn't even considered counting the alleya leaf. They had always crossed over in small numbers in the past, and she worried they might not have enough of the leaf to counteract the poison in the elbagrass on the other side of the Window.

"I don't think so," Taggerty admitted. "I've been counting the leaf on the full moon, and as long as the men spread around the field, we should be able to find enough. The only problem is that we need them to go in single file so they can all find the pond in the center, and we can't collect the leaves into a pile because they start to wither and dry the moment they are picked."

"Then they will have to eat the leaf and line up right away," Avalon said. "I just hope they take your warnings seriously."

"It only takes seeing that field of grass turn blue one time to believe in anything," Taggerty said reverently.

They were back at the campsite too fast, and Taggerty fell into step just off Avalon's shoulder, but he didn't say anything more, and she didn't look at him. She was looking into the field of elbagrass that glowed blue under the full moon. She had experienced the sight a handful of times, but it still struck her as amazing. Avalon was too short to see over the tall reeds of grass, but she knew the small rectangular pond lined with rectangular stones waited for her within, and she was both excited and afraid to again look at her reflection in the Window.

As she neared the group of soldiers, she noticed that every man was on his feet staring at the blue anomaly. She could tell who had been here before and who was new by the expressions on their faces. Some held the hilt of their swords at the ready, remembering when the Runners came across, and others stood awestruck with their mouths agape.

"As you were," Avalon said to the few who had noticed her and bowed. They met Chylyn and the small group of Guides and soldiers that stood with him. Jakon and Davev bowed as Avalon approached. She never looked back at Taggerty, and he didn't join the circle but remained behind the King. If Taggerty felt as awful as she did, she understood that he wouldn't want to face her either. She put all that had taken place between them away, and she turned so he could hear her command.

"Please carry on," Avalon said to him.

"Jakon, prepare yourself," Taggerty said. "You will accompany the King to Cormicks, and we will follow in two days." Jakon nodded to Taggerty and bowed to Avalon.

Avalon saw Jakon look at Davev with a knowing smile, goading his cousin. These two George men were true to the core, and Avalon was starting to enjoy their competitive drive.

Avalon smiled and turned to Jakon's shorter cousin. "Davev, you will wait here and cross over with Taggerty. He will be focused on our plan for the battle with the enemy, and I need to know that you will be at his back to make sure nothing happens to him as he leads the rest of the soldiers. Can I count on you?" she asked. Avalon expected Davev to rally against his cousin right on the spot, but instead a very serious look crossed his face.

"Of course, Your Highness," Davev said with all seriousness, and then Avalon noticed the twinkling smile on Davev's lips as he bowed to his King with all of the self-satisfaction he could muster.

"Jakon," she said in a deep voice, and he snapped to attention. "You will obey my every order when we are in Cormicks, whether you agree or not."

"Yes, Your Highness."

Avalon turned to Taggerty. "We don't have much time. Prepare Jakon for the trip, and I will meet you back at the tent for final planning."

Taggerty squinted at Avalon, and she could see that he expected to stay by her side until she left, but Avalon needed time to prepare herself too, and being with Taggerty wouldn't help her focus.

Avalon finished eating the little she could put in her stomach while her nerves were twisting in her gut. She fed Jackie another grape and checked her small pack for the tenth time. She tucked a knife in her boot as Nugget had taught her. She was glad that it was warming up in Cormicks at this time of year because it meant that none of them would have to carry the bulky blankets to keep from freezing at night without a fire. She wondered if they would be able to have a fire if they did gain control of the Anthracites. It seemed to work that way within the castle walls, and Avalon hoped it held true on the outside too.

"King Avalon, it's Taggerty," she heard from outside the tent.

"Enter," she said, checking her weapons again. The night was calm and the tent was dark in the candlelight. Taggerty entered and bowed to Avalon.

"I have questions on strategy," Avalon said making comfortable talk. "I assume you have thought of everything already, so I won't bore you with my battle plans but to say that we will meet in two sunrises at the base of the mountain where the Anthracites first found us."

Taggerty nodded. "I have a backup plan," he answered slowly, "just in case things don't work out with those monsters."

"The everreds?" Avalon shuddered at the memory of the thousands of tiny, bloodthirsty red spiders that had appeared and devoured Brick and the other dead Runners.

"We will be going through the walls of Cormicks. The Anthracites will destroy anything that stands in our way," Avalon said more confidently than she felt.

"About the everreds," Taggerty said quietly. "They don't go into the elbagrass, and when I was there six months ago, there were bodies everywhere."

"I will be okay," Avalon reassured him.

"You have seen death, Avalon. Sonrah, Nugget, and Cincin have not."

"They know the score," Avalon said, but she didn't look at him. "They taught me how to communicate with the Anthracites, Taggerty, but they don't think that I can."

"Don't," Taggerty replied.

"I can, and I will." Avalon was adamant.

Taggerty stepped forward and grabbed Avalon's shoulders. "I know you can, that's not what I'm saying. I'm saying, don't do it. Leave it to Chylyn and Sonrah to make contact. You are lucky that when you sleep at night, all you see is blackness. You are lucky that you don't dream. When I close my eyes, all I see are the bodies of the men that I chopped up in the woods with Walthan. I trained and practiced and wanted to be the best, but when it comes down to it, Avalon, you don't forget." The bags under Taggerty's eyes got deeper and darker in that moment.

Avalon grit her teeth wanting to rip herself from Taggerty's hold and start into the elbagrass. She didn't have time for even a hint of indecision. She remembered that night, seeing them hacking the limbs apart, and she knew that was his first time killing someone. It had been disgusting to see, but she hadn't imagined how it had felt to commit the act.

"You trained to protect the King, not to advance on an enemy. I'm sorry that you have those memories, Taggerty, but I'm not sorry that you and Walthan stopped Brick from showing the enemy where we live."

They stared at each other and then Taggerty's grip released and they both took a moment.

"We have to get to Hawker. It's a miracle he hasn't come here already," Avalon said. Taggerty pursed his lips and nodded.

Avalon took Jackie off the table to tuck him in her pocket, but first she pet his back and whispered to him, "Be good, Jackie. I don't know what's going to happen over there, but be safe." Avalon had no idea if she could make Jackie stay with her on the other side, but she was going to take him with and see what happened.

She tucked Jackie in her pocket and grabbed her pack.

"I'm ready to go," Avalon said. She didn't mean to sound angry but she was nervous on every level. She had no idea what she could possibly say to Taggerty to make him understand how she felt and then walk away to face whatever waited for her on the other side of the Window. She hoped he knew.

"Allow me, Your Highness," Taggerty said, grabbing the pack from Avalon and pushing the tent flap aside.

Avalon walked to the clearing and stopped to talk to Chylyn who sat next to three small packs and the larger square one that Avalon had noticed him carrying from Fontanasia. She was curious but didn't ask what was inside.

"We are ready," Chylyn said with all seriousness. He stood as Taggerty placed the small pack next to the others.

"I am ready," she replied.

"Let us hope they are not," Chylyn said looking at the elbagrass that cast a blue haze around the clearing.

Jackie squirmed in Avalon's pocket. Avalon told herself that she would eat the same alleya leaf and it would be the same journey through the elbagrass, but she knew that this wasn't anything like her first time through. She was a child back then, filled with wonder, wanting to learn about this world. She knew nothing of Taggerty at that time, aside from the fact that he was a snobbish King's Guard. And this time through she was in love with him and she was not going through to a world of wonder. She was going through and would one way or another face death.

"You will cross over with the men tomorrow night and on the second sunrise we will meet at the hill where the Anthracites first found us," Avalon repeated her plan.

"You mean where they almost killed you the first time?" Taggerty retorted.

"And you drew them away with your fire," Avalon said with an attempt at a smirk, but her heart was pounding. She was still scared when she thought about the Anthracites, but this had to be done.

"Yes, well, let's hope they don't harbor a grudge," Chylyn offered.

Taggerty cleared his throat. "And if you are not there, should we wait for you?" Taggerty's face was grave, and Avalon knew he didn't like her plan.

"We will be there," Avalon said with more confidence than she felt. "And if we are late, move in with your men and find Hawker," she said quietly so that only Taggerty and Chylyn could hear.

"And do what with him?" Taggerty asked.

Avalon looked into Taggerty's green eyes and enjoyed the moment of strength that his gaze brought her. "Stop him," she said, unable to word her true thought, but Taggerty understood her intention. They were putting everything on the line during this mission, and they both knew that this would be life or death for them or Hawker.

"Understood, King Avalon."

"Goodbye," Avalon said, her heavy heart squashing anything else she might have said. Taggerty's face flattened to the most solemn expression Avalon had seen, and his lips trembled into a half-smile.

He then turned to Jakon offering his hand and they grabbed at the wrists. "Are you ready?"

"I'm always ready," Jakon replied, turning to Davev and slapping his cousin on the back before stepping to the elbagrass and carefully pulling three of the alleya leaf from where they had sprouted on the elbagrass in the last hour.

Taggerty and Chylyn nodded at each other and then Chylyn turned toward the grass, carefully picking several alleya leaf. He handed three to each of the girls who stood behind him, and then handed four to Avalon. Avalon tucked one leaf into her pocket for Jackie and ate the other three. The taste of the leaf was death on her tongue. It's bitter flavor brought back the memory of Walthan's dead eyes.

Jakon's face had puckered at the bitter taste, but the Guides seemed not to have noticed the flavor as they chewed and donned their packs. They traveled light with one small blanket and two days of food each. Chylyn heaved his large square pack on his shoulders and then without a word, he stepped into the blue elbagrass.

Taggerty took one last look at Avalon and turned away. As she melted into the tall blue sea of grass, she could hear him calling, "These are our men in the grass, do not fire!"

Chapter 9
First Blood

Chylyn had looked back several times to make sure that everyone was still following him. Avalon realized halfway into the field that she had been following Jakon and not Chylyn. Jakon towered above them as Walthan had, and he could actually see over the tall reeds of blue elbagrass.

"Nugget," Chylyn said, and Avalon saw the glint from the tip of the warrior spear wave above the grass.

"Everyone is here," Jakon said.

"Give me a ride, beast," Avalon heard Nugget say to Jakon, and Cincin and Sonrah giggled at the comment. They had gotten to know each other enough in the short hours spent waiting for darkness to fall.

"I'm not your pet," Jakon replied, but Avalon could hear a smile in his tone.

At his comment, Avalon patted her pocket and Jackie scrambled in a circle. He couldn't see out, but he was agitated and he had tasted the alleya leaf. Avalon was sure that he knew what was to come. She just hoped that Jackie wouldn't give their position away to the enemy.

She was breathing hard when they arrived at the center of the field. Avalon looked around in the night to see if she could notice the lookout towers, but the constant blue light on her eyes blinded her to the rest of the night. Avalon stopped short of the rectangular rock outline, and she grit her teeth when she saw the small pond outlined in the dim light.

"The enemy may be waiting, so we need to go fast. Look at your reflection," Chylyn was saying. "Look into your eyes." He made sure that they all understood, and then he leaned over the water and disappeared.

Jakon managed to choke back the expletives that unconsciously uttered forth when he saw Chylyn there one moment and then gone the next.

"Don't be afraid," Nugget teased him, and then she stepped forward and leaned over the water. She didn't disappear right away, and Avalon thought she saw Nugget's small hand grip tighter to her spear. There was fear inside even Nugget, but Avalon could only empathize. Then Nugget too was gone and Cincin stepped forward, leaned over and disappeared.

"Jakon, go now," Avalon commanded before Sonrah could go next. Jakon was a fierce protector and had proven himself trustworthy, but Avalon could see indecision playing out on his face. The Guides were raised around magic and faith in the unseen, but Jakon was not, and Avalon hoped that her command coupled with his manly need to show Sonrah that he was strong would make him move faster.

He stepped to the side of the pond and hesitated so Sonrah stepped up next to him. She put her hand on his back and Avalon could see that the distraction helped his resolve. Jakon looked down at Sonrah who was only slightly shorter than him. She pulled her hand away and then he leaned over and was gone. Sonrah leaned over and disappeared, and Avalon didn't hesitate. When she saw her own eyes in the pond, the world became dark, and she knew that she was in Cormicks.

The night was much the same temperature and she could hear the chirp of insects, but it was the absence of the moon and the blue glow of the elbagrass that was the obvious clue.

"Let him go," Avalon heard Chylyn's voice whisper, and when she felt Jackie poking at her side through her pocket, she knew he was talking to her.

"Go," Avalon said to Chylyn, and he started walking away from the pond in the opposite direction than they had gone last time. She reached into her pocket as they moved, and grabbed hold of Jackie who was now squeaking and squealing, his tiny, immeasurable weight already growing in bulk. He was almost larger than her pocket already, and she had to tug him out.

Avalon wanted to keep him with the group, but she and Chylyn had discussed this before the trip, and the noise he would make was too dangerous to chance. She took four steps and he was already the size of a small dog, and Avalon stroked his head with her whole hand as his body jerked and flailed.

"Go now, Jackie. You will find Taggerty here in two days, or you can find me by the castle where we met before. Be quiet, and be well," Avalon whispered, wishing that he understood her words. She put him down in the grass and paused to watch as he ballooned in size, his front and back legs alternating kicks.

He had been terrified the first time and he looked much the same now, and as much as she wanted to calm him, Avalon knew there was nothing she could do. Jackie would grow to be larger than a horse, and he would either choose to follow her out of the grass, or he would again run off in terror. She was worried about him alone in this place, but they couldn't afford the noise. The others were still on the move and already out of sight, so she stepped away from Jackie and heard his body rustling in the grass behind her as she walked away.

She saw the gray outline of Jakon's head bobbing up and down as she quickened her pace to catch up. The sky was dark, and she tripped over something hard and put her hands down in front of her and found a rock to push herself up on. It took her a moment to realize that she was actually falling over the remains of the dead Runners Taggerty had mentioned. She wasn't touching rocks but the petrified remains of bodies. Avalon gagged and was glad that they would clear the field in the dark. She didn't want to see what Taggerty had seen. She pulled herself together as she finally caught up to the others.

It was a long time before they were out of the elbagrass, and when they made it to the clearing they shuffled across to the cover of trees before stopping to rest. Avalon's legs burned from the exercise of trudging through the thick grass, but no one wanted to sit down and rest. Chylyn was the only one who had been in this world enough times to truly have his wits about him.

"No one has been in these woods for two generations, so I don't know where they lead. We will skirt the field back to where I know it leads toward the castle," Chylyn whispered. "Does anyone need to rest?" he asked, and when no one spoke up, he turned back to the edge of the woods. His hands snatched tiny, shimmering bugs from mid-air, and he wiped one on each of their backs as he had last time Avalon was here.

Avalon felt Chylyn's strong hand rub down her back and then he moved to the others, and she could see the faint glow smeared on the girls' clothing.

When Chylyn moved to Jakon, the soldier held his hand up. "You don't need to see me, I need to see you," Jakon said snatching up a bug from the air and rubbing it down Chylyn's back.

Chylyn nodded and then moved around the low brush that skirted the field. Avalon, Nugget, Cincin, and Sonrah, followed with Jakon at the back. Chylyn went slowly, stopping often to listen. Avalon was listening, too, for any sign of the enemy, and she was surprised to find the field left unprotected. She realized that Hawker must not have thought she would be so bold as to send soldiers here. He had been utterly condescending the last time she had seen him, and Avalon hoped that this meant his defenses were down.

The going was actually easy, and she heard one of the girls sigh as they walked. The hyper-anticipation of the trip was wearing off and they were settling in to their new surroundings. A long time passed before they heard something that was out of place, and Chylyn led them back into the cover of the trees.

They watched in the gray light for a long time. Just as Taggerty had said, there was a wide opening where a section of trees had been cut down.

"We go in here," Chylyn whispered before they came to the downed area of trees, and Avalon followed him into the woods. She squinted her eyes, remembering the small branches that scratched at her face and hands last time. They went excruciatingly slow because they knew that at some point on this journey, they would see the Runners.

The three girls were quiet, but once in a while Avalon heard Jakon grunt and she knew that his muscular bulk was scraping between the tightly packed tree trunks.

After an hour of sneaking and trying not to make any noise, they were out of the woods. As they tried to pull the sticks and leaves from their hair and clothes, Chylyn urged them on. In a while they were in the rock clearing that Avalon remembered sleeping in. She thought that they would stop, but Chylyn kept walking so Avalon followed.

She was tired, but her adrenaline kept her going. Every step she remembered the voracious everred spiders, and when they crossed through a cluster of trees, Avalon wondered if that was where Walthan and Brick had faced off.

They had covered a lot of distance in a short time. Last time, they had traveled very slowly, constantly hiding to make sure no one happened upon their stealth reconnaissance group. This time Chylyn walked quickly and had only stopped twice so they could each drink some water before moving on, but no one complained.

"We will rest here," Chylyn said when he came upon a group of small boulders. Avalon climbed on the rocks and the girls followed. Chylyn climbed a tree to get a better look, and Jakon stayed on the ground.

"You will want to get on the rocks," Avalon whispered to Jakon. "The ground here lives in some places, like in the ravine." She couldn't see his expression, but Jakon's boots scrambled onto the opposite rock, and Avalon fought the urge to laugh. Jakon was disturbed by the suggestion and it shouldn't be funny in this serious hour, but the harder she tried not to think about it, the funnier it got.

She laid down on the rock and put her hand over her mouth so the others wouldn't hear her chuckle. When she saw the carpet of stars in the sky, her mind turned serious. She couldn't see the gray moon from her position, but it didn't matter. She had looked up at the moon each night in Fontanasia and knew Taggerty was looking at the same moon. It had made her feel close to him in some way, but even if she could see the moon in this place, it wouldn't be the same moon that Taggerty was seeing tonight.

Avalon listened to the trees as they swayed in the breeze and she took a deep breath. There was no turning back now, but she didn't fear the thought. This was her destiny, to be King of Fontanasia and to stop the enemy. She had trained for this exact moment her whole life, and it felt right to her now as she lie under the stars in Cormicks.

There was no indecision left in her, and Avalon felt the confidence of the kings before her squaring her shoulders and strengthening her resolve. She had made the decisions that had brought her to this moment, and there could have been no other way.

Avalon closed her eyes and breathed deeply. There were no more questions within her. She remembered Walthan and the way his head was held high and his eyes seemed to look across the horizon and see everything. Avalon saw the future on her horizon now, and although she had no way of knowing the outcome, she was not afraid. As she drifted into sleep, she felt the joy of personal presence for the first time in her life.

Avalon was climbing a small mountain, and although in her mind it didn't seem very steep, she was sweating and breathing heavily. She pulled her hands away from the ground and saw black dust on her palms. The mountain moved under her feet, and then Avalon's ankles slipped below the dirt. She stood up as the ground evened itself out, and she realized then that she was standing atop an Anthracite. She was sunk in ankle deep, and small rocks flowed around her legs like water in a river. The Anthracite was more alive than Avalon had ever known.

She looked down to the ground, and Jakon looked terrified. Avalon knew that he was more worried that she would die on his watch than he was that the Anthracite would crush him.

"Rooooooookk-aaaaaaaaa," Avalon yelled although she was already on the Anthracite and she didn't need to be so loud. With her command, the Anthracite started to walk, and she fell back on her butt as the beast started its slow stride forward. She tried to stand and slowly repositioned her feet so that one was out in front of the other. She could keep her balance now, and although the sensation of the rocks slowly pulling on her ankles was a little terrifying, Avalon was on top of the world.

"King Avalon!" she heard Jakon yell. His voice sounded far away and she looked down, but she couldn't see him. She felt a sting on her cheek and wondered what might have caused it. Then the Anthracite began to melt away from under her feet, and Avalon fell into darkness.

Avalon woke up on the boulder as the wind whipped leaves around her. She felt the grip of the Anthracite on her ankles and then realized she had been dreaming. It was Jakon pulling on her legs to get her off the boulder.

"He is awake," Cincin told Jakon. She had been shaking Avalon's shoulders trying to wake the King up. Avalon had never been woken during a dream before, and she wished they had left her alone. Riding the Anthracite had been so vivid and thrilling, and she wanted to know how it turned out, but she would have to find that out at a later time. Right now, they were caught at the edge of a bad storm.

"I'm fine," Avalon said to Jakon as she shook his grip off. Her legs were dangling over the side of the boulder and she could see that he had been ready to pull her sleeping body down onto his shoulder.

"Yes, Your Highness. We couldn't wake you up. I'm sorry," he said. Avalon could hear the embarrassment in his voice and she was glad that it was still dark so she didn't have to see his discomfort.

"We have to go now," Cincin said as a large tree branch bent and then snapped under the force of the wind. Avalon reached for her pack and patted her pocket out of habit before remembering that Jackie wasn't with her. She worried for her pet in this storm and hoped that he would find shelter.

"Where are we going?" Avalon asked as she slid off the boulder behind Cincin and they met the rest of the group.

"We make for the hill next to the Anthracites. As soon as the storm lets up, we will call them and move away from Cormicks."

"Is there any shelter left there?" Avalon asked. She had almost been killed there when the rocks caved in on them.

"There is enough for us to stay safe from the storm," Chylyn said. Avalon could hear worry in his voice. "King Avalon, back with Jakon, please," Chylyn said and then started walking.

Nugget and Cincin moved forward and Avalon was forced to the back of the pack. She was the King and she could do what she wanted, but Avalon trusted Chylyn implicitly and she wouldn't allow her pride to cause a mistake this late in the game.

Walking was more difficult in the wind, and leaves and small objects caught in the air pelted their skin. She had to squint and looked down to focus on Sonrah's green robes that whipped in the wind, and she hoped they would make shelter before the rain came.

When they made the rock outcropping, dawn was upon them and they could see a little better. The air was full of dust as thunder crashed around them, the lightning fully exposing them in blasts of white and blue light. Avalon was relieved to be out of the darkness, but with the light came the danger that they would be spotted by the enemy.

"We are here," Avalon whispered to Jakon and Sonrah who walked with her a few paces behind the others. Avalon's muscles ached, and her mind was ready for rest. She covered her mouth with her collar to keep the dust from her lungs and jogged the last short distance to shelter.

Chylyn had slowed his pace and Avalon was even with him when she turned the corner and stepped under the shelter of the indentation made in the side of the hill. She pulled her collar down, and was immediately shocked by the presence of two Runner soldiers who were holed up in the small space. She should have been tugging at her sword hilt, but Avalon froze and stared, eyes wide.

The massive brutes were on their feet and stepping forward before she could draw her blade. It would have cost her if Jakon and Nugget hadn't been so quick.

"No!" Avalon heard Chylyn call behind her, and then she saw Nugget's spear run through the neck of one of the soldiers while Jakon's sword cut diagonally down across the chest of the other man. Their eyes went wide as blood spewed from their wounds.

Nugget's acrobatics landed her on a rock on the right side, and she swiftly pulled her spear out of his neck with a twist and the soldier fell to the ground. Jakon had placed himself in the small space between Avalon and the other soldier and most of the blood spatter hit his uniform as the soldier crumpled.

"No killing yet," Chylyn complained. Avalon was stunned, her mouth hanging open. She had been stupid to assume this place would be empty, and her haste could cost them the element of surprise.

"They are the enemy," Nugget said. In the flash of lightning, Avalon thought she saw the hint of a smile on Nugget's face. Avalon watched Jakon and Nugget wipe their blades on the dead soldiers' clothing.

"You should not have done that," Chylyn said to Nugget.

"We do as we will," she replied. Nugget acted swiftly and didn't halt when Chylyn had yelled, and Avalon now wondered if this girl could be trusted to control a powerful weapon such as the Anthracites.

"You are right, we do as we will, but that was the wrong choice," the Guide answered.

"They were a liability to us and to our brothers who will pass in a day," Nugget said confidently.

"Yes, they were," Chylyn answered. "But if they are noticed to be missing, we will be in danger," Chylyn complained.

"We were in danger the moment we saw ourselves in the pond," Sonrah said in defense of Nugget's actions, and she was right.

"They saw me. There was no other recourse," Avalon said regretfully.

The rain started and the five of them pushed into the small space, the two soldiers' bodies taking up much of the standing room. The wind pushed the rain into the outcropping, and they were all wet within a minute.

Chylyn climbed up on the rock next to Nugget and gestured for the rest to do the same. "This is all hard ground, but we can't chance the everreds," Chylyn said. At his words, Cincin, Sonrah, and Avalon hurried atop the rocks. There were only three feet between the rocks and the roof of the shelter, and they all had to half-lay huddled together in the space.

"I'm fine," Jakon said.

"Climb up, Jakon. You don't want to be on the ground right now," Avalon commanded. Jakon kept his sword drawn and didn't move. He was too large to be comfortable on the rock shelf. "It's not safe on the ground right now. Stay up on this rock. That's an order, Jakon," Avalon said as she tugged at his solid arm. Jakon nodded and ducked his head as he climbed up just in time.

Avalon felt the ground under her feet shake and then she heard a familiar rustling sound. She knew it was the everred spiders cleaning the men's flesh from the bone and she was glad that she wasn't able to see the carnage. The memory of the wave of spiders devouring Brick was enough to disgust her now.

"Don't leave this rock, but look at the soldiers," she told Jakon, and he and Nugget leaned over to look. Avalon could see disbelief on their faces, and in a moment the everred spiders were gone and so were the soldiers, the stain in the ground the only evidence that they had been here.

Jakon turned to Avalon with a tight frown on his face and nodded, and even Nugget had nothing to say after the grotesque spectacle. Jakon found two smaller rocks off to the side that he could stand on without having to bend over. He looked to Avalon for approval, and she nodded in the coming light of day. This place was more dangerous than Jakon had imagined, and he hadn't even seen the Anthracites yet.

Wind and water whipped around them, and the rolling thunder didn't let up. Avalon hoped all of the Anthracite dust had washed out of this area because she knew the lightning could set it ablaze. This storm was one of the most violent that Avalon had ever seen, but she had always been within the protective stone walls of the castle when it rained.

The light of day was a comfort as she watched the trees bend under the onslaught of the wind. Avalon saw a red freckled paiche bird fly by the opening, but for all of its frantically flapping of wings against the storm, it was flying backwards in the wind.

She closed her eyes and reviewed her dream. She knew that her dream would come true because her dreams always came true. She would survive this storm to ride an Anthracite, of that she was certain. As terrifying as that thought should have been, the waiting was more difficult because the waiting meant she had time to deconstruct her plan and question its validity, and it was much too late for that.

Avalon looked down at the stain left behind where the dead soldiers had been sucked into the ground, and she thought about her own soldiers who would be following her to war for the first time in Fontanasia's history. She wondered if her people had ever been at war before. They had been attacked at Hawkerness and overrun, but that was not a declaration of war, it was a tragedy that changed her people's fate.

Dead enemies piled up in Avalon's mind into a hill of spent flesh as Avalon added Walthan and Brick's bodies to the tally, and she wondered how many others would die. She imagined Taggerty among the dead and it was a horrible thought, but not worse than the thought of Zaria and Myra and the whole of Fontanasia sacrificing their blood to Hawker's madness. She was right to come here, but it didn't make her mission any easier.

She opened her eyes to Nugget's watchful stare. The small but powerful Guide wasn't much younger than Avalon, and she had killed a man already. Avalon met Nugget's gaze, and there was still the hint of a smile on her face, the look of utter confidence and self-righteousness not wavering under the heavy blanket of what she had done. Avalon hadn't drawn her sword, but between Nugget and Jakon, Avalon's conscience seemed to be suffering the consequences, and she didn't know how much longer she could sit here in silence.

In time the storm blew over, and she felt some relief in the daylight. They climbed down slowly into the mud. It would not be easy to travel now, and they would leave tracks, but they couldn't stay here.

Chylyn handed Jakon a cloth. "The everreds smell blood as you saw, and if we have blood on our hands they will devour us all. Let's hope those men aren't missed this morning, and if this spot is found, let us hope the enemy assumes they were devoured and not slain by an enemy first." He pointed at Nugget. "You and Jakon make sure you are clean of blood."

They took turns using the cloth, but Nugget had remained clean so that left Jakon to wipe the blood from his chest plate.

"It was a bad storm," Nugget said. "I'm sure it will take some time for anyone to think twice about them missing."

Avalon hoped that Nugget was right.

As they walked away from the protection of the overhang, there was the sound of collapsing rocks behind them. Avalon turned to see Jakon using his strength to push half of the rock shelf they had all been perched on over the red stain. It sounded like wet sand thudding into the ground, and though it wasn't perfect, it would serve to hide the area.

"Step as one," Chylyn said, and he walked away taking stunted steps. Nugget followed in his tracks, and then Cincin and Sonrah. The print was deep in the mud, but it did look as though one very large person had walked away from the hollow. Avalon followed, the squish of the mud sucking at her boots as she lifted her feet with each step. She knew that Jakon's large boots would press all of their footprints into one, and she marveled at Chylyn's continuous cunning.

Chapter 10
Branded

Chylyn moved to the trees and circled around to the place where Avalon had first seen the Anthracites, and they were easy to pick out on the landscape. The first time she was here and before she knew what they were, Avalon only saw three hills of rock and grass. It must have been a long time since they had been called upon before then, because they looked like any other hill of stone and foliage. But now she saw the unmistakable black outline of what she knew to be Anthracites.

"What's in there?" Jakon asked as he pointed to the black hills.

"You speak of those tracks into the mountains?" Sonrah answered.

Avalon saw what Jakon had noticed. There were huge trenches in the ground where the Anthracites had dragged their legs along before crumbling into their resting form.

"There is nothing in there. It is there," Sonrah's deep tones sang, and Jakon's brow curled up in thought, but he didn't understand.

"Chylyn, we have made it here safely, but we know that we cannot remain hidden forever." Avalon's words stung them both. Chylyn had been to this world countless times on reconnaissance missions to watch and learn and to make sure that no one knew about Fontanasia. He had watched these people and reported back to the King alone. He had not been found out until the traitor Brick turned on them under Hawker's orders. And now Hawker was here, the leader of these brutal people, and he knew how to get back to Fontanasia. The status quo could not stand.

Chylyn looked at the sky. They had been traveling in the daylight and Avalon knew that he was used to the cover of darkness. It was still hours until dusk, but Chylyn nodded. It was now or never.

"Use these," Chylyn said, and he knelt in front of the square pack he had been carrying from Fontanasia. Avalon's jaw dropped as he produced two large metal boots.

"You don't need those," Nugget said.

"King Avalon, we don't know for sure what happens when you try to get on top of an Anthracite, and I don't want the rock to crush you. You should put these on," he told her.

Avalon looked back at the mountains of black. "Thank you, Chylyn," she said, stepping next to the metal boots to see if they would fit.

Cincin reached into her bag and pulled out a bell the size of Avalon's head and a short bow with a metal string pulled tight across it. Avalon knew this kasic bell from her training, and she tried to steady her shaking hands as she took it from Cincin. It was heavy, the sides built thick with a metal that she hadn't encountered anywhere else. She had made the sound three times before, after two months of trying, and she hoped she could duplicate it today.

"Move away and spread out as we discussed. I will give you twenty minutes," Avalon commanded.

"This won't work," Nugget protested to Chylyn. "The Anthracites will not take the command of a male. No offense, King Avalon, this is just a fact." And although Avalon knew the same facts that Nugget did, there was still a preemptory tone in the Guide's voice that Avalon knew well. It was Nugget's typical 'I'm better than everyone' tone, and Avalon was no longer bothered by it. Nugget had proven herself when she had protected Avalon by killing the Runner. She was quick, trained to perfection, and had a confidence that Avalon needed near her if she was going to survive. Plus, Avalon reasoned to herself, it wasn't Nugget's fault that she didn't know Avalon's secret.

"It will work," Avalon said confidently. "I am the King, they will respond." Nugget blinked fast and bit her lip, nodding her head and then shaking it because she didn't believe for a minute that this would work.

Avalon jumped when Chylyn touched her shoulder, and she was almost as startled by the touch as she was at the instigator.

"The thing is not to fight your fear, it is to put the fear itself aside," Chylyn said, all the time looking off at the living mountains.

"Thank you," Avalon said with a shaky voice. Then Avalon remembered her dream and that she would be on the Anthracite. She took a deep breath and whispered to herself, "I will, therefore I can."

"Go," Avalon said, and the four Guides turned and walked quickly away.

"Go," Avalon said to Jakon.

"Begging your pardon, King Avalon. I would rather keep this post with you." He wasn't looking at Avalon, he was staring at the black hills and trying to deduce their secret. Avalon wasn't sure what all Taggerty had told Jakon about this place, and she wanted to order him away to keep him safe, but she realized that would be a ridiculous order for a King's Guard.

Avalon shrugged as casually as she could. "Stay if you want. When it happens, follow as fast as you can."

"Yes, Your Highness," Jakon said, and she had to admire his unwavering commitment.

Avalon silently counted as they watched from the edge of the woods. She kept her eyes open for the small white and red freckled paiche birds, remembering how they would flock around a bush of berries and eat before moving away, but there were no paiche birds or other animals stirring in the trees. It felt ominous. When the wind blew, she could smell the Anthracites. The smell was a noxious mix of mold and rotten eggs.

She pulled Chylyn's clunky metal boots over her own and sprung back and forth on her feet. Her legs felt like lead weights with the boots on, but Chylyn's comment about not knowing what the rock would do had made Avalon wonder herself, and she'd decided to wear the boots.

Finally, she counted what she thought would have been about twenty minutes. She stepped out of the woods and inhaled deeply. Wordlessly, Jakon stood next to her and reached for the hilt of his sword but Avalon shook her head.

"If this goes as I think it will, follow the path. If it doesn't, find the others and meet Taggerty at dawn tomorrow." Jakon meant to protest, but Avalon didn't give him the time.

She held the heavy bell out in front of her and pulled the bow up to the side of the bell that had scrapes along the bottom edge. Avalon pressed the top of the metal string to the bell and pulled the bow toward her, but nothing happened. She took a deep breath and loosened her grip on the bow, closing her eyes to create the right amount of pressure to make the bow vibrate the bell. Halfway up the next stroke the bell began to vibrate in her outstretched hand. She pulled the bow back and continued to press gently. Her hand on the bell tickled with the vibration, and as she caressed metal to metal, a loud sound began to ring across the grove.

The ground unfolded in front of them, and Avalon pushed the bow three more full revolutions before stopping. The metal was vibrating hot and continued to chime out the tone to the Anthracites. Once the bell went silent, Avalon turned to Jakon.

His mouth fell open as the first mountain came to life and stood up in front of him. The black stone flowed within itself like water taking shape, and each mountain became a two-legged creature. There were no arms or eyes, but when the first Anthracite took a step in their direction, Jakon knew that they were more than mere rock.

He looked to his King for direction and Avalon tried to smile, although she too was terrified. She had ridden an Anthracite already in her dream, so she knew that she would, but she didn't know if it would be today, or if the outcome would be a success. Cincin and Jakon had pulled her from the dream before she could see the ending.

"Take this bell and follow us and watch your back in case the Runners decide to follow too." She handed the bell and bow to Jakon who put them in the sack and slung it over his shoulder. Avalon stepped out of the clearing in the bulky metal boots and pointed in the direction that the others had gone.

"Heeeeeeeeeeee," Avalon sang out from the back of her throat in a high-pitched rasp. The sound hurt for her to make, but like the bell, she needed her voice to vibrate in a way the Anthracites would understand. She struggled to make the harmonic that Sonrah found so easily.

The Anthracite shook the ground beneath her feet, and Avalon wanted to run, but she stood in the heavy metal boots and watched as the black dust spread around her like a fog. Avalon gulped back her fear and squared her shoulders, hoping she wouldn't be crushed.

The charcoal beast stepped within ten feet of Avalon and the pounding noise jarred her bones. Just when she was sure that it would crush her, it stopped, and the heavy dust settled as they both stood like statues.

Avalon put her arm over her face to cover her mouth and nose. She took a deep breath in and then called, "Sheeeeecraaaaaah!"

Avalon yelled at the top of her voice. Her throat hurt with the tone of the last sounds she made and she realized that in her excitement, she was yelling louder than she had ever practiced these sounds. The language was grating and it hurt her throat and it was all she could do to not cough the words.

She looked up at the Anthracite, and to her amazement, it slowly moved its rocks into a kneeling position. It pounded its foot twice on the ground, and Avalon took a tentative step forward in the boots. They were loose and heavy and she felt like an oaf walking in them, and at the last second she made the decision to take them off.

Avalon heard Jakon unsheathe his sword and she called out to him over the rumble of the third mountain of black rock unfolding from the ground. "No, Jakon!" Avalon cautioned him back with her hand, and then she pointed again and yelled at the top of her lungs. She thought her throat would break and she would lose her voice if she had to continue with this sound much longer.

The Anthracite was dangerously close to Avalon and she coughed in the black cloud of soot that enveloped her. She tied a scarf around her face wishing she had told Jakon to do the same. There was no time to help him now.

Just when Avalon thought she might be flattened, the second Anthracite turned and started it's ground crushing steps in the direction that she had pointed. The third Anthracite followed, and in six long strides they were out of the clearing.

Avalon hoped on all hope that the Guides had enough time to spread out. They needed to lead the Anthracites far enough away from Cormicks that it wouldn't be easy for the Runners to follow. No one knew what the Runners would do. The last time Avalon was here, the charcoal beasts had torn from the ground when they had sensed fire. Under no specific direction from anyone, they had chased the fire down. She hoped that the Runners would have enough experience with this phenomenon not to question the motives of the rocks.

Avalon chuckled a frantic laugh. She knew that her Uncle Hawker would be utterly paranoid, but she also knew that he wouldn't give any credit to the Runners, much less expect intelligent action from a rock. The end of her laugh was fear coming to the surface because she was about to attempt the impossible.

She raised her hands over her head and yelled, "Roooook-jaaaaa!" There was not much of her throat left after the first command, and the faltering tremolo of her voice could not sustain in the black cloud of dust, but she had given the proper command. The Anthracite oozed out a bridge of rock that rippled around her and gripped her ankles and swept Avalon off her feet. She fell back and the rock caught her and Avalon grabbed at the moving form, but she was upside-down and being pulled by her ankles higher and higher off the ground. Her calves were inside the beast now, and Avalon wondered if she would be swallowed whole and pulverized to death by the moving stones.

Hawker could hear the cracking sound of the Anthracites ripping out of the ground. It had been months since he had bothered with the giant rocks, and he was surprised to find them moving now without his command. He took another bite of meat and chewed slowly, staring at Triangle who was waiting to see how Hawker would react. The table shook, liquids rippling in their chalices, the carved plates rattling on the table.

Hawker chewed slowly as he listened, and when he heard the second Anthracite rip from the ground, he jumped up and let his chair crash to the ground behind him. Triangle straightened but didn't say anything. His two servants tried to remain still, but Hawker could tell that they were shaking in place, wondering what their King would do next. They had all learned to wait for his command and obey his every order. Some of them had even inherited burn scars for their trouble.

Hawker half-smiled at the thought of torture by fire but then the crack of the third Anthracite shook the table and his blood boiled.

"I did not give the command!" he yelled at Triangle. The White Robe turned and strode out of the room, and Hawker already knew what he would report when he returned.

The Anthracites had just left. They did that every once in a while, and it was assumed that they would have detected fire somewhere and had gone to squelch it. The Runners knew that they were not to light fires outside of the castle grounds, but some of them had gotten cold on their overnights out in the damp weather and had disobeyed the rule, and they had been crushed for their troubles.

Still, Hawker was King and he liked to use these moments to remind the counselors and servants, and the massive tattooed Runner guards, just who they answered to.

His servant righted his chair, and Hawker sat to finish his meal. A few minutes later he heard the tone of the bell that called the Anthracites, and he knew the girl was on the parapet trying to call them back. He didn't expect it to work, it never did when they were so far away. Hawker marveled at the tone that traveled so easily through the rock walls of the castle. He appreciated that someone had the knowledge and patience somewhere back in time to communicate with the dumb black rocks, and he relished to use that power for his own rule.

Hawker wanted to take the Anthracites to Fontanasia and tear the place to bits, but he didn't know how they would possibly cross over. They were alive in some ways, but really consisted of dead rock. Some days he wished he had an army to move on Fontanasia, but the forces had been cut in half when the Monarch had failed, and Hawker wanted to rebuild the troops so that he could surge into Fontanasia and utterly destroy Avalon and his King's Guard. That would take more time than he wished, but Hawker had always played the long game, and he could wait.

The ringing stopped and Triangle returned and bowed, holding the bell and bow that called the Anthracites. Hawker kept these tools on hand, not wanting the girl to use them against him to call the Anthracites of her own volition.

"My lord, they would not come back."

Hawker stared at the counselor who lowered his eyes. "I told you how to address me and I will not tell you again!" he snapped, pounding the table. He would not be addressed like the Monarch. His father and brother were addressed as 'Your Highness', and Hawker would accept the same courtesy.

"Your Highness, of course. Yes, Your Highness," Triangle stammered. Triangle's small tattoo was ink before Hawker had arrived, and now it was a large triangle brand burned into the skin in the center of his forehead, outlining the smaller triangle tattoo within.

The words calmed him, and Hawker's nose twitched when he remembered Birch. His brother was so naive, but in the end as Birch had choked on the poison, he'd seen Hawker for who he truly was. Hawker would never have to act polite to anyone ever again. He'd never have to be subservient. He was finally the King.

Still, he shouldn't have broken Triangle. He was the most trustworthy of counselors and was very intelligent, but as the months passed, his exposure to Hawker's temper had made him less reliable. He seemed to be trying to do the right thing and to find the right answer for the King, but those weren't always one and the same.

"Take me to the girl," Hawker commanded. Triangle bowed and turned, bell and bow still in hand. He led Hawker down several corridors to a staircase. They climbed one level and approached a door that was guarded by one of the tattoo-faced brutes who stepped aside. Triangle swung the door in on its hinges and Hawker entered the suite of rooms.

The girl was on the couch, her eyes wet from crying. She tried to wipe the tears away, standing to bow to the King.

The sight of her crying made Hawker smile. He was breaking her, too.

Chapter 11
Rock Tamer

*A*valon looked down to see Jakon watching mouth agape in the black dust. He held the bag with the bell and bow in his left hand and was reaching for his sword, but there was nothing to be done.

The slow stomping of the Anthracites beat in Avalon's ears, and she was surprised that she wasn't jarred by the impact, but the rocks that swirled around her ankles had pulled her to the top of the black mountain and cushioned each blow. She had flailed upside-down for a moment, but she was able to grab her knees and curl into a ball and then thrust her weight forward to pull herself to a standing position. There was a steady wind at this height that pushed the cloud of dust away, and Avalon could finally breathe.

Avalon looked to the castle off in the distance to her right. The Anthracites stood well over the wall and could easily crush through it as she had assumed. She was sure that their height would reach to the third level of the castle, and Avalon nodded to herself. Her mad plan to attack Cormicks might actually work.

Avalon looked closely at Cormicks. She was surprised to see more structure here. There were stone streets, and sturdier housing surrounded the castle than when she had been here last, and Avalon thought she could see the beginnings of real boroughs instead of the ramshackle wood huts and tents. Hawker must have ordered these improvements. Of course, he wanted to be King of Fontanasia, not a slum like Cormicks. She wondered for a split second if her uncle was actually making this place better for the inhabitants, but Avalon knew she couldn't leave him installed as ruler of Cormicks. He would turn his wrath toward Fontanasia as soon as he deemed fit.

Avalon turned her attention to the task at hand. They stomped by the small figure of Cincin on the ground who was yelling and pointing off into the distance. The two other Anthracites crashed through the trees leaving a path of destruction that wouldn't be difficult to follow.

Avalon had been half-crouched, and she took a minute to feel her balance on the beast. She had ridden Jackie once, and she had ridden horses and felt their muscles moving just under the skin on both animals, and although the Anthracite's rocks swirled around her ankles to keep her locked on top, she didn't feel muscles per se. It was solid rock just underneath.

This was a moving mountain, but she didn't sense any spirit like she did in the other animals. This was a sentinel, coal and stone, and it was trudging on after the others because it had been summoned. It had no more soul than the ground they tread on.

Nugget didn't call to the Anthracite when Avalon crashed out of the trees. She pointed after the other two beasts and actually stepped in to get a closer look as the giant rock feet smashed into the ground. Avalon didn't need to see Nugget's face clearly to know that the Guide was jealous and incredulous. The King had summoned beasts that would only answer to females.

They were soon upon Sonrah and Chylyn. Sonrah's gown flowed in the wind and she was graceful moving her arms up and down like a bird while calling a word. The voice projected the brute song, and the Anthracites were reacting to her words. They slowed their pace but didn't stop.

Avalon took deep breaths and looked out over the landscape. She tried to see the wood that hid the field of elbagrass, or a hint of red on the horizon that might be Jackie, but the same brown dirt and greenery moved beneath her. Avalon needed the beasts to get far enough from Cormicks to not be ambushed, but to stay close enough that the others could catch up. She counted slowly to fifty and then took in the scenery before drawing in a deep breath.

Avalon pulled her leg from the rock and stomped three times before yelling at the top of her lungs. "Kooooor-eeeeeee!" The others didn't hear her, but her Anthracite slowed to a stop and then crashed to it's knees. Avalon thought she would be thrown clear, but the outer layer of rock flowed forth like water and as the beast curled down into mountainous form, Avalon was left to easily slide down the side to the ground. As soon as she dismounted, the rest of the rock solidified, and she stood at the base of a black hill. She could feel the ground pounding as the other two Anthracites turned back and crashed to stillness next to the one she had ridden.

She was exhilarated. Riding on the Anthracite had been like nothing she had experienced. Riding a horse to her was a necessity, and she had felt a bond with them, but that was a part of her everyday life. Riding the Anthracite was dirty, scary, uncommon, and the most exciting thing she had ever done. She was still scared that they might turn and trample her, but that had been a risk worth taking. She could defeat Hawker with the Anthracites. She was sure of it now that she knew they would respond to her call.

Avalon watched the mountains, eyes wide, heart pounding. She knew that they wouldn't move unless they sensed fire or the vibrations of the calling bell. Still, she could hardly believe she had done it. She looked down at her clothes smudged black, and with a sense of utter gratitude, Avalon threw her hands in the air and then started to cry. Years of indecision flowed out of her, and she knew that this was her place. She was grateful to be King, but she couldn't puzzle out her history and how it had become so, and yet she knew that she had been delivered to this moment on purpose and that purpose was to save her people. She was overwhelmed as the pieces unlocked in front of her, and without dreaming of events to come, the future became clear.

The tears ran their course, and Avalon pulled a clean rag from her pocket and wiped her face. The rag was black when she was finished, and Avalon took a moment to brush the Anthracite dust from her clothes. She knelt down in the dirt and drew a map of Cormicks from memory. She closed her eyes to concentrate on her plan once more. Avalon remembered the gold braided map from her father's study, and she couldn't help thinking of her father in the process.

He couldn't have known that his decision to make her a prince would have brought her to this place. She remembered her father saying that she might want something different someday, and she knew now that he had meant what she felt for Taggerty and the impossible future she wanted with him. Her father knew her body would change, and she felt the change within herself, both physically and emotionally. She was in love with Taggerty and she wanted a life with him. Maybe if she lived through the next day, she would have that chance. Avalon daydreamed for a long time, and when she heard crunching steps behind her, she shook the thought from her mind.

She turned to see Jakon running from the clearing that the Anthracite's steps had caused. His face was red and drenched in sweat, and she could tell that he had run the entire way from where she had called the Anthracites. When he saw his King alive and out of danger, the sack with the steel boots and the bell and bow crashed to the ground, and he bent over to catch his breath.

Jakon looked at his King with wide eyes. He had accepted the sand eels and the crossing over the Window without a question. He had even seen the hellish feast of the everreds without comment, but seeing these giant crushing monsters answer her call had been too much to take in.

Avalon didn't wait for Jakon to come any closer. She tipped her head back in the direction they had come and said, "You take first watch."

"But King Avalon," Jakon said. Avalon knew he was worried the King would die on his watch. She stopped his protest with her hand. He had come to protect Avalon in this place and found it impossible, and Avalon understood his plight.

"You said that if I brought you here you would do exactly as I say, and I'm telling you to take the first watch. I need you between me and the Runners if they come."

He took a deep breath and then turned in the direction he'd come.

A little while later she heard movement through the brush, and Nugget approached. Avalon could tell by the look on her face that Nugget was not pleased. The girl thought that in all of her years of training it was her right to call the Anthracites. And in came this man, this King of Fontanasia, to override the training she had undergone her whole life.

Avalon understood the impulse. Over the last months, she had been leaving the day-to-day operations of Fontanasia to Zaria and Kensington. That was her right and her future, and they had taken it over so easily that it had sometimes frustrated Avalon. She had been short with Zaria at times, and she recognized now that her mood was because of this preemptive assumption that no one could run Fontanasia but the King. The look of veiled contempt on Nugget's face drew her own feelings forward and made Avalon aware of her own behavior. She wasn't mad at the girl, if anything she was endeared to her, and Avalon smiled.

Nugget found level ground and then cartwheeled over to Avalon, and Avalon was glad that she had sent Jakon on watch. He would have drawn his sword if he had seen the Guide's approach. It was aggressive, and the girl's arrogance would have made a bystander think there was contempt in her movement toward the King. But Avalon had trained with Nugget for six months, and like an owner to an aggressive puppy, Avalon felt no harm in the girl.

Nugget landed five feet away and snapped to attention before smiling at Avalon and bowing her head. "May I speak freely with my King?" She asked. Avalon let one side of her mouth creep into a smile.

"You may," Avalon said.

"Was it fun?" she asked, twirling her staff in practice. Anyone in Fontanasia would have been appalled at Nugget's talking to the King this way, but they rarely spoke without moving during training, so Avalon still didn't take it as a slight.

"Yes, you could call it fun," Avalon said, wondering if this girl ever tired of motion.

"I am happy that my years of preparation were of service to my King," she replied, obviously jealous. Like all the Guides, even a young girl like Nugget was serious about her responsibility. It was the same intensity Avalon had found in the way Taggerty took to his calling as a King's Guard.

"Do you know why queens don't rule Fontanasia?" Nugget asked. Avalon had heard the story from the Guide chief, and she nodded her head, but Nugget continued as though Avalon hadn't responded.

"A Queen who controlled the kingdom and the Anthracites would have utter power over the people," Nugget said calmly, and Avalon nodded. Nugget's insinuation was the same fear Avalon had of Hawker being King and controlling such beasts. The combination would only bring destruction and abasement. Avalon knew Nugget was now referring to her.

"Since females can call the Anthracite, it was decided long ago that only a king could rule the people. It keeps a balance of power," Nugget continued.

Avalon didn't comment. She wasn't certain if Nugget was commenting on Avalon's control of both the people and the beasts, or if she was commenting on a male's control of the Anthracites, or if she was wondering if there was a chance Avalon was a girl.

"I shall control the Anthracites here in Cormicks, and rule the people at home in Fontanasia then," Avalon said.

Nugget moved toward the black hill and poked one of the rocks with her staff but nothing happened, and Nugget continued on as though Avalon hadn't spoken. "Because of the original destruction of Hawkerness, the Guides decided to carry on the study of the language, but not to share it with the Hall family. In this way, no Queen could rule both man and beast, and no woman could betray her King again and cause the destruction of a city."

"I heard the story from your Khee," Avalon said to Nugget. "The girl who served the Queen of Hawkerness learned the language of the Anthracites, and she used that knowledge to betray the Queen. She used the Anthracites to help the man she loved." Avalon looked at Nugget and put her hand up, and although the girl was not facing Avalon, she stopped her movement and turned to the King.

"What would you like to say to me, Nugget?" Avalon asked. Avalon both feared what Nugget would say next and at the same time longed to tell this girl her secret. She thought that Nugget might like her better if she knew that Avalon was a girl; a girl in control of Fontanasia, and a girl in control of the Anthracites. At that moment the others arrived and Nugget moved away as though she had been practicing her fighting motions and not talking to Avalon at all, but she continued in a low tone that the others couldn't hear at a distance.

"I think girls can do anything, but then no one ever told me I couldn't. I was trained to be quick," she said somersaulting away from Avalon and twirling her staff. She stopped suddenly and bowed gracefully to Avalon. "And I was trained to serve the King if needed. I have fulfilled that training, but I didn't think that my King would be able to actually use this instruction by himself. So you can see, you caught me off guard when the Anthracites actually answered your call."

The others were getting closer and Avalon's heart beat fast, but she wouldn't offer Nugget any information unless the girl asked her a direct question.

Nugget curtsied slowly. "And I was trained to be the lady that I will grow up to be," Nugget said more graciously than even Sonrah. Avalon saw a devilish smile cross the girl's face as she sat on the dirty, black rock of the dormant Anthracite and pulled out a snack.

Avalon could feel exhaustion creeping in on the peripheral of her mind, but she shook it away and took deep breaths to pull the adrenaline back to the front. Taking the castle at Cormicks was the only agenda that mattered, and she didn't need to explain herself to Nugget or to anyone.

Sonrah and Chylyn approached, but Cincin remained near the woods. Chylyn noticed Avalon's far off gaze and he walked up to Avalon and bowed which startled Avalon. Chylyn was always respectful, but he was a man of the business at hand. Since she had started training, he had cut short the proper courtesies shown a King, so his bowing now stood out.

"King Avalon, you are fearless," he said with excitement.

"This was the plan," Avalon said.

"This was legend come to life," he said with a smile. "No one has ridden an Anthracite in hundreds of years, and even then, we only had the stories told by our forefathers. It has been myth until now."

Avalon stood taller at Chylyn's compliment. She had done what she had come to do, and riding the Anthracite had been extraordinary.

"Should we get to the business at hand?" Avalon asked.

"It is almost dusk, and we leave before dawn," Sonrah answered.

Avalon looked at Sonrah who even in the day's exercise still looked beautiful. Her green robes were stained with the black chalk she had walked through following the Anthracites, but her deep red hair flowed free and there wasn't a bead of sweat on her brow. She had a way of making everything look effortless. Avalon tried to imagine Sonrah on the undulating beast of the Anthracite, but she knew that Sonrah would not ride.

"I want to talk to the Anthracites to try to convey our plan. I need to make sure that they understand and they follow us."

Sonrah nodded. "And what would you say to them?"

Avalon's eyebrows rose and she cleared her throat. She had been puzzling that out for weeks, and it sounded clever in her mind, but she hadn't spoken a word out loud, and now that there were onlookers, she felt foolish. The

Anthracites were big rocks, not humans. Still, she needed to explain to make sure they didn't betray the plan.

"Well, I want to say to come with us and if they help us win Cormicks back, we will make sure to treat them fairly. Hawker is obsessed with fire, and I can't believe that he hasn't already set one of them ablaze just to see the outcome."

"I wouldn't tell them that," Nugget said from atop the Anthracite.

"No, you're right. But I should tell them something to make sure they stay on our side."

"You already know how to speak to the Anthracites," Sonrah said in her deep tone. "All they need to hear is 'Come with us'."

Avalon was baffled. "And that will work, just like that?"

"It did for you today. Your Highness, these rocks are somewhat animal, like dogs. They don't understand full speeches, and we can't fully communicate with them, but they understand come, and sit, and stay," Sonrah said matter-of-fact. Her smile was not smug, and she wasn't mocking Avalon. Sonrah was very practical, and she knew what was at stake.

"If they are like dogs, can they smell us? Do they know that we aren't their masters?"

"They're rocks, not actual dogs. They don't smell." Sonrah wasn't having fun at her expense, but Avalon was embarrassed to not have worked that out for herself.

"Obviously not," Chylyn said with a smile. "They would have kicked Nugget off by now if they were." They all looked over at the smallest yet most confident of Guides. She had finished eating and was getting her blanket ready for the night. Avalon realized that Nugget was going to sleep right there on top of the Anthracite. She looked away and noticed Cincin on a small rock outcropping off in the distance.

"I'll be over there. We leave before dawn." Avalon moved toward Cincin and wondered if anyone would sleep tonight.

When Avalon was close, Cincin stood and bowed. Where Nugget showed only a basic amount of decorum and a good amount of sarcasm around the King, Cincin made up for it by always doing the right thing around Avalon.

"As you were," Avalon said, holding her hand out to the side of the rock that was open.

"Please, Your Highness," Cincin said.

Avalon climbed on the rock and sat, looking around at her surroundings and hoping that Hawker hadn't sent anyone after the Anthracites. She needed these last few hours to try to rest and regain her courage. She patted her pocket in habit, but remembered that Jackie wasn't there. She hoped to see him again, but in her heart she didn't want him to return until the battle was over.

Avalon ate some of the dried beef jerky and sipped water that Cincin offered. It was a long time until dusk. She stretched her limbs and ran the plan over and over in her mind, trying to plan for all possible outcomes.

"King Avalon?" Cincin asked when the sun fell behind the trees and the sky began to gray.

"Yes, Cincin?"

"How did you ride the Anthracite?"

Avalon sat up and looked over at the Guide. She was a teenager and almost Avalon's age, her body fully grown. She was studious and respectful with the practiced skills of a young warrior, but Avalon could see that Cincin was having a hard time grasping the Anthracites, much less riding on top of one. She had prepared for this moment, and the moment had come. If Avalon would allow herself to admit it, it was terrifying.

Avalon took a deep breath and squared her shoulders. "I knew that I would, so I did," she told Cincin. The Guide nodded her head, but Avalon could see she didn't truly understand.

"I don't think that I can do it," Cincin whispered. Cincin had seen the beasts in real life for the first time, and even with all of her training, they frightened her. Avalon remembered the first time that she had seen them as they tried to crush her, and she couldn't imagine what she would have felt back then if she knew that she was expected to actually make contact with the giant, black creatures.

"You will do it when the time comes," Avalon said.

"Yes, King Avalon," Cincin mustered.

"No, Cincin, I mean you will overcome your fear and do as you have trained to do. It's not easy, believe me, but it can be done. You saw me do it, so you know that it can be done. You will, therefore you can." Cincin nodded, but Avalon could see that she wasn't convinced.

"Did you know that Kings of Fontanasia can sometimes see the future in their dreams?" Avalon was smiling as Cincin's head darted up. "It's true. We can't control it, but Cincin, I can sometimes see the future in my dreams. So you see, I was going to ride the Anthracite no matter what, but I did see it in a dream ahead of time, so I knew that I would do it." Avalon nodded at Cincin's incredulous expression.

"Is that true, or are you just trying to make me feel better?"

Avalon laughed out loud. "It's true, but it's a secret, so I need you to keep that to yourself."

Cincin nodded.

"Let's try to get some rest. We all need to be as clear minded as we can be tomorrow."

"Well let's hope you have a dream tonight," Cincin said, and they both smiled.

It was all Taggerty could do to wait until the next night to cross over. He thought of Avalon constantly and worried that they had missed something in their planning. When she and Chylyn and the others disappeared into the elbagrass, Taggerty almost ordered his men to follow directly. It would have put Avalon in more danger though if he had. Six in a group would be easier to hide than a hundred soldiers. He didn't know where he'd hide that many men in daylight, and so he waited until the sun set on the next day before calling his men to order.

They all knew what the mission was and what was expected of them, and they were as well-prepared as men could be who were going to travel to another world and fight an army that few had seen first hand, with giant creatures no one would believe existed.

Taggerty was on one knee tightening his pack when he heard the whistle of the lookout. He and his men immediately stood to face the field of elbagrass and Taggerty slowly pulled his sword from its sheath.

"Some soldiers you are," Taggerty heard a familiar voice behind him. He swung around to see men of the King's Guard streaming from the woods.

"Prince Kensington!" he said to his friend, and the two grasped arms and smiled in the blue light of the elbagrass.

"My son is a prince. I am simply your humble servant." Kensington smiled and Taggerty hugged his friend.

"You have a son?"

"Yes, Prince George Hall of Fontanasia," Kensington said with pride.

"But there was more time," Taggerty said.

Kensington's eyebrows rose. "I know that King Avalon doesn't want me in harm's way, but I took my baby's early birth as a sign that I was to be here instead of in

Fontanasia." He smiled and lifted his arm and more soldiers streamed from the wood. The men who had not been here before were staring mystified at the bright blue field of tall grass.

Taggerty and Kensington stepped to the edge of the field and out of earshot of the other men. "King Avalon didn't tell me you were coming, and I was beginning to think you weren't going to make it," Taggerty admitted. "We were about to cross over without you."

Kensington sucked in a deep breath. "I tried to convince him, but he commanded me and the rest of the men to remain in Fontanasia."

Taggerty's mouth dropped open. "You disobeyed the King?" Taggerty asked incredulously, joking with his friend, but Kensington didn't smile.

"And half of your men were to remain behind to guard the Window, so it seems that I'm not the only one disobeying orders." Kensington smiled and Taggerty bit his lip and looked at the men who were waiting for his command.

"In truth, I wasn't going to come. King Avalon has a plan, and we must trust it," Kensington admitted.

"What changed your mind?" Taggerty asked.

Kensington smiled and shook his head. "Princess Zaria. There will be no living with her if something happens to the King." Kensington looked around. "Where is King Avalon?" Kensington asked sheepishly, knowing he had disobeyed an order.

"Cormicks," Taggerty answered, kneeling down to finish tying his pack. "Ten minutes!" he yelled to his men.

"Cormicks?" Kensington asked in disbelief. He stood frozen for a moment and looked all around him in a panic at Taggerty's men who were readying themselves. There were many men here, too many men. "Who went with King Avalon? How many men?" Kensington asked.

"Four of the Guide and Jakon, that is all the King would allow, and I had to beg for even Jakon to escort them." Taggerty stood and pulled on his pack, stepping away to check on his men.

"King Avalon lied to me then," Kensington said to himself. Then he called to Taggerty, "I would never have agreed if I knew what he was planning."

"I know," Taggerty called back.

Kensington nodded slowly, firming his resolve in his mind. He knelt and started to pull items from his pack to lighten it. He watched his men, some resting from the journey, others still staring at the blue grass that lit the air around them. "Men!" he called. "Lighten your packs to one day's ration. We go to war tonight!"

Chapter 12
Steel Resolve

No one slept very well that night. Avalon drifted in and out of a light sleep, but any sound brought her back to the reality of Cormicks. This wasn't home.

She saw Chylyn's outline moving away from the Anthracites. He was going to find Jakon to take over the watch, but Jakon didn't return and Avalon was concerned for him. The King's Guard was either worried about the enemy showing up, or he was more shaken about the Anthracites than Avalon had realized, and commanding him away from his King certainly didn't help.

The night in this strange place under it's black sky and browned moon seemed to take forever, but when she noticed the first gray light of dawn creep over them, Avalon felt panic rising in her chest. They would leave now and her fate would be decided before the full light of day.

The moment Avalon stood, the four Guides rose. They had been awake and ready, waiting for their King. Cincin had rolled her blanket and threw the string over her shoulder, but Avalon didn't bother tidying her area. She dropped down from the rock and led Cincin over to the lifeless form of the Anthracites. They stood in a loose circle, Nugget rolling a short staff in her hands, unable to stand still. She pulled a second short staff out of her belt and cracked them together twice. Avalon's eyes went wide.

"To bring Jakon back, Your Highness," Chylyn said. "He knows the signal and will be here in a moment."

"Thank you," Avalon said. It was right that Jakon hear his orders from his King. It took him a few short minutes to find the group in the dark. He bowed to Avalon and cleared his throat, his hand on the hilt of his sword, ready for his orders.

"Sonrah must stay back to call off the Anthracites," Avalon commanded.

"I can handle myself, King Avalon," Sonrah said with respect.

"I mean no disrespect, Sonrah. I have trained with you and I know your capabilities. But I don't know the outcome of this battle, and I need to know that someone can call these beasts away, and if it becomes necessary, to drive these beasts away so that they can't be commanded by anyone again." Avalon pointed at the sack that held the bell and bow, and Jakon slid the bag off of his belt and handed it to Sonrah.

"This battle is not about today, Sonrah, but the outcome will dictate the future. You have the cleanest dialect of any of us, so it is most important that you are held in reserve."

Sonrah nodded in acceptance. She took the bag and smiled. "Thank you, King Avalon. I am honored to carry the future for you, but just for a little while. I will stay at the back and will call off the Anthracites if that's what it comes to."

"Thank you, Sonrah," Avalon said with all due respect. She was glad that Sonrah had not said the word that had been at the tip of her own tongue: retreat. For Avalon there could be no retreat, but she had to plan for anything. She took Sonrah's open hand and bent forward to kiss it as a gentleman would do, and Sonrah bowed. She shared a look with Cincin and Chylyn for a long moment, and then hit Nugget in the arm and stepped back from the circle.

"King Avalon," Chylyn broke into Avalon's quandary. "Will you allow Jakon and Sonrah to begin their trek ahead? It will take much more time on the ground to get to the castle."

Jakon cleared his throat, but he didn't say a word as Avalon looked over at Cincin. It was hard to see her face in the darkness. She was a trained warrior, and she would not shirk her duty, so Avalon would command her elsewhere.

"Take Cincin," Avalon said. "Nugget and I will be easy targets on the Anthracites, and I need to make sure that if something happens to us, we still have a fighting chance."

"Very well, King Avalon," Chylyn said. Cincin bowed her head to Avalon, and where Avalon thought she would see relief she only saw humiliation. No one else had heard their talk the night before, and Avalon didn't mean to offend.

"Cincin," Avalon said to the girl, "Sonrah will remain back, but I want you with Jakon in the battle. You have spent some time with these creatures too, and you will need to be up front to command them if we cannot. I am counting on you."

Cincin's eyes brightened, realizing that the King hadn't lost faith in her.

Avalon turned to Chylyn and Jakon. "We will take the Anthracites a bit further out to get used to their feel before turning back. The light of day will be here soon enough. Take Sonrah and Cincin as fast as you can and go back to where we found the Anthracites. Taggerty will be there with the men. When he hears the Anthracites, the men will begin their attack."

"Yes, King Avalon," Jakon said. She could see the regret on his face, but she would be riding the Anthracite into battle, and he couldn't come with her. Jakon bowed deeply and turned to leave.

"Go now," Chylyn told the three. "I have some other business to handle. Sonrah, get clear and then sound the bell in five minutes."

They picked up their packs and moved away from Avalon and the three mountains of black rock that would soon be alive and hopefully under control. When they were out of earshot, Chylyn explained himself.

"Nugget, you said that the King would not be able to control the Anthracites, and yet he did."

Nugget was still anxious about that detail, and for a moment, Avalon thought Chylyn had learned her secret and was going to call her out right then and there.

"Men rule the land, and women rule the Anthracites, correct?" he asked Nugget.

Avalon was sweating in panic, knowing that Chylyn was about to expose her. Did it really matter anymore? She would do anything she had to in the course of regaining Cormicks, and she knew that could mean losing her life. The detail that she was a girl was losing its significance in the scope of things.

"We should start," Avalon said.

Chylyn's lip pulled up in a sideways smile. "And we will, when Sonrah rings the bell." His grin told Avalon that he had a secret to tell, but by his expression, she knew it wasn't her secret, and she let out a sigh. Avalon had seen this expression before when they were training. He was about to teach Nugget a lesson.

"Women control the Anthracites. Correct, Nugget?" Chylyn asked again in a tone that made Nugget roll her eyes. She too knew that a lesson was forthcoming, and although Nugget liked to dish it out, she couldn't take it when someone was bold with her.

"Yes, correct," Nugget said in a hurry. She checked her weapons and pulled her short cape tight. She turned toward the Anthracites, discarding the rest of her pack on the ground. Nugget tied a scarf around her mouth, and the gravity of the moment took Avalon.

They were leaving for battle now, and Avalon wasn't prepared. She checked her own weapons, feeling the hilt of her sword and two knives tucked into her belt. She pulled her pants around her boots, hurriedly pulling the laces tighter than usual so that bits of Anthracite would not make their way in. She also checked her jacket and tied the scarf around her mouth to block out the cloud of dust that would envelop them as soon as the charcoal beasts stood.

"Well, that's not completely true," Chylyn said, turning to the Anthracites. "I believe that the beasts will listen to whoever knows the language. They didn't listen to King Avalon just because the King is the King, no disrespect meant, King Avalon."

"None taken," Avalon said, her first command swirling around in her mind. She was trying to keep her head straight, but the Anthracite language was escaping her thoughts, and she didn't fully comprehend what Chylyn was telling them.

Chylyn dropped his square pack on the ground with the tang of steel bow on steel bell beginning to ring out. He pulled out the steel boots that he had offered to Avalon and held them out. Since there were no takers, he pulled them on his feet. They slipped on easily, and weren't loose like when Avalon had put them on, and Avalon wondered why he would have made these boots for himself. Then his statement reverberated in her mind like the burgeoning ringing, and she understood.

Chylyn was standing between Avalon and Nugget, and as he stepped into the metal boots, Avalon saw Nugget's eyes widen into shock. She turned her head to look at Chylyn. They heard the building timbre of the kasic bell and the bow off in the distance, and Chylyn laughed.

"May I?" Chylyn asked Avalon, pointing to the Anthracite. Avalon's mouth fell open. He really thought that he could control the charcoal beasts, and for a moment she wondered if he could.

"Of course," Avalon said, stepping back.

Chylyn smiled and then his laugh built with the look of utter disbelief on Nugget's face. The ground shook and black dust enveloped them, and he faced the Anthracite that had started its tear out of the ground. The noise this close was immense, and Avalon pulled the scarf tighter around her mouth and then covered her ears for a moment.

"Roooooj-Kaaaaaaaa!" Chylyn screamed at the top of his lungs with his arms outstretched. Avalon and Nugget took a few steps back when the Anthracite turned toward him. Avalon took several more steps backward and waited for the Anthracite to respond to Chylyn. She'd never heard him try the words, but his pronunciation was actually as good as hers, and yet the outer layer of rock wasn't turning to the flowing pebbles that had pulled Avalon up last time.

"Roooooj-Kaaaaaaaa!" Chylyn screamed again, the double vibration of the tone weakening his vocal chords. The Anthracite was fully unfolded and the second mountain was beginning to rumble to life.

Then Chylyn turned to Avalon and smiled. He had to yell over the crunching sound of the unfolding beasts. "I have wanted to try that for a long time, but it was just a theory. I thought you proved me right, but I guess not." He turned to run, but he was stuck in the heavy metal boots, and he tumbled sideways as the Anthracite lifted its leg.

Avalon shrugged at Nugget, a part of her wishing that Chylyn had been successful. "I will never understand his sense of humor," Avalon said before yelling, "Roooooj-Kaaaaaaaa!"

The Anthracite's leg slammed back on the ground, and Chylyn pulled his shoes from the boots before turning to run. The Anthracite's outer rock layer swirled for a moment before its rocks reached out for Avalon. She stepped up onto the waiting surface, balancing on the undulating pebbles and for the second time, she rose to the top of the Anthracite.

Kensington had seen the bright, blue elbagrass, and he'd talked to Taggerty about crossing over to Cormicks, but there was nothing to prepare him for the actual moment. Taggerty and the Guides had walked among the men to prepare them. They were to wade through the grass together and then one at a time, look at their eyes in the pool, and then move aside for the next man to pass through.

It was almost midnight when Kensington bit into the three bitter alleya leaves that were given to him, and he grimaced as he chewed, but he made sure to swallow. The Guide had warned everyone that they would need the leaf to counteract the poison on the other side. None of the men was sure what "on the other side" meant, but they knew what poison was, and they all followed the instructions.

The grass was well over Kensington's head, and he followed close behind the Guide. When he stepped up to the small rectangular pool of water lined by stone, he couldn't believe that was where the warriors who had burst from the elbagrass less than a year ago had come from.

The Guide in front looked at Kensington, leaned over to look into the water, and then he was gone. Kensington gasped and hoped the men following didn't hear his surprise. He gulped back his fear and stepped up to the pool, first glancing at the man behind him and then down at the water.

He saw the moon's reflection and then looked into his own eyes, and all at once the bright blue glow was gone.

He was still leaning over, and the Guide who had disappeared was there again, and he grabbed Kensington's arm and pulled him away from the water. A moment later, the man who'd been behind him appeared, and Kensington pulled him away from the pool before turning to notice his surroundings.

It seemed to be the same field of tall grass, but it was dark and there was no moon to be seen. Kensington felt as though he was still in Fontanasia, but he sniffed the air and knew that he was no longer home. His eyes adjusted quickly to the light, and he could hear the movement of tall grass in the wind around him and see the black figures of men in the bit of gray light that the night afforded them.

"Come," the Guide said when he saw Taggerty appear at the pool. There were fifteen men across, and it would take a long time to get the rest of the men over, but they had to start moving before the rustling of a hundred men in the elbagrass could be heard and alert the enemy of their presence.

Taggerty patted Kensington on the shoulder and the new Prince of Fontanasia followed the Guide out of the field. Kensington didn't consider himself above anyone, but he was the head of the King's Guard and he understood his new duty, and he was ready to lead these men until they found the King. Then Kensington would relay any battle orders that Avalon gave, and he would make sure they were followed. Taggerty had said there would be no orders though and that Kensington would know the moment to attack. He'd wondered if his friend was toying with him, but there had been no sideways smile on Taggerty's face to accompany the comment.

The grass on this side of the Window was just as tall, and the Guide went slowly so even in the darkness the men could stick together. When they reached the edge of the field, the Guide stopped and searched the gap between the grass and the wood for any movement. Kensington and the men just behind him stared into the darkness too, but there was nothing but the sound of the trees and grass in the breeze.

The Guide said nothing, standing and stepping out into the clearing with confidence, and Kensington followed. They moved to the edge of the wood and waited for the others to collect behind them. As more men came, they formed two rows alongside the trees.

Exposed in the middle of the clearing, it was a long wait, and Kensington constantly moved his eyes in search of the enemy, but no one was there. He couldn't believe that the moon could just disappear as it had. He'd been under a full and bright moon when he'd stepped into the blue glow of the elbagrass. The pointed diamond light on the moon beamed from the spots on the circle, lighting up the night. But here it was pitch black, as though the moon had been extinguished in an instant. Kensington wondered if he'd traveled to a completely other world.

Davev came to the front of the line and whispered to Kensington, "That's all of us, sir."

Kensington tapped the Guide's shoulder and they moved forward. They had to move fast, and all of the men were constantly at the ready, but there were no guards at the elbagrass, and the large group moved quickly around to where they would cross through the trees.

When the Guide stopped, Kensington held up his hand and his men behind followed his lead. They were crowded close, on top of each other in the pitch black, and it was a fool's errand if there was an enemy close by because they could easily be picked off. Kensington wished they could spread out, but the dark seemed to suck the light out of the air and if the men split up in this foreign place, they would be lost.

Taggerty moved forward and whispered, "Davev and I will go first."

"I will go," the Guide said.

"These men need you more than anyone. You know the way to the castle. Give us ten minutes and then follow through where the trees have been cleared. It will be faster."

"Go," Kensington whispered into the black night and then the Guide plucked an insect from the air and smeared it down Taggerty's back, and a faint light shown where the bug had been.

Taggerty moved into the tightly packed trees and Davev followed. "Guard your face," Taggerty said, warning Davev of the branches and bark that their bodies and faces would be exposed to as they went through the forest. Davev was a stout form, much like Brick and Kensington, and the trees would be harder to get through for him than Taggerty who was wiry strong but not bulky in mass.

For Kensington, the waiting to move forward would have been the longest ten minutes of his life had his son not already been born. Hearing Zaria's screams from outside their bedroom was excruciating for him, and it had gone on for several hours. This ten minutes was anticipatory, but not agony.

The Guide led them on when the time came, and they stayed in two long lines, one on each side of the clearing, single file over the stumps. There was a lot of ground to cover before dawn and they were still unprotected, but this was a better way to go than to have all of the men try to fit through the tightly packed trees. They moved methodically over the tree stumps, trying not to trip or sprain their ankles when they could barely see the ground before them.

When they reached the other side, Taggerty and Davev stood on the flat ground beyond. Their swords were still drawn, but they were relaxed.

"Six guards, all sleeping," Taggerty said with a hint of regret in his voice.

"And sweet dreams to them," Davev said, a hard edge to his voice. It was dishonorable to kill these men while they slept, but there was more than a kingdom at stake. Their mission held the lives of every Fontanasian in its grasp, and there was little time for regret.

"Good," the Guide said, and he moved forward.

They didn't leave anyone to guard the clearing. They were all in now, and the Guide on the other side of the Window would know what to do if the enemy returned instead of King Avalon. They would burn the elbagrass again and pray that it would grow back as it had last time Avalon had set fire to the field. They would make for Fontanasia at all haste, and then prepare the city for the coming battle.

Kensington tried not to think about this outcome. His King was his duty but his wife and son were his love. This attack could not fail.

They walked endlessly, sending Taggerty and Davev out ahead to scout the terrain. They passed another section of woods, several areas with boulders stacked together, and then hours later, when he thought he could see the slightest hint of gray light in the sky, they stopped.

"We will meet here," the Guide said. "We will go to battle within the hour."

"One hour," Kensington said to the soldier closest to him. "Tell the men to rest and prepare."

The men lightened their packs, but no one ate. They had snacked on the journey this night, but no one was hungry but for the outcome of the approaching battle. Kensington recognized Taggerty as his friend approached, but he didn't see King Avalon anywhere.

"We go soon," Kensington warned Taggerty. "And we go with or without the King."

"What are we waiting for?" Kensington asked. After many conversations with Avalon, he knew that this place was close to the castle and that they could make it there in less than fifteen minutes at a run and with no obstacles. There would be an outer wall to contend with, and the low ground meant death, but Taggerty didn't seem worried, and Kensington knew that he hadn't brought the men here to die at the base of a wall.

"You will know the moment to attack, I promise you, Kensington. We will go without King Avalon if we must, but we should wait until daybreak as promised.

"Where is the King?" Kensington asked. He knew part of the answer. All Taggerty had said was that Avalon and the Guides had gone to search for a secret weapon, but he'd never said what that weapon might be.

Just as Kensington had finished his question, all of the men around them drew their swords and stood at the ready. There was someone approaching on horseback, and the sound of the gallop came over the hill before the figure did. It was a strange sound, four legged like a horse but not exactly the pattern horse hooves made.

"It's alright," Taggerty said, and he sheathed his knife and took several steps out in front of the line of men. They all tensed as the patting sound rose in the dark. Then the steps slowed to a stop, and Kensington squinted through the gray light of dawn. It was Jakon and two of the Guides on the back of a giant, red lizard.

"Is that Jackie?" Kensington whispered, incredulous that the King's tiny pet could turn into a reptile larger than a horse.

"It is," Taggerty said as the lizard stepped forward and knocked his nose into Taggerty's head.

"Okay, boy," Taggerty said, running his hand gently along Jackie's neck.

"He's already a giant. That's going to do nothing good for his ego," Davev said when he noticed Jakon, and he too sheathed his sword.

Jakon swung his leg over Jackie's head and jumped down and then turned and offered his hand to Sonrah. She took it and slid from Jackie's back gracefully. Davev gawked at her tall, slim figure. Cincin ignored Jakon's hand and slid off of Jackie's back, barely making a sound when she hit the ground.

"Wow," Davev said aloud.

"I know," Jakon answered his cousin, and he hit Davev in the chest. It was more than a friendly greeting, and Davev had to step backwards to stop from falling over. Still, he continued to stare outright at Sonrah. She'd been beautiful the first time he'd seen her at the ravine, and he found that he still couldn't take his eyes off of her.

"Where is King Avalon?" Kensington asked.

"He will be here any minute," Jakon answered. At that moment, the ground vibrated and everyone looked around in the coming light. It shook again, and Jackie ran frantic circles around the group.

"Tell the men to hold fast. No smoking and no fires. Now!" Taggerty commanded. Davev turned his attention away from Sonrah and relayed the order, taking the pipes out of a few of the men's mouths and crushing the tobacco underfoot.

"Hold fast," Kensington ordered again to reassure the men, but the shaking ground was tickling his bones, and he wondered what was approaching. They all heard an immense crushing noise getting louder and louder until it was on top of them.

Just then, Chylyn appeared next to Taggerty as though born out of midair. He was panting and sweaty, and Taggerty could see he'd been running full out for a while.

"They're here," Chylyn said. "Do you remember what it felt like to get chased by an Anthracite?" he asked Taggerty with a smile.

"Very funny," Taggerty answered.

"Anthracite?" Kensington asked.

Taggerty held Jackie still so Sonrah and Cincin could mount the large, red lizard again. Jackie's skin bristled with nervous energy as the ground shook and Taggerty could feel the leathery skin slithering under his hand. "Jakon," Taggerty said, and Jakon moved away leading Jackie without hesitation.

The dawn darkened again as three giant, black beasts came stomping out of the trees, crushing the tree trunks like Kensington might crush the flowers in a field. His mouth was open as he stared up. From a distance they looked like solid rock, but as they came closer he could see that they were made of rock and stone that somehow stayed together to take this form. He looked for a face with eyes and a mouth on the giant but couldn't find one. The creatures were just two huge legs crushing the ground with each step. His instinct was to turn and run, but he'd just told the men to hold fast, and he trusted Taggerty.

The giant monsters stopped in front of the line of soldiers, and as the sun crept a little closer to day, Kensington saw the figure of a man on top of the charcoal beast. The figure slid closer to the front of the rock, and Kensington watched in wonder as King Avalon waved down at the men.

"It worked," Taggerty said, on the edge of laughter.

"This was part of the plan?" Kensington asked in awe.

The black dust settled all around as Taggerty and the rest of the men stared up at their King, riding on top of a massive creature they'd never seen before. The sight took Taggerty's breath away. He wasn't beyond being worried about Avalon's safety, but he was in awe of her fortitude under the weight of such magnificent and insurmountable odds.

Avalon drew her sword, and Taggerty noticed Nugget on the second Anthracite holding her staff over her head. There would be no last conversation, no speech from the King.

"This was part of the plan?" Kensington asked again.

"Have the men follow me, Kensington. They must stay to the left and stick together."

Taggerty took a deep breath and steeled himself for the coming battle. Butterflies filled his stomach, and he was overwhelmed with respect for his King, but he grit his teeth when he thought of Avalon in danger with no way to protect her. There would be no hiding, no skirting the trees or ducking under thorny bushes to watch over Cormicks. They would take the castle or they would die. He looked up at the Anthracite but he could no longer see Avalon. It was better that way, he thought.

Kensington's mouth was open, and Taggerty had to pat him on the arm to rouse him. Taggerty held his arm out, and Kensington stepped forward.

"We go to battle now, men!" Kensington yelled, and he turned and started to run next to Taggerty. The men called out as they followed, and the sound of more than a hundred soldiers beating a path to Cormicks filled the morning air. It didn't matter though; it would hardly give them away. When the Anthracites rounded the men and crushed through the protective wall surrounding Cormicks and allowing the invading army inside the city, the surprise would be total.

Chapter 13
Jackie's Climb

Hawker had always been a night owl, and during his reign in Cormicks, little had changed. He liked to study late in the quiet of night when he felt more awake. This night had been little different, and he'd just gone to bed at the first sign of gray light in the window. He usually slept late into the day and he'd been asleep for very little time when the bed shook, and he could feel the Anthracites returning. He sighed in satisfaction. They were not easy to control, but he knew they would be back. They always came back.

Hawker rolled over and closed his eyes, but he didn't fall back to sleep. He knew what the rumble was, but it wasn't tapering off like it usually did as the giants curled up into stagnant mountains. They should have gone dormant by now, but the pounding steps that vibrated everything within a mile continued, and they weren't slowing down.

He'd already sat up when there was a knock at the door. Hawker pulled on his boots and his long, black robe. "What?" he yelled at the closed door, and when Square-Dot burst through, Hawker thought he already knew the answer.

"It's an army, Your Highness," the White Robe said. "At least that is what the men are reporting." Square-Dot bowed his head, but Hawker had seen the utter panic on his face. This was a cunning counselor, and although Hawker had broken the man's confident demeanor into one of subservience, he was still shrewd, and Hawker didn't like to see concern on his face.

They stood listening to the rumbling for a moment and then two Runners and Triangle burst into the room.

"We must leave, Your Highness. I must take you to a safe place," Triangle said, but Hawker swept past both White Robes into the hallway.

"Stop your sniveling. This is Hawkerness, and I am King Hawker. We aren't going anywhere." Hawker moved down the corridor to where a heavily tattooed Runner stood guard. At the sight of the King, the soldier opened the door.

"Bring her," Hawker said. He moved down the hallway, his cape trailing behind his tall, swift frame.

When King Hawker had burst in, Mandetta was ready, but the Runner still pulled her by the hair all the way up to the parapet. The guards did as they were told, but they also relished adding punishment of their own and the King didn't seem to mind as long as his order was carried out in the end.

When they stepped into the light of day, the guard twisted her arm and Mandetta was thrown out in front of him. He made sure she would remain on her feet though. Once he'd pushed too hard and Mandetta had fallen, the kasic bell clanging in front of her sprawled figure. The King strode to the careless guard and stood face to face with the brute Runner as he heated the metal of his knife in the flame of a torch. Then he burned the guard's flesh with the heated steel of his knife.

Mandetta had been treated a little easier since then. She doubted the burn had hurt under all of the layers of tattoo, but it had scarred the guard's ego, and he hadn't let it happen again.

Triangle appeared clutching the bag with the kasic bell and bow, but Mandetta knew it was too late. She'd heard the rumbling of the Anthracites and had been counting the seconds, and when she looked up at the orange haze of sky, her breath caught in her mouth. The three Anthracites were pounding in a line on her left and they were almost upon Cormicks. They would soon hit the wall that protected the castle, and they made no hint of stopping.

The orange light became yellow and Mandetta could see the figure of a person on top of the first Anthracite. She wasn't the only one to see it because the counselors were pointing and speaking quickly to the King about leaving. Mandetta's heart leapt in her chest, and the thought of freedom whispered the hint of possibility in her mind.

King Hawker turned on Triangle and backhanded the small, bald man who stumbled back into the wall of the castle and fell to the stone floor. The bag with the kasic bell and bow clattered to the ground.

"Call them!" King Hawker screamed at Mandetta, and she had the kasic bell and bow out of the bag before she knew what her hands were doing. King Hawker terrified her, and her hands shook as she raised the bell. She knew that her own father had beaten men. He was a strong ruler, but he had civility at his core. King Hawker had not been predictable in the time he'd ruled Cormicks, and he was not above lies, games, torture, and mutilation to get what he wanted. He frightened her to the core, more than the Anthracites did, and she tried to steady her hands as she pulled the bow to the bell.

Mandetta heard the explosion of stone as the Anthracites crashed through the protective wall followed by the roar of men, and she realized that behind the beasts was an army. She kept the bow gliding over the bell as she moved to the edge of the parapet. When she looked down, her heart sank. The enemy was a much smaller army than her father's had been. Many of his men had been cut down on the day that her father had died, and Mandetta no longer knew the strength of Cormicks.

The Anthracites had stopped their forward motion, but the invading army streamed through the open wall and clashed with the Runners who'd been alerted. Mandetta could hear the clanking of steel as swords flashed in the sunlight.

"I want all of the men pulled to the front," Hawker commanded to Square-Dot, and he ran off to give the command. Mandetta looked back, but Triangle was gone too, and there was only she and Hawker and the guard left on the balcony.

"No need to fret," Hawker said to Mandetta with a smile. Her skin crawled as he loomed over her. "It's just my nephew come to call this morning." Hawker pointed at the approaching Anthracites. "Call them off," he hissed, and her muscles snapped to.

Mandetta hesitated though, as she looked at the outlined figure riding on top of the Anthracite. This invader was the Prince that her father had kept in the dungeon. This was the new King of a place called Fontanasia. This was the boy who had taken Hawker's place and driven the man to an insane fury. Mandetta saw only one possible chance at freedom, and she made a decision then and there that she would help this King kill Hawker, the man who had killed her entire family.

Avalon heard the vibrating tone that called the Anthracites. It pulsated through the rock and up into the bones of her feet and legs, and the Anthracites suddenly stopped their advance. Avalon looked over to Nugget who was still atop the Anthracite next to hers. Nugget had her tall staff at the ready, and when she noticed Avalon looking at her, she pointed the staff at the castle and nodded her head forward. Avalon pulled the scarf down from her face and squinted, and she could tell by the way his long hair danced in the wind that the tall form on the parapet was her Uncle Hawker. She wondered if he knew that it was his own nephew coming to unseat him, and the flutter in her heart told her that he must.

The vibration moved from the Anthracite up into her legs again, and Avalon heard the deep drone of the kasic bell. She could see someone near Hawker, and she knew that it was the caller at the castle ringing the bell. Avalon didn't know what to do. If Hawker was able to regain control of the beasts, she would be dead on the spot.

"No," Avalon whispered as the third Anthracite halted. She could see her men moving out ahead of the black beasts now. They were exposed, swords clanging with the Runners who had taken the field, and Avalon could see enemy archers forming a line off to her left. A loud cry came from the parapet, and Avalon didn't recognize the command. Her Anthracite didn't move, and Avalon looked to Nugget who shrugged and shook her head.

"Jzuuuuuuu-aaaaaaaa!" Avalon heard again from the castle, but it was no call that she had heard in her training. She could see that it was not a command Nugget knew either. She waited for her Anthracite to throw her off or to fold up and crush her, but it just remained planted where it was.

Avalon tried to slide her feet to wake up the Anthracite. She had to get to Hawker. If she could stop him, she had a chance of winning this battle early and before any of her men were injured.

Avalon called to the Anthracite to move, but it wouldn't, and she could hear Nugget trying at the same time. The beasts stayed still though, waiting for the command from whoever had rung the kasic bell on the parapet.

"I'm going to call them from the ground," she yelled to Nugget. "Do what you must!" Avalon didn't wait for Nugget's reply. She pulled her feet from the rock and dove to the edge, grabbing a rock for balance before sliding over the side. Avalon tried to get footing again, but the side that she hung over was solid, and she knew she would break bones when she hit the ground if she let go.

She let out a scream as the rock she was holding onto sank beneath the outer layer of the Anthracite. Her hands started to plunge into the rock as her feet had before. She felt as though she was trying to grasp sand as the Anthracite slowly lowered her to the ground. Arrows ricocheted off the rocks and Avalon was glad that she had dismounted away from the archers. She stood on the ground and pulled her hands out of the Anthracite, looking at her skin. It was red, but there were no cuts.

Another arrow flew past her head, and Avalon looked around at her soldiers who were sprinting around the Anthracites, scarves pulled down from their faces now that the black dust had stopped clouding around them. Jakon found her first in the fray, and Avalon was relieved to see Cincin at his side. They could hear Nugget yelling commands to no avail.

"Get Sonrah to ring the kasic bell," Avalon yelled. Cincin nodded and when their eyes met for a moment, Avalon knew that the girl understood the seriousness of their predicament.

"Go!" Jakon told Cincin, pointing back to the tree line.

Avalon's head darted all around. She had to find a way to get up to the parapet. She had to get control of the kasic bell, and she had to put an end to Hawker. Her sword was drawn, but Jakon cut down the few Runners who came near. She spotted fire to her left, and Avalon could see a row of enemy archers lining up and a torch moving down the row of arrows. Then she and Jakon lost the cover of the Anthracite as it started to move on its own.

She heard the crunch of rocks as the Anthracites moved, slowly but ferociously, and in three giant steps they were on the enemy fires. The black dust that moved around the Anthracites like fog crackled to life when it came in contact with the archer's flames, and Avalon was horrified that Nugget would be blown to bits. There were a thousand sparks before the Anthracite's feet stomped on the enemy soldiers. Explosions rocked the ground, but the Anthracites didn't seem to be harmed. They had suffocated the embers under their mass.

Blood curdling screams of men could be heard now as the injured and half-burned bodies lay in the wake of the giant black shadows. Avalon could see Nugget trying to call to her Anthracite, but as quickly as it had moved, it had stopped, and all three beasts remained still again. Finally, Avalon saw Nugget being lowered to the ground. She was closer to the main enemy line than anyone else, but she wasn't immediately in danger because none of the Runners wanted to go near the Anthracites.

Nugget twirled her staff and then ran screaming into a group of the enemy. The Runners towered over her, but Nugget didn't seem to notice that she was outnumbered. The Guide moved fast, spinning and cartwheeling and kicking, her staff and her feet connecting with the enemy. Avalon had never liked Nugget's inflated ego, but in that moment of sheer bravery, Nugget would earn endless praise from Avalon, assuming they made it out of the battle alive.

The vibration of the kasic bell behind her met Avalon's ears, and she knew it was Sonrah calling to the Anthracites, but at the same time, the vibration came from the castle and the charcoal beasts still didn't move. Avalon looked to the castle, but from the ground she couldn't see onto the parapet. She knew that Hawker was there though, and she had to stop him. Avalon watched the battle unfold for another moment, wondering how she could climb the wall, and then the answer presented itself.

She saw the body of a Runner that had been blown into the side of the castle when the Anthracites snuffed the fires. It hung there, splat on the rock like an insect. Avalon was glad that she wasn't close enough to see the details, but his figure triggered the answer in her mind. For three years, Jackie had been climbing up and down Avalon's jacket, all over the furniture, and onto any table that had fruit on it. Jackie was the answer, and although she didn't want to put her pet and companion in danger, there was no alternative.

She recognized the black curl of Taggerty's hair and the silver wrist plates he never removed. She wanted to call to him, but it would cost him his concentration and would be a deadly mistake. They had promised each other to stay focused on the plan so they wouldn't be blinded in battle by their feelings. It would be a weakness neither could afford, so instead she turned to Jakon.

"Tell Taggerty that I need Jackie right now."

"Yes, King Avalon," Jakon said. She pointed in Taggerty's direction and Jakon nodded but said, "I can call the red monster. We're friends now."

Avalon smiled half a smile hearing her friend, who spent most days riding around in her pocket, described as a monster. "As you will, Jakon."

Jakon didn't hesitate. He put two fingers in his mouth and whistled three short bursts. Davev appeared next to Jakon in an instant, and the two cousins exchanged merely a nod before Davev took a post in front of Avalon. Jakon ran back into the crowd of fighting soldiers and within two minutes, Jakon and Jackie appeared at Avalon's side. Jakon slid down and Avalon accepted a boost from Davev to mount Jackie's back. She could feel the reptile skin move under her legs, and it was a strange sensation.

"I'm going for the parapet to put an end to this," Avalon said to Jakon and Davev, and then she patted Jackie's side and the red lizard sprinted forward. Soldiers looked at their King as he mounted this foreign, red beast. They were focused on the fight and were tough soldiers, but their eyebrows betrayed their cold emotion with question as to what this animal was, and why their King was riding it.

Jackie ran frantically through the battling soldiers, and his immense size and his tail that whipped side to side saved Avalon from being cut down. She'd rode horses, but this was much different. Jackie wasn't used to being this size or in battle, and his typically anxious manner was tenfold. Avalon coaxed him with words and used her hands to push Jackie's head in the direction where she wanted to go. He ran in circles for a moment, but eventually he made toward the Anthracites.

"Kaelan!" Avalon called as she closed in on Nugget. After the courage she had seen Nugget display, Avalon would never use the nickname aloud again. "Kaelan, I need some of the black rock!" Avalon yelled.

For her part, Nugget's fluid movement didn't miss a beat. She stabbed a Runner in the eye with her staff and then twisted under an oncoming blow to turn and unsheathe her knife. In a fluid uppercut, Nugget ran the knife through the neck of the muscled man that towered over her, and as he fell to the ground, Nugget pulled the axe from his hand. If it weren't for the blood, Avalon would have equated the precise movements to a dance.

Nugget ran to the nearest Anthracite with the axe and Avalon was afraid that the metal end would ignite sparks if it struck the charcoal beast. Nugget had the same thought though, and she found a head-sized rock that had blown off in the explosion. She placed the wood handle against the black stone and pounded the top of the axe on the large rock, breaking them into hand-sized pieces.

Nugget put the rocks in a pouch that she had strapped over her shoulder. She pulled the bag off and waited for Avalon who was barely controlling Jackie. He was barreling through the Runners and constantly changing direction. Three times Avalon was certain she would get pummeled, and then an arrow through the neck or head would cut down the enemy. She was sure that was Chylyn's true aim, and she would have to thank him when this was over.

Jackie turned left and Nugget ran to his side, using her staff to boost her up onto his back. Before Avalon could say anything, Nugget looped the bag around Avalon's neck and then she flipped off the lizard and landed feet first into the tattooed face of a Runner. His neck snapped back with a crack and he crumpled.

Just then Avalon looked up and saw a fiery boulder cross over the side of the castle and out onto the battlefield. It missed the Anthracites and crashed down into the dirt. Avalon swallowed hard. She slid forward to where Jackie's neck started and she could properly hold her legs around his writhing skin. Her feet moved in rhythm with his front legs and it strained her muscles, but she didn't try to reposition herself. Avalon didn't mind heights, but she had to stay on Jackie's back once they started up the castle wall.

Jackie bowled through the last of the Runners and they were fully behind the enemy line. Avalon moved his head left to right and then back left as he scampered back and forth in front of the castle wall. She was trying to get him to go up.

Another fiery boulder flew overhead and this time it hit the side of one of the Anthracites and exploded into a thousand pieces. Chunks of rock landed all around, and then the sky began to rain pellets of fire as the black dust fell down and crackled into nothing. Jackie was terrified and he scrambled in circles.

"Up, Jackie. Up!" Avalon yelled. He stopped next to the wall, his mass pushing Avalon's right leg into the brick. She leaned forward and grabbed his neck with her left hand and patted the wall with her right.

"Go up, Jackie!" Avalon yelled, and then he understood. Avalon barely had enough time to grab on with her right hand when Jackie arched his back and put his front pads on the wall. He tested the brick for a split second and then jumped ten feet in the air. Avalon's heart dropped as she held her breath. She tightened her grip on his neck and Avalon screamed but she wasn't sure if it was in terror or exhilaration. They were ten feet up and suspended by Jackie's sticky pads, hanging from the castle wall.

The soldiers had run full out for ten minutes and yet no one had slowed. Kensington had been on the front line next to Taggerty as they'd rounded the corner of trees and crossed the dirt and coal tracks left by the Anthracites the day before. King Avalon had moved the immense rock beasts away, but Kensington could hear them coming now, closing in behind him. He ran faster, afraid that the Anthracites would trample him. The hair on his neck stood up but he didn't dare turn to look. Three arrows flew from behind and over his head, but he was too close to the wall to know what they'd been aimed at, and he hoped they had hit their target.

The wall was just ahead and he had no way to go over or under it, but he didn't worry for long. In two gigantic strides, one of the Anthracites moved around on his right and smashed through the outer wall. Kensington followed Taggerty, climbing over the rubble and through the opening.

The men poured through the opening as fast as they could. It was almost daylight, and Kensington could see across the barren ground to the castle. There was a small village to his left with several cook fires started, and stables to his right. Kensington wondered if they would make it to the castle unchallenged, and then he saw the enemy.

The Runners were tall like Jakon and muscular, their chests bare but for the straps that held up their black pants. Tattoos covered any skin that was exposed, even their faces. Kensington had seen some of these men when they'd crossed over to Fontanasia, and he wasn't intimidated. He'd trained to be a soldier and one of the King's Guard even before he knew there was a real enemy, and yet he felt like he'd been preparing for this moment all of his life.

He raised his sword and charged ahead, clashing into the first row of Runners. His men moved around and through the pack, running ahead toward the castle. Kensington slashed and punched and kicked and tasted his own blood in his mouth after being knocked down, but he was up again quickly.

The fight had moved ahead of him as more Runners emerged and his small army met them. Kensington saw a few of the Guide who had come across in the fight as well. They were very different fighters than his own men, but very effective. They moved with a fluid motion, taking handfuls of dirt and blinding their attackers before sweeping their legs, or throwing rocks hard at the forehead of the defenders. Chylyn was deadly with his bow and arrows, and his black hair flowed as he worked his way forward, always keeping himself in the same area of battle as Taggerty.

The Anthracites had all moved through the wall, but they'd stopped, frozen in place for some reason. The battle enraged around the stationary rocks as more Runners came to join the fight. Kensington saw a line of archers to the left beginning to light their arrows, and the Anthracites came back to life moving on the line of archers and exploding them underfoot. The concussion shook the ground, and minutes later Kensington saw Chylyn fire an arrow toward the Anthracites. That's when he saw Jackie running haphazardly all over the field with King Avalon on his back.

Kensington's eyes widened as he saw Chylyn loose another arrow in that direction, and he watched it sail over Avalon to hit a Runner in the chest. Chylyn was helping to clear a path for King Avalon, and Kensington felt dread as he watched his brother-in-law, the King of Fontanasia, ride into the oncoming Runners. Avalon was on his left, but Kensington moved to his right and tried to get around the fray. His one objective was to protect King Avalon, and he would die trying.

He saw Jackie zig by the Anthracite and then zag back toward the castle wall. Avalon was looking up now, and so Kensington looked up and saw a tall, slender figure with long, straight hair watching over the edge of the parapet. The head bent to the right, and Kensington knew that it was Hawker Hall.

Kensington had spent over a month with the exiled Prince of Fontanasia when he and Taggerty had placed the fallen traitor as far from the city as possible, and as far as had seemed necessary for a helpless prince who knew nothing of the outdoors. It had all been an act, and Hawker had somehow made his way here and taken over. He was a dangerous man, and Kensington knew that he had to get to the parapet before Avalon.

He ran further out to the right where there were fewer skirmishes, cutting down several Runners as he sprinted by on his way to the castle. Kensington had a straight shot to an arched door that led into the building just to the right of the castle. He saw horse and cart there alone under the right parapet, but no soldiers.

Kensington looked back toward Avalon and saw Jackie jump onto the castle wall, and some of the fighting stopped for a moment as men who had cut down the enemy turned to look at the anomaly. They hadn't seen a huge, red lizard before, and they certainly hadn't seen an animal climb the side of a castle wall.

Unbridled adrenaline carried Kensington across the courtyard and through the archway. He drew his knife and had a blade in each hand as he found the nearest staircase and ran up. He got to the top and ran down a hall before finding another staircase. There were very few people in sight, and the ones he came across dropped to the floor and cowered or moved into side rooms to get out of his way.

Kensington scrambled up the staircase to the exit and was shocked at what he saw. The morning sky was lit up with fiery boulders that were coming from somewhere on the other side of the castle. He looked over the stone parapet and saw men crashing into each other with swords and hammers, their battle cries and screams of death curdling his own blood. He looked at the battle below and saw the Anthracites coming to life again, and he saw Jackie scrambling back across the field, but King Avalon wasn't on his back anymore.

More fiery rocks were being launched from behind the castle wall. Most missed the Anthracites, crashing into the debris of the outer wall or the forest behind them and starting to burn the trees. A fiery boulder hit its mark, and one of the Anthracites cracked like fireworks, a chunk of his rock body both fracturing off and blowing up at the same instant.

Kensington ran to the sidewall, and then he looked down and saw Avalon and Hawker on the next parapet over. The King was seated on the brick floor and Hawker was reaching for a torch.

"Get up," Kensington whispered, and then Avalon rolled to the side and Kensington could see that Hawker was about to burn King Avalon alive.

Kensington shook his head and grunted because he knew that what he was about to do was very stupid. He stepped up onto the bricks and took a deep breath. It looked to be two stories down, but that wasn't the worst of it. There was a long gap between the outside patios, and Kensington didn't know if he could make the jump.

The girl was useless. She'd been yelling commands at the Anthracites, but they hadn't responded at all. When he'd seen the Anthracites crush his archers, Hawker had cleared the guards from the castle. He wanted all of his men on the field. He would crush Avalon and the invasion, and then he would storm across the Window and burn Fontanasia to the ground.

Hawker had seen Avalon standing on the Anthracite, and his blood boiled. He should have killed his nephew when he'd had the chance. No matter, he would finish the job today.

The girl was yelling again, and Hawker took three strides and then backhanded her. She wasn't prepared for the blow, and she stumbled sideways and fell, the bell and bow clanging at her feet.

For her part, Mandetta lay on the ground and didn't try to get up. She'd been making the call with the bell, but she'd been yelling sounds that weren't close to any command she could remember, and the Anthracites had frozen in place. When the wind came in, she could hear the enemy's bell resonating, but there was no call yet, so Mandetta had continued to act the charade.

Hawker could kill her now. Her family was gone, and it didn't matter. She held satisfaction that the boy King had come with his army, and he would crush the Runners, and kill King Hawker.

Mandetta touched her lip and it was bleeding. The side of her head was sore where he'd hit her, and she half-expected him to kick her or beat her, or worse, burn her as he'd burned others over the months. He'd turned away though, his long cloak sweeping past her face. She thought the blow must have damaged her mind when she looked over to see a giant, red lizard appear over the side of the wall. It's front legs found the floor and then it's back legs found the top of the wall. Mandetta saw someone riding on the back of the lizard.

Hawker was laughing when Avalon came over the wall. She'd known he was here when she was on top of the Anthracite, and she was glad he hadn't left, but it was disconcerting to see him laughing. She almost fell head over heals when Jackie's back legs caught on the top of the wall, but he must have sensed this because even with his back legs still up on the wall, he snaked his body down to a level position.

Hawker looked at Avalon, and in an instant, even covered in the black powder and dirt, she knew that he recognized her. An evil smile crossed his face. Hawker took a step forward, and Jackie flipped his tail around and hit Avalon's uncle flat in the chest. The tail cracked like a whip and the laughing stopped, but Hawker stood his ground.

Hawker's nose twitched and he drew his sword, but Avalon had her knife drawn already and she slid off Jackie's back and lunged forward, slicing Hawker's hand. Hawker didn't pull away though. He trapped Avalon's blade in his left hand and drew a knife with his right, slashing at the back of Avalon's hand. She reacted by letting go of the blade, and Hawker awarded her stupidity by throwing her knife over the wall and down to the ground below.

Avalon cursed under her breath and stepped back, watching Hawker's maniacal face. He didn't strike though. He was enjoying his moment too much, and Avalon intended to use his arrogance to her benefit.

"Go!" Avalon yelled at Jackie, and she pushed the lizard's face toward the wall they had just climbed over. Jackie didn't hesitate. His body brushed against Avalon as his large mass went face first over the wall. The end of his tail hooked the bricks for a moment, and then he was gone.

Avalon turned back to Hawker and noticed the girl lying on the ground next to a kasic bell. She drew her sword and moved between Hawker and the girl. Hawker didn't react right away. He was clutching his bleeding hand inside his cape. When Hawker saw the sword he had given Avalon as a gift, a soft smile crossed his face.

"I thought you might have melted that down, but it seems you are more sentimental than I knew," Hawker said. "Have you missed me, nephew?"

"I kept this sword, Uncle Hawker, to remind me that I should trust no one. It is meant for this very moment, to finish what I should have done last year."

Hawker hissed. "Strong words for such a weak boy."

Avalon glanced at the girl who was still crouched on the floor. Caught between the two kasic bells, the Anthracites had frozen in place because this girl hadn't given a true command. "Leave," Avalon said to the girl, and she hoped the girl would understand.

"Stay," Hawker countered, and he looked over Avalon with eyes that could kill. The girl looked between them and then picked up the bell and bow and ran as fast as she could back into the castle.

"Bold move, nephew, attacking like this. I didn't know you had it in you," Hawker sniveled.

It was Hawker's face twisting and sneering in condescension, but it was not her uncle looking at her now. Her uncle's tall, reedy frame was always bent over a little, but this man stood straight, his shoulders squared like royalty. The Hawker who had helped raise her was dead long ago, and still Avalon felt regret.

"You left me for dead. I should return the favor," Hawker said, flinging his black robe open, and Avalon saw his arm whip forward. She saw the glint of steel and raised her sword to block, and then a sharp pain struck her front foot. Avalon dropped her sword and crumpled, grabbing at her ankle. Hawker had thrown a knife through the front of Avalon's foot.

Avalon let out a yell and fell back slowly, trying with every muscle in her body to keep her foot where it was. It was the most excruciating pain she'd ever felt. She could hear the cold grating of her uncle's laugh, and anger flooded her body.

"Did that hurt, nephew?" Hawker taunted.

Avalon grit her teeth and reached for the knife, but Hawker flicked his arm again and a second knife went through the back of her hand and into her boot. Avalon screamed, frozen in place, and Hawker watched her, toying with her like she was a mouse. There was a loud explosion behind Hawker as one of the flaming boulders met their mark, and an Anthracite let out a piercing squeal.

Avalon pulled the knife out of her hand, but her foot was still pinned by the first blade. Her arms shook, and she thought she might throw up. She needed time to think. "That's right, I am your nephew," Avalon yelled over the battle raging below the balcony. "My father loved you. You were brothers."

"We were half-brothers, and our father couldn't even see me," he spat back at Avalon. "Birch was always best, Hawker didn't exist. What do you know?" he yelled.

"Why else would he make you my advisor?"

Avalon could see by the rage on Hawker's face that he might run her through right now, but his nose twitched and he leered at her. She sat bleeding on the stone floor and grabbed the handle of her sword, but she didn't pick it up.

"Advisor," he laughed. "What garbage. Your father was blind and weak and you are the same. I am a King now!" he exclaimed as he held his arms out wide and looked up at the castle before him. "This is my land, and when I'm finished with you, I will take what has always been rightfully mine." Hawker took a few steps closer and then looked at Avalon with more hate than she could imagine possible, and it made her sad.

"You people," Hawker spat, and his face curled up in distaste.

As much as Avalon tried to put Hawker behind her this year, she still knew in her heart that they were family. No longer. No matter what was in their blood, the exclusionary words "you people" had finally cut the history between them clean in half.

"Look at it, Avalon. This is my kingdom," Hawker said, turning to the parapet and holding his arms out to the battle below. "It took me years of planning, and I never really expected to come here until I had taken Fontanasia. And then you left me in the wilderness."

Hawker was already celebrating a victory, and Avalon had to make a move now. As his back was turned, she grit her teeth and sucked in a breath before pulling on the knife that was in her foot. The pain was debilitating, and the blood held back by the blade began to pool around her foot so Avalon stopped removing the knife.

Avalon's eyes watered and she felt the pain burn up her leg and into the pit of her stomach. The ground shook again, but she couldn't see what was happening below. Hawker watched the battle for a minute, and when he turned back to face her, he didn't comment, but she could tell how the battle was going by the look on his face, and she smiled through grit teeth. The rumble was the

Anthracites, and her people had gained control of them again.

Hawker pulled his sword hand from under his cape and like a wounded animal he licked the blood from the back of his hand. "Your father was easier to kill, but the end result will be the same for you, Avalon."

"My father was a great King."

"Your father was a liar!" Hawker yelled and then he laughed and Avalon wondered what he knew. Hawker's nose twitched. "Your father was a liar," he said again, and Avalon squirmed. "Or didn't you read the note that he left for you with the map? What was it he said, 'Do the right thing, no matter the lies I have told?' What lies were those, Avalon?"

Hawker raised his eyebrows as though he expected the truth, but Avalon had no intention of answering. She was born a girl, that was the lie, but she had been raised a King, and today she would prove that was the truth.

There was a huge crash and some of the castle wall collapsed. Black dust wafted over the parapet and crackled in the air. Another crash sounded and more of the parapet wall fell off the castle and more black dust clouded the air, and Hawker turned away from Avalon to see what had happened. Avalon remembered the bag that Nugget had put around her neck, and she reached her hand inside and grabbed a hand full of the black dust before Hawker turned his attention back to her.

"We are right back where we started, nephew. You should have let me finish this last time." Then Hawker walked to the side of the balcony and reached for a torch, and Avalon's stomach turned.

Avalon was covered in the Anthracite dust, and she knew this was the end. The moment a flame touched her, she would crackle and explode. She unconsciously looked down at her clothes and found a moment of relief. The front of her body had been wiped clean of the powder when she was riding on Jackie's back. Avalon knew that the black dust was still caked on the back of her clothes, but it didn't matter. She had to put an end to Hawker no matter the consequences.

Hawker walked toward Avalon with the torch in front of him, and Avalon knew he would light her on fire. Her eyes darted around and then she looked up and saw Kensington on the balcony above. He was looking down at her from the opposite parapet, helpless to make a move at this distance. He stepped onto the wall to jump, and Avalon yelled, "No, don't!" as loud as she could.

Kensington froze where he was, but Hawker never looked up. He kept moving toward Avalon with the torch, a sneer pulling at his lips. Avalon leaned forward and with her bloody left hand, pulled the knife from her foot, screaming in pain. More blood began to pool under her, but she didn't move. Her right hand had the Anthracite dust, and she needed her uncle distracted.

Hawker's nose twitched and then his face filled with an evil smile as he stood over Avalon. He leaned down, and at the same moment, Avalon cupped her hand in front of her face and blew the black dust up toward Hawker. The air between them came to life. The black dust crackled and sparked as it caught the flame from the torch and made its way up into Hawker's face.

Hawker jumped back in pain as the sparks popped. His eyes burned and turned pink and watery, the air thick with smoke. He couldn't see Avalon through the sharp crackles of light as the powder continued to make tiny explosions in his face.

Avalon took another breath and blew across her hand, and Hawker stumbled back and screamed. Some of the crackling beads fell down onto Avalon's legs, and she swatted at her pants as they caught fire. She had to roll over onto her stomach to smother the flames, and when she rolled back over she could see Hawker reaching for her sword.

Avalon scrambled to her knees and looked to the archway fifteen feet away, and she wondered if she could get through the door on one leg. Her boot was soggy with blood and her stomach was queasy. She tried to inhale her last breath, but the air was thick with smoke now and it stuck in her throat.

Hawker rubbed his eyes and stood to his full height, towering over Avalon. He scraped the blade of her sword over the ground as he stood, leaving the torch burning at his feet. He was holding a hand over his left eye, and Avalon could see that his face was burned.

"How dare you," Hawker barked. "I am the King here. I am the King of Hawkerness."

"You are insane," Avalon said. "You are nothing." She was kneeling in front of Hawker trying to buy a moment. She was reaching in the bag, relieved to palm a chunk of the black rock.

"That's right, Avalon. Kneel before your King," Hawker snarled.

Everything slowed down for Avalon then. Avalon looked up at Kensington who was frozen on the edge of the parapet wall, a look of horror on his face. Hawker drew her sword across his chest to spin the blade into a head-chopping blow, but she was waiting for his movement and she was ready. When his arm was over his head, Avalon pulled the black rock from her pocket and found the patience to ever so gently roll it towards the torch at his feet.

She dropped to the ground just ducking below Hawker's killing blow, and then she used her one good foot to dive away from Hawker and roll her body toward the arched entrance into the castle. Avalon knew it was futile. She had seen a small explosion from just a tiny amount of the black rock and she'd just used a full palm size chunk.

Avalon turned and tried to run on her bloody foot. Anger burst from Hawker's mouth but there were no coherent words. Avalon looked back and saw his twisted expression as he swung the sword over his head to throw it at Avalon, but he'd realized what she had done with the black rock piece of Anthracite, and his realization came too late.

They both saw the black rock roll into the orange flame of the torch. She heard Kensington scream her name as she hobbled toward the doorway, but he was drowned out by the deafening white blast that consumed her and everything else on the balcony.

Chapter 14
The King is Dead

Kensington watched while Avalon stood up on one leg and tried to walk toward the doorway, dragging the other leg behind. And then the white-hot explosion came, and he watched Hawker die in a million explosions as the Anthracite dust burned and crackled around him until the concussion and flames tore him apart. It was the utter disintegration of Hawker's flesh and then Kensington was hit by the heat of the blast and thrown back from the parapet to the floor of the balcony. He was lucky to be higher up because the stone wall of the castle shielded him from the bulk of the blast.

He shook his head and stood up checking his limbs, but aside from small cuts, he wasn't hurt. He could taste the black smoke, and when he moved back to the side parapet and looked down, the front of the castle was gone.

Kensington's heart dropped, and he wondered how he could possibly tell Zaria that Avalon was dead.

Kensington heard a cheer erupt and he moved to the front of the parapet. He looked down on the battlefield to see his men reveling in victory. He would hear later that the enemy, though fierce, had no real leadership. They were taken off guard at dawn, and aside from the fire cannons, they hadn't regrouped after the Anthracites destroyed the archers.

Taggerty's plan of giving small groups of men specific goals and led from within had worked well, and with the help of the Anthracites, only eighteen men had perished. Even with the sheer mass of their soldiers, the Runners took a much harder loss, and without King Hawker or any real leadership, they fought until the front of the castle exploded and then retreated.

Kensington turned to go back into the castle. He had to find King Avalon. He saw the explosion, but he couldn't bring himself to believe that the King was dead. Inside the castle he weaved his way down two flights and then tried to find a way to the area where Avalon had been. Parts of the castle had been sectioned off from each other, and Kensington was frustrated with the maze until he found a staircase that was covered in bricks and rubble. He picked his way up the stairs and when he reached the top, half of the wall and floor were gone and he could see through to the hall below.

Kensington searched the rubble closest to where the balcony had been, calling for Avalon and turning over brick after brick, but there was no answer, and there was no Avalon.

Kensington thought about Zaria and his search became more random and more frantic. The worst didn't seem possible, but as each minute went by, Kensington found himself losing hope. In that moment the voices from outside quieted, and the Anthracites became still, and utter quiet descended on the room.

"Where are you?" he yelled to the empty room. And then a brick fell from the opposite wall and down through the open floor to the hall below. He looked across where the brick had fallen, but there was only a pile of rubble.

"King Avalon, where are you?" he called again. He squinted and watched, and as the sun rose slowly into the room, he saw a glint of metal in the pile of brick on the opposite wall. He leaned in, and Kensington realized he was seeing a red stone gleaming in the light of day. It had to be the ring that King Avalon wore.

He realized that Avalon had made it through the balcony entrance and must have been blown clear across the room in the explosion, somehow landing through the archway in the opposite hallway, and miraculously avoiding falling through the floor in the outer room. Kensington prayed that was the red gleam he saw, and he prayed that Avalon was still wearing the ring.

"Ha!" Kensington yelled, excited but wondering how he could make it across where the floor was missing. He thought of going back downstairs and trying to find another way up, but then he saw an archway full of bricks where this room went back out into another hallway. There was an outer alcove that snaked all the way around the room that had collapsed.

Kensington moved away from the stairs he'd come up and pulled bricks from a side doorway that he hoped led into the alcove. He stepped over the pile that remained and gingerly put weight on the floor. It was in fact a hallway that ran down the side of the room, and with each step he grit his teeth and hoped the floor wouldn't fall out from underneath. He was able to turn the corner to the right, and there he saw the pile of rubble at the end of the hall. He dismissed the alarm in his mind and threw caution to the wind, running down the hall to the bricks and concrete piled there.

"King Avalon," he said where he'd see the glint of red stone. "Can you hear me? It's Kensington." There was no reply, and Kensington knelt and started pulling the pile apart brick by brick. He pulled on a tapestry that had landed on the pile and was caked in dust, and when it fell away, he could see King Avalon lying dead in the center of the debris. Avalon hadn't been blown to bits like Hawker, but the explosion had decimated him and the fire scorched his body. His arm was twisted overhead and legs were splayed in the debris.

Kensington pulled the last bit of stone away and knelt next to the body. His hand moved to cover his mouth. The King was dead. His wife's brother was gone. He couldn't believe they had won the battle and lost their King. Kensington choked back tears. He had sworn to protect King Avalon, and he had failed.

Avalon was lying on her back, but the black powder that was on her clothing had burned up in the explosion, and the outer layer of clothing was partially burned off. Kensington was surprised to see a full layer of underclothing that was only partially tattered. The King's hair had mostly singed off, and there were cuts and scrapes on all exposed skin. Kensington half-heartedly continued to clear an area around Avalon. Tears made hazy work of his progress, and he didn't notice Avalon's eye open.

"You disobeyed me," Avalon croaked and then coughed, and Kensington jumped at the sound of Avalon's voice. "I told you to stay with my sister."

Kensington grabbed his chest, wiping away his tears. Then he laughed. "It's easier to disobey a King than it is a wife," he replied. He pushed the bricks away from Avalon's head and slowly pulled the jagged arm down to Avalon's side. Avalon groaned at the movement but Kensington continued clearing stones from Avalon's legs. The left boot was soaked red so Kensington left it alone for now.

"Can you sit up?" he asked.

"No," Avalon moaned. She turned her neck to the left and pain shot through her head. Her joints might move, but everything hurt, and Avalon wondered if she would die. She closed her eyes.

"Avalon?" Kensington asked.

"It's okay," Avalon said. "Hawker's gone," she whispered. "Hawker's gone, and Fontanasia is safe forever." Avalon let out a breath and her mind went blank. There was nothing else for her. She had protected her people, and for the first time in her life, she felt a burden lift from her shoulders.

"You will heal," Kensington said, reassuring himself more than Avalon. Kensington removed Avalon's blood-soaked boot and ripped cloth from his jacket to try to stop the bleeding. Avalon could barely feel what he was doing, but she was uncomfortable with Kensington being this close to her and touching her clothing. Still, she knew that she was hurt very badly and she needed his help.

"You will be a legend," Kensington said, "and I will tell your story to my son, George."

He tied the rag tight around her foot and Avalon took in a sharp breath. "You have a son?" she asked.

Kensington smiled. "You have a nephew. We named him George after Myra. He was early and he is small right now, but he's healthy." Kensington continued his work on Avalon, and she clenched her teeth as sensation slowly returned to her body. She wished it hadn't though, because every inch of her hurt.

"I have a nephew, and I will be a legend," Avalon said. A sharp pain ran up her skull and Avalon winced. "The King is dead," she said and closed her eyes again.

"Stay with me," Kensington begged. He pulled the small canteen from his side and poured some water slowly into

Avalon's mouth. It ran down the back of her throat and she drank it and then coughed, and the muscle spasm made her whole body hurt, and she blacked out for a minute.

"Taggerty," Avalon said, when she came to.

Kensington looked down at Avalon and smiled at her as though she was a child. "I should go find him before he tears the castle apart looking for you."

She took her brother-in-law's hand. "Find him, Kensington," Avalon said. "I will be a legend," she said, and then her eyes closed. Now that her body was clear of the bricks, Kensington could see Avalon breathing so he didn't panic.

"I will bring him here, King Avalon," he said. He gingerly walked out the way he'd come in still worried the floor might give way underfoot.

Kensington reached the bottom of the stairs and saw Davev coming through the collapsed hall at the bottom.

"Davev!" he called, and Davev ran around the piles of rubble that had fallen from the floor above. He was ready to storm up the stairs but Kensington stopped him. "The King is upstairs, but the floor could cave in at any moment. He has asked for Taggerty."

"We've been looking for you both. Taggerty went down that corridor." Davev pointed to the way Kensington had entered the castle. "I'll get him."

"I will get him," Kensington said, remembering the maze he'd gone through earlier. "You wait here and block these stairs. No one goes up, Davev, and I mean no one." Davev nodded and squared his shoulders, and that's when Kensington realized the soldier's arm was bleeding.

"Are you okay?" he asked.

"It's just a scratch. It's going to be a great story to tell the ladies," he said with a big smile, and Kensington knew that Davev was fine.

Kensington turned and pulled a knife from his belt before running into the next part of the building. He could see footsteps in the dust on the brick floor, and he followed them up two flights and down a hallway, and there he heard Taggerty call out for King Avalon.

"Taggerty!" Kensington yelled.

"I'm here!" Taggerty stopped moving and called back. Kensington rounded the corner and Taggerty grabbed him by the shoulders. "It's gone, Kensington. I saw Jackie climbing up with Avalon, and the whole balcony is gone."

Kensington could hear the panic in Taggerty's voice. "The King is alive, but he's hurt badly, Taggerty."

Taggerty bit his lip. "Show me."

They ran back down the stairs and along a corridor, and Kensington stopped so fast that Taggerty almost ran into him. Kensington's hand went up and both men instinctively took a step backwards. There was a door ajar that hadn't been open before, and Kensington readied his knife and stepped in and pushed the door open. They saw a short girl in a white robe jump back, but she didn't scream. Taggerty recognized the kasic bell and the bow on the side table.

"Bring her," he said to Kensington. He didn't know if she even knew how to use the bell, but he couldn't take the chance, and he didn't have time for a conversation. They each grabbed an arm, but she didn't fight. They pulled her along to the staircase where they found Jakon waiting with Davev.

Davev moved aside so Kensington and Taggerty could go up the stairs. Kensington pointed up at the ceiling that had caved in. "The floor isn't stable. No one comes up." He pulled on the girl's arm and she followed him up the stairs, but he had to wait for Taggerty.

Taggerty saw Davev bleeding, so he turned to Jakon. "Jakon, go get the men. Tell them to come inside the castle or stand on any rock. They have to get off the dirt. There are spiders here that will consume any blood."

"Of course," Jakon said, remembering the everreds.

"Spiders?" Davev asked.

"They are tiny spiders that come out of the ground like waves," Jakon said, and Taggerty nodded and then ran up the stairs after Kensington.

"Spiders that eat blood," Jakon said to Davev, patting his cousin on the arm that was bleeding. He smiled at Davev and then turned and ran outside. Davev waited at the bottom of the stairs and tried to use his sleeve to stop the bleeding. He felt itchy then and scratched his arm and his neck and rubbed his other sleeve, wondering if the spiders could smell his blood. He was a battle-tested soldier, but spiders gave him the creeps, and he decided to take a few steps up away from the stone floor.

When they had reached the top of the stairs, Mandetta gasped. Piles of debris were everywhere, and the balcony was gone along with the side of the castle. She put her hand over her mouth and stared. She'd been on that balcony, but she'd been saved.

"King Hawker," Mandetta said.

"Your King is dead," Kensington spat.

"He was not my King. He was a devil," Mandetta told him. "Your King is dead," the girl said, and then Kensington knew who she was. It was the girl on the parapet with Avalon and Hawker.

Kensington pointed across the gap in the floor and nodded at Taggerty. "Over there, but go that way," he said, nodding to the left. "Over the rubble and then the hallway goes around."

Taggerty fought the urge to run. He could see the building wasn't stable, but he was impatient as he climbed over the pile of bricks and through the doorway. He walked as fast as he dared around to the corridor to where Kensington had pointed. He didn't even notice Avalon's body laying in the rubble, and when he finally made out the form of a human in the gray dust, his heart sank. He stopped several feet from Avalon and his mouth fell open. Avalon had been decimated in the explosion, and it would be a miracle now if she lived.

He knelt next to Avalon and took her hand, and she opened her eyes.

"Taggerty," she rasped and the flicker of a smile crossed her face.

"Avalon," Taggerty choked, but he couldn't say anymore so he bit his lip.

"Kensington says that I will be a legend for today," she said.

"You already are, Avalon. You already are."

"Then I want to die here and now, Taggerty. I want to lay King Avalon to rest and start my life over."

He didn't understand what she was saying at first, and then he realized she was telling him that she didn't want to be the King anymore.

"I want to start my life over, Taggerty," she said again. Avalon knew that the only thing in the world she couldn't control was time. Time would just keep ticking on, and she knew that she had to make a change for her life here and now.

Taggerty touched Avalon's cheek. "You can't do this. You are the King." Since he could remember, he had dreamt of a lifetime serving his King, and in the past year he had thought of a future with Avalon, but he couldn't have her give up the throne.

"And you are the King's future. You are my future, Taggerty." Avalon reached over and put her hand on his, and she knew she was right.

"You are the King," he said, leaning closer to Avalon. "You can't give this up for me. You are the greatest King that Fontanasia has ever had. I won't be the one to destroy that."

"I'm giving this up for myself, Taggerty. I don't want to live that way, alone forever. I want to be with you. Don't you see? This is the only way we can be together. You are the King's future, Taggerty. This is the way you fulfill what the Guides have prophesied for you."

It was Avalon's daydream coming to pass. She could run away with Taggerty knowing that her people were safe. She had done her duty, and it was her turn to choose, and she chose Taggerty this time, now and forever.

She felt love, but it had never been easy for her to say exactly what she was feeling. She always thought before she felt. She always thought before she spoke. Avalon knew she loved Taggerty, but she had allowed herself to doubt for so long. She had doubted that he even looked at her in any romantic way, and she had doubted that a future with him could ever be possible. As long as she let the doubt seep through her, there was no chance to hope.

She had to tell him now. She'd never said those words before, never. She would have said it to her father, but looking back now, she realized that they were in the business of kings. She had heard Myra George say it, but Avalon had never learned to say it back because of the guilt she felt from her mother's death. Avalon had never been taught to say it, so she was surprised how easily it slipped out when she told Taggerty, "I love you."

They had both been loved by the parents in their lives, but they had both in some ways been pawns of destiny. Whatever lies and confusion they had in their growing up, they were free to make their own choice for the first time, and Taggerty could see that this was their chance.

Avalon squeezed Taggerty's hand and pulled, and Taggerty leaned down and kissed her ever so gently. She could see tears in his eyes and she held her breath, and when he smiled, she allowed herself to breathe in for the first time as a girl.

Kensington waited for five minutes, and then he pulled the girl around the rubble and over to Taggerty and Avalon. When Taggerty leaned back, the girl gasped. Avalon was in very bad shape, and Kensington understood her reaction, but he was surprised when she spoke.

"I pledge my life to this King who has destroyed King Hawker," Mandetta said.

"You be quiet," Kensington told her, and Taggerty turned to face them.

"We need medicine," Taggerty said to the girl. She pulled her arm away from Kensington and approached Avalon.

The girl put her hand over her mouth. She could see the burnt tattered ends of clothing around the King, and Mandetta knew that there were burns over most of the back of her body, and the King's hair was almost all singed off. She'd had experience with burns since Hawker had killed her father and took over as Monarch of Cormicks. These men would not trust her yet, but she owed this King a debt.

She turned to Taggerty and lifted up her sleeve. The flesh of her arm was pink and white and patterned where the skin had tried to heal from burns.

"I know this pain," she said. "Bring the King to my room. I have medicine."

"The King is dead," Avalon said.

The girl turned back and looked at Avalon's face, knowing that this was the one who had rode the Anthracite through the wall. This was the one who had been dropped on the balcony climbed to the parapet on a giant reptile, the one who had saved her from Hawker's rage.

"The King lives until the King is dead," Mandetta said. "I can help you heal."

"You can help me heal," Avalon said. "But I will not be the King. The King is dead."

The girl stared at Avalon for a long moment and then nodded and turned to walk away, and Kensington let her go. They had no choice but to trust her. Kensington looked through an opening in the wall and called through the hole in the floor.

"Davev, the girl is coming down. Go with her to her rooms and bring three blankets back with you."

"Yes, sir," Davev called back.

Kensington knelt next to Avalon and checked the bandage on the King's hand and foot. The hand looked okay, but the foot was soaked with blood. Aside from the burns, there were no other open wounds to be seen.

"You will live, King Avalon," Kensington said. "You will return to Fontanasia and meet my son."

"It was your idea, Kensington. I will be a legend, and legends don't need their life to live." Avalon fell asleep then.

"What was my idea?" Kensington asked Taggerty.

"Kensington, I have to tell you something, but first we need to get Avalon downstairs and behind closed doors, and then you need to tell the men that the King is dead."

Kensington crossed his arms. "And why would I do that?" He watched Taggerty who rocked from foot to foot, squirming under his friend's gaze. He didn't know quite how to tell his closest friend that Avalon was a girl.

"Well?" Kensington asked. "Are you all right? You look a bit banged up." Taggerty had gotten through the battle with some bruises and scrapes but no open wounds.

"I'm fine, Kensington. You're not listening to me."

"You're not saying anything, but that's okay. Zaria is my wife, and we don't keep secrets."

It took a moment for Taggerty to catch on to what Kensington was saying, and Taggerty was shocked. He wondered if his friend already knew about Avalon.

Kensington's demeanor toward Avalon had never shifted, and he'd not once said something to Taggerty.

"When?"

"Shortly after we were married."

"But you never said anything."

"Well, you left right after my wedding, for one," Kensington said with a smile. He slapped Taggerty on the arm and became serious. "Avalon is my King, and it wasn't for me to say. Zaria is my wife, and I am not going to jeopardize her family."

"So, you will go along with this?" Taggerty asked.

"It's better than having you live in the woods alone for the rest of your life," Kensington jibed.

"You can say that again."

"I have to send someone ahead to Fontanasia to tell Zaria. I won't have her suffer unnecessarily."

Just then there was a deep rumble, but it wasn't like when the Anthracites moved.

"It's the everreds," Taggerty said. He nodded his head to the opening in the wall where the balcony was. Kensington walked back around the corridor and over the rubble to look outside. The sky was partly cloudy, and when he leaned against the opening and looked down, there was plenty of light to see a wave of red ground roll over the dead and pull them under the dirt. It was like a lost wave from a red sea leaving a black stain in its wake. The red wave moved over the entire battleground, devouring the dead, and Kensington thought it both very efficient and tragic at the same time. Any of his men who had died or was left bleeding on the field in the wake of the wave would be eaten by the ground and gone, and he hoped all the men had been cleared from the field in time.

"The blankets," Davev said. He was standing in front of Kensington, and when he looked out at the field he scratched his bloody sleeve. "Those are the spiders?" he asked, but Kensington didn't answer. He didn't understand this place, and the day was taking its toll on him.

"Follow me," he told Davev. They walked around to where Avalon was lying in the rubble. Taggerty was leaning over the body, and for a moment Davev thought he saw Taggerty kiss the King. Davev was close enough to see Avalon. The bulky clothes were burned and torn, and Davev clearly saw the outline of a girl's figure. He blinked and looked again and noticed the way Taggerty knelt and doted over the body, and Davev saw for the first time that King Avalon was a girl. He dropped the blankets and Taggerty and Kensington wrapped Avalon's body as gently as possible, rolling her into the blanket.

"I must talk to the men," Kensington said. He looked at Davev. They were the same height, and Kensington stepped in close, right up to Davev's face.

"The King is dead," he said. Davev looked at Kensington and then at the blankets and shrugged. He'd seen the arms and legs move when they were wrapping Avalon, and he'd seen the King's lips move when whispering to Taggerty, but he didn't question Kensington. The King was still alive for now, but the body was charred and Davev didn't think King Avalon would live through the day.

Kensington walked down the stairs and saw Jakon and the other soldiers standing inside the castle. The rumbling outside had stopped, and he knew the everred spiders had moved on. He lifted his hand and pointed two fingers outside, and the men cleared a path for Kensington and then followed him outside.

Kensington wasn't sure how he would lie to his men and tell them that Avalon was dead when she wasn't, but when he saw the wounded and the exhaustion on some of his soldier's faces, and the places on some faces where the dirt had been cleaned off by tears, it wasn't hard to be emotional. They walked to the center of the field and met the other bands of men who had taken safety on the rocks of the fallen wall. Kensington looked around the group.

"King Avalon is dead. He died killing the Monarch of Cormicks, and so ended this battle that you all fought so bravely." Kensington cleared his throat. He needed to keep it together. These men needed someone to lead them, and here on the other side of the world, it was his job now.

At the words, all the soldiers took off their helmets and bowed their heads. They would not speak the words, but they would show respect to their deceased King.

Kensington choked back his emotions. They had fought a hard battle and lost good men taking the castle. He wished these men would have the knowledge that Avalon had lived. The King's Guard especially would feel the dishonor of losing the King they were supposed to be guarding, and he wished he could tell them all the truth, but it was impossible. The truth would reverberate back through King Birch's reign and cause a crack in the foundation of the Hall family, and he couldn't do that, not even for these men.

King Avalon Hall was already a legend, riding an Anthracite into battle and leading the men to victory. They saw the brutality of the Runners with their own eyes, and they could see what the King had done to keep their families safe, to keep Fontanasia safe. They had paid a price being away from their families, and the King had paid with his life. What came next though, Kensington did not expect.

Jakon turned to Kensington and knelt in front of him, and then the men started to kneel down one by one. Jakon put his fist to his chest and the rest of the men followed suit, and in that moment Kensington knew that his men were pledging themselves to their new King, Kensington's son, Prince George.

Kensington shook his head and tried to keep the world from spinning. He didn't know if that would be true, if his son would be the next King. He'd never given it a moment's thought.

Kensington nodded and told the men to stand. He was more concerned with the next two weeks before the Window to Fontanasia opened again. They still had many things to do to secure Cormicks.

Chapter 15
Long Live the King

Two weeks had gone by, and the Window to Fontanasia would open tonight, but Kensington would not go back just yet. The girl, Mandetta, had helped to nurse Avalon back to a point where they thought for sure Avalon would live, but even if she'd continued to be King, life would never be the same. There were burns over most of the back of her body. The double layers of clothing had helped to protect her from the blast, but the black Anthracite dust had done it's worst, and she would be in pain for a long time.

Mandetta had also been helpful in telling Taggerty and Kensington the hierarchy of the counselors and a little about each tribe, and Taggerty and some of the soldiers had escorted each counselor back to his village because Taggerty wanted to take a look at the enemy for himself.

Some of the villages were clean and had some advancement, but others were dingy and unkempt like the areas had been around the castle. All Runners who were soldiers were sent back to their villages, and to nail the point home that they had been defeated, Taggerty rode on Jackie's back with Nugget on an Anthracite in tow as a show of force.

None of the counselors were interested in becoming monarch anyway, and they were content for now not to be executed. There might be time for peace talks in the future, but all Kensington and Taggerty were concerned with was getting rid of the Runners and fortifying the castle as a base in Cormicks.

Avalon spent all of her time with Mandetta who seemed trustworthy. She was happy to be free, glad that Hawker was dead, and she had vowed to honor King Avalon with her service. She had lost everything: her father, her family, her position. Avalon didn't know if this was a centuries-removed relative of hers or a descendant of the servant girl who had stolen the Anthracite's song from the Queen and betrayed her people, but she would not come into this new friendship with prejudice.

She had explained to Mandetta her history and her hopes, and Mandetta had simply nodded, and said, "What will you be called?"

And without thinking, Avalon had replied, "Samantha." It was the 'S' she had been given as a baby when her father had named her S. Avalon Hall, and she would be called by her mother's name for the rest of her days. "Call me Sam," she said in afterthought. Better to separate herself a bit from King Avalon's history.

Avalon spent some private time with Kensington and Taggerty. Taggerty hadn't left her side for the first two days, but once color returned to her face, she convinced him to see to the men.

Taggerty returned each evening asking Avalon questions about how she wanted everything set up in Cormicks, and on the full moon two weeks hence, she smiled and said,

"Do you realize that I am going to turn this place over to you, if you will have it?"

"Yes," Taggerty said, his salty green eyes alight again with Avalon's recovery.

"Then stop asking me these questions. These are your decisions to make."

"King Avalon, this is your vision. Once your vision has been created, then I will make decisions on my own."

"I have other visions now," Avalon said and smiled, and they both blushed.

She was in pain all of the time and could barely walk. The back of Avalon's hands and the back of her head had been burned the worst because there had been no clothing to protect her skin. In two weeks time, most of her blisters were gone, and she was able to sit up.

On the day before the men left for Fontanasia, Avalon asked to see Jakon. He had been an honorable King's Guard, and he'd felt personally responsible for Avalon's death because he'd been sent to Cormicks with the King. It was Avalon's decision to see him, and she was glad that she did.

Avalon hadn't seen her own reflection yet, but she could see how bad she looked in everyone else's eyes. Taggerty, Kensington and Mandetta had learned to control their repulsion because they were getting used to it, but when Jakon came in the room, all he saw was a wounded girl. He sat down next to the bed and looked around the room and at his fingernails, and anywhere but at the poor soul on the bed who was wrapped almost fully in bandages.

Avalon cleared her throat and lowered the tone of her voice as she had for the last ten years. "You were told that your King is dead, but I am not."

Jakon's head jerked up and he looked at Avalon's face. He squinted and his mouth fell open, and then he slid to one knee and bowed his head.

"Please, Jakon, sit with me," Avalon said, and then she relaxed her voice and told him her story. She saw the epiphany on his face when it had struck him that she was a girl and that she had been a girl all this time, but he remained quiet and listened. When she was done talking, he'd knelt in front of her and bowed. He'd reacted like Walthan, accepting her no matter the circumstances. She told Jakon that he'd reacted just as Walthan had because she wanted him to know that she saw greatness in him.

Jakon was an imposing figure, taller than most men and massive in size, but she could see that this trip had shaken him to the core. He's seen things that he never could have imagined. She asked him to go back to Fontanasia with the knowledge that he'd not lost the King on his watch, and he had not shirked his duty.

For her last order, she told Jakon to gain an audience with Zaria through his Aunt Myra. He was to tell only those two that she was still alive, but that she would not come back. She had asked him to protect her sister and her family, and she hoped that would be enough of a reward for his part in helping her win Cormicks.

"My aunt knows?" Jakon asked, and Avalon smiled. That wasn't half of the story, but she wouldn't tell him Myra's secrets.

The next night on the first full moon, she sent Jakon back with some of the soldiers who could travel but were injured. Jakon would bring Zaria news that Kensington would be back in a month or two, once he could be certain that the new settlement in Cormicks was safe, and in turn that Fontanasia was safe.

They also sent one of the men who was the most vivid storyteller of the soldiers so he could properly pass along all news about Cormicks to the families of the soldiers who had died, and then to the rest of Fontanasia. Cormicks would not be a secret any longer, and in time many men and some of their families would cross over to Cormicks, others staying at the elbagrass to create a small village on the Fontanasia side of the Window.

It was six months before Avalon returned to Fontanasia, and she wasn't concerned anymore that anyone would recognize her. The heft of her athletic body had thinned out because she wasn't wearing bulky clothes anymore, and she hadn't been training with the sword and building her muscles as she had every day for years.

Her seventeenth birthday had passed, and she had a female's figure now. Her hair was below her shoulders, and her proud stance had moved in on itself with her injuries. She walked with a slight limp, and she kept her left hand in a ball when she wasn't using it because she still felt pain when she needed to use her fingers. Hawker was gone, but for this and many other reasons, she would think of him every day for the rest of her life.

Avalon and Taggerty made the journey together, and as they walked around the deteriorating bodies in the elbagrass, and walked across the new footbridge that went over the ravine and sand eels, Avalon realized how much time had gone by since she had left Fontanasia.

Sitting in the back of a wagon, she saw the city again, her city, and tears came to her eyes. It was so foreign to her now: the beautiful, clean streets, the children running in play, and the shop owners selling their wares. This place was wonderful and so far removed from the dinginess of Cormicks that Avalon longed to return here to live out the rest of her days. She couldn't hide anymore though, and while changed enough that no one would even suspect she was the King, even the thought of coming back as a girl left Avalon weary of pretending.

It was a small traveling party, and most of the men went further up into the Fingers, but Taggerty steered their wagon left toward the village of Guides outside the walls of the city. They would only be there three days before returning to the elbagrass and crossing back over to Cormicks.

Avalon and Taggerty would stay with Chylyn's family. Chylyn knew that she was Avalon. She had told him months ago in Cormicks. They had shared a laugh when he recounted to Taggerty his trying to call the Anthracite because King Avalon had done it successfully.

Here, Avalon would simply be Sam from Cormicks, and no one in Chylyn's family knew her true identity. Chylyn had said that the only way to keep a secret was to never tell, and so the less who knew, the better.

Avalon ached to see her family and it was hard to wait any longer. They had decided that it would be best for her to wait until the weekend when there were less people in the castle, so there would be less chance of anyone recognizing Avalon. She enjoyed her time in the Guide's village though. She didn't go outside the home because the Guides all knew King Avalon and she still didn't want to get found out, but she could hear the people in the streets talking, and she loved to hear the day-to-day activities. She spent most of her time reading from the small books that Chylyn kept in the house. They were very old, and she suspected he'd placed them there just for her visit.

After delaying for two days, when Avalon could barely stand to wait anymore, Taggerty came for her. She'd traded the white robe that she wore in Cormicks for a brown robe of the Guide's so she would blend in. They walked up the path outside the castle wall to the small gate, and Taggerty knocked the sheath of his sword on the metal. Just on the heels of the clanking sound, Avalon could hear a key opening the locks, and when the door opened, Kensington stood in front of her with a big smile on his face. Avalon almost put a finger to her lips, but his smile was gone as fast as it had come, and he wouldn't give her away to the other King's Guard that stood with him.

Avalon lowered her head in the brown hood and stepped through the small opening followed by Taggerty. When Kensington was satisfied that the gate was locked behind them, he led them up a flight of stairs. They had thought it best not to be seen together, so Avalon and Kensington stopped on a parapet to look over the city, and Jakon led Taggerty up to the King's suite.

As Avalon looked over the city she loved, she was proud and nostalgic but resolved in her future.

"I never get tired of looking at it, you know?" Kensington said. "When I think back on those black monsters, I couldn't imagine them coming here and crushing this place."

"I could, or rather I did," Avalon replied. Kensington nodded. He couldn't understand what had driven Avalon all those months until he'd seen Cormicks with his own eyes. The Runners, the Anthracites, and even the everreds were living nightmares for Avalon.

"Shall we go up?" he asked.

They walked up to the King's suite. The King's Guard eyeballed Avalon, but it was out of suspicion and not recognition. They didn't guard her anymore, they guarded her sister's family now, and she was a stranger here to them. The irony wasn't lost on her, and Avalon kept her eyes on the floor and tried not to smile.

Jakon was alone at the end of the hall, and he pushed the large wood door open so that Avalon could pass through. When she saw Zaria and Myra, she lowered her hood and they converged on her with hugs, all three breaking into tears of joy. Myra doted on Avalon's wounds and was clearly affected by the scars, but Avalon assured her that she was just fine. Stories of the battle had come back with the wounded, but after Kensington arrived and told them of Avalon's injuries, neither of them knew what to expect. Just seeing Avalon alive was a miracle.

Avalon looked around the room at the table and couches and her mouth opened in surprise. It was beautiful and much different than Avalon had remembered it. There were white flowers on the tables and the windowsill, and garlands of green with flowers were hung around the room, filling the air with a wonderful scent.

"Wow, Zaria, this place looks great. I can't remember it having a woman's touch."

"Your mother kept flowers, but not this many," Myra said. "This is Taggerty's doing."

"Taggerty?" Avalon asked. Just then she heard the cry of a baby down the hall.

"Come, Avalon, meet your nephew." Zaria led Avalon and Myra down the hall to the King's room.

Avalon took a deep breath in. This was the room that she was born in, and it had been her parent's room and the room of the kings before her. She expected a wave of emotion to crash over her, but she was left with fond memories of spending time with her father in the suite, and this room held the same joy. She closed her eyes and remembered jumping off the bed into her father's arms as a small child. It was sad to know that she might never return to this space, but Avalon smiled because she knew that if she closed her eyes, the memories would keep her company.

Avalon moved to the side table and took the carved box that Jackie used as a home and placed it in the pocket of her robe. She didn't know if she would ever see Jackie small enough to fit in the box again, and she was glad that he had found a home in Cormicks. Avalon wondered if someday she might use the box to give a jakkow lizard to her nephew.

Zaria crossed to the far corner where there was a large crib, and within was a baby boy trying to sit up on his own. He cried again when he noticed them, and Zaria picked him up and he quieted at her touch. He was already sitting upright in his mother's arms, and Avalon couldn't believe everything she had missed. She would be a stranger to her nephew, George. He would grow up without her, but it was a comfort knowing he would grow up with stories of her.

"Here, hold him." Zaria said. She turned George toward Avalon who had never held a child before in her life. Myra stepped closer and they made a circle around him, Avalon's unsure arms holding him upright. His big, black eyes stared back into hers, and the joy in Avalon's heart filled her soul.

"This is George," Zaria said, gently rubbing her hand over the back of his soft head.

"Amazing," Avalon said. "And you don't even look like you had a baby." She studied Zaria. She was the same beauty that she'd always been, and motherhood seemed to be good to her.

Avalon put her nephew on her right arm and moved her other hand around to his back, holding him steady with her left hand in a ball to ease her pain. His legs gripped around her waist on their own, and she felt comfortable holding him. She smiled at Zaria and Myra and then moved to the window with her nephew. She talked to him in a low tone, telling him what great adventures he would have as King, and she believed he would. Cormicks was no longer a secret, and it would take years to build a society there, but it would be done in his lifetime. Avalon wondered if he would travel there someday.

She ran her hand through his feather-soft hair and kissed her nephew on his head. She said the words that she was to never speak, the words she was never supposed to hear again.

"The King is dead, long live the King." Tears came to her eyes and she swallowed them back out of habit, but in her heart she was crying for the whole life she thought she would live, and how wonderfully different everything was working out.

Avalon would return to Cormicks, and Zaria and Kensington would act as advisors until their son grew to be fourteen, and then this little baby would be King of Fontanasia. Avalon didn't feel mad at her fate just then. She wasn't angry at her father, she never had been. Some strange twist of fate had brought her to this moment exactly where she was meant to be. Avalon could hear Myra's words in her thoughts, and she was grateful to have had such a good mother. She didn't know what was to come, but she was taking the life that Myra and Zaria had been hinting about, the life that her father knew she might someday want.

Myra on the other hand looked like she had aged ten years in six months, and Avalon knew that was due to her absence. Myra's hair had turned mostly gray and there were lines on her face that Avalon knew were due to worry. Of course, some of the tired look was certainly due to baby George, but there was an overwhelming melancholy underneath, and even in Myra's smile there was a hint of sadness. Myra had lost Queen Samantha and King Birch and now Avalon was going away. She would love Zaria's family as her own, but life would never be the same.

Avalon realized then that Myra's nephews had gone away and only Jakon had come back. Taggerty had told Avalon last night just how much Jakon had changed since Cormicks. Kensington sometimes caught him staring at objects, and he thought Jakon might be wondering if anything inanimate might come to life.

Myra's other nephew, Davev, hadn't returned yet from Cormicks, and Avalon wondered if he ever would. Avalon hadn't taken the time to talk to him like she had Jakon. Davev was resilient and the loss of the King hadn't gripped him as it had Jakon. Taggerty told Avalon that Davev had been the one to carry her down to Mandetta's room, and he wondered if Davev had guessed she was alive. He'd never asked though, and in the few times she was in his presence, he had not so much as looked in her direction.

Avalon handed George over to Myra, which immediately perked her up. Myra was a nanny to the core, and Avalon and Zaria joked for a while about all the things George would have to go through under Myra's tutelage. Zaria spent a lot of time with her son, but she was also busy working with Kensington and the King's Council on the future of Fontanasia, and she told Avalon that Myra was ready to turn over most of the care of George to her niece.

Avalon watched her family closely as they spent some time together doting on George. He chewed on his fingers and giggled, and the sound brought pure joy into the room. Kensington came in and held his son, and Avalon could see unequaled pride on his face.

"Ladies, your presence is requested," he said, and Avalon moved to the door, missing the silent look that Myra and Zaria shared with Kensington.

Avalon walked down the hall and her mouth fell open when she stepped into the main room. Candles of different heights were already lit throughout, although it was still midday and the suite built into the side of the mountain wasn't dark yet. Light from the candles mixed with the flowers to form a gorgeous setting, and for a moment she wondered what was happening.

As if on cue, Taggerty stepped from her childhood bedroom dressed in full King's Guard uniform that was decorated with ropes and patches. For all of his consistent cockiness, Taggerty had a look of utter clarity on his face. He crossed the room to Avalon and took her hands in his, and Avalon looked up into his fiery, green eyes.

"I asked you to marry me when we were in Cormicks, and you said that you would. I thought you might want to do that with your family present."

"Yes," Avalon whispered, and she sighed loudly realizing what all of the decorations were about. Zaria clapped her hands together and she and Myra approached Avalon.

"Come and get dressed," Zaria said, and she pulled Avalon away from Taggerty back to Zaria's old bedroom. Avalon could hardly believe what was about to happen. She had accepted Taggerty's proposal, but the actual wedding day seemed a lifetime away. She could hardly believe that she would be getting married today.

"There is a dress for you, Avalon," Zaria said as Myra closed the door. "It took Myra the last two days and nights to get it ready."

Avalon walked over to the wood closet where she had reluctantly been made to put on Zaria's dresses over the years. She saw the silver and yellow dress that Zaria had worn to the ball last year, and after years of not understanding why anyone would want to wear such a garment, she found herself wondering if she would look good in it.

"Myra, you shouldn't have."

"Oh, pish posh. Of course I should have," Myra said as she began to ready the garment for Avalon to put on.

Avalon removed her robe, and then the dress underneath. It was a cotton dress, light and loose and nothing like the dresses that Zaria wore. It fell easily from Avalon's slight frame, and she could hear Zaria stifle a gasp.

There was a burn scar on the back of Avalon's neck and the scar left by Hawker's knife on her left hand, but that was all they could see when she was dressed. Now in her underclothes, they could see the patchwork of rough skin on Avalon's back and legs, and when Myra turned around and saw Avalon, she pulled her hand up to her mouth.

"My baby, Avalon. What did they do to you?" Myra asked, and it was the first time that Avalon had ever seen Myra cry. The tears fell quick, and Myra wiped them away.

Zaria took Avalon's hand. "You did it, Avalon. You saved Fontanasia, and you are a legend," Zaria told her.

"I'm happy just to be alive."

"They're working on your statue for the Hall of Kings. Would you like to see it while you're here?" Zaria asked. Avalon shook her head. Although she would like to see the statue of her father one more time, that life was over.

"I've heard stories, Avalon," Myra scolded. "Did you really climb up the side of a castle on the back of a giant, red lizard?"

"It was Jackie. He gets really big in Cormicks, but it was perfectly safe," Avalon answered.

Myra shook her head, and they shared a smile.

"Kensington says that you are to leave tomorrow. Can't you stay longer?" Zaria asked Avalon.

Avalon shook her head. "It's not a good idea. I could be recognized."

Avalon wished that she could tell Zaria and Myra how she felt and how her life had changed in some ways for the better in Cormicks, but they wouldn't understand. Davev had decided to stay in Cormicks to court Sonrah, and to everyone's astonishment he had won her over. Neither the people of Fontanasia nor the Guides would accept them as a couple, but in this strange new place, the Runners didn't know it was a new situation. For Avalon, Cormicks was a place to be her new self without worry or recognition, and in the last six months she'd enjoyed her freedom.

"Now, how about that dress?" Avalon asked, stepping up to admire the garment.

"You've changed so much. And to think I used to have to fight to get you in a dress," Myra said, smiling, but Avalon noticed again the years of worry that had been added to Myra's wrinkled face. Myra touched the swirled skin on Avalon's back. "How is it that this is the same sky I was under yesterday?" Myra asked, and she gently hugged Avalon.

Myra had done a wonderful job on the dress in height, but she couldn't have accounted for Avalon having lost so much weight, and it hung loose on her shoulders and around her waist. Zaria fixed Avalon's hair and pulled it up in a comb. Then she placed her own tiara on Avalon's head.

There was a knock at the door.

"I think I'm ready," Avalon said, and Zaria and Myra stepped back to look at her, and both flushed with joy and pride. Then Myra turned to open the door, and to Avalon's surprise, Counselor Creighton was waiting at the threshold. Avalon blushed. She was immediately worried that she would be found out, and by the smile on his face, she knew that she was already.

"Ladies," Creighton said with a slow bow to Myra and Zaria and then very intentionally to Avalon. "May I have a moment with the bride-to-be?"

Avalon thought that her heart had stopped. He knew who she was, and he was here to call her out. Zaria turned to leave, but Avalon grabbed her sister's hand.

"It's all right," Zaria said. "He is here by invitation. He knows, Avalon, and he asked for a moment with you before the ceremony."

Myra took a parting look at Avalon and then moved outside, and Creighton bowed again as Zaria moved out of the room. Creighton held his hand out as though asking permission again, but Avalon didn't say anything. She was frozen in place, and she felt exposed.

He walked slowly into the room, playing the part of the old man at all times. His hands were folded together and his magenta robe swayed with his steps. He reached out his hand in greeting, but instead of offering her hand, Avalon fumbled with a curtsy. Julius Creighton reached his hand forward and softly touched Avalon's chin, tipping her head up to look into his eyes.

Avalon should have taken a step back or protested, but her mind couldn't decide what to do, and she was shocked into submission. When their eyes met, she could see that his were half-filled with tears.

"Your father would be so very proud of you, Avalon," he said softly. "You have saved Fontanasia from destruction and have forever sealed our peace."

Avalon stood silent and allowed herself to hear his words and believe them again. She had thought that it was her fault for making Cormicks aware of the presence of her people. He was right, though. If it wasn't for Avalon's first trip to Cormicks and Hawker's treachery, they might still be sending the Guides to reconnaissance. Her nephew and future kings could now live in perfect self-assured peace knowing that there was no enemy evident to Fontanasia.

"You knew," she said.

"Yes," Creighton marveled at Avalon's transformation into a girl.

"You knew all this time?" she asked, and Creighton nodded.

"Your father confessed to me when you were a young boy, and I have kept his secret. You made that easy to do. You studied so hard all of these years, always so focused on the task. No one suspected, Avalon. You must know that."

Avalon was very surprised to hear that her father had told anyone the secret. She sighed, happy to rid her mind of all thoughts of inadequacies and paranoia, and she realized again just how free she felt in Cormicks.

"You make a beautiful young lady. Dare I say that no one would recognize you as King Avalon." Creighton smiled softly, and Avalon couldn't ever remember seeing that expression on his face. She wondered if she was just now seeing the real Julius Creighton.

"Well, I need a little work with my curtsy," she said, and they shared a laugh.

"You will learn," Creighton promised.

"You will keep a new secret then," Avalon said. Creighton nodded, still smiling at Avalon, his old face replaced by his true, young complexion. He would be one of only seven people who knew that King Avalon was not dead.

"So you go to Cormicks with young Taggerty?" Creighton said as he clapped his hands together.

Avalon nodded. She wasn't following Taggerty, nor was he following her. They were going to Cormicks together, tasked to pick up the pieces where their ancestors had been driven out. It was her intention to teach the Runners a better way of life. Avalon would work behind the scenes with Taggerty and the others to ensure that Cormicks was rebuilt into a city like Fontanasia, and that the Runners were dealt with by stern diplomacy.

Creighton smiled into Avalon's eyes. "I have asked Taggerty to write often about Cormicks and about your progress. I may be of some assistance to your sister Zaria who will want to know how you are doing. I daresay you should not write to her yourself."

Creighton was giving advice, and she would take it. She wished that she'd known her father had trusted this man's counsel enough to tell him the full truth. Perhaps she wouldn't have been suspicious of him for so long.

Avalon nodded. "You are right again," she said sarcastically.

"I have one more question for you, then." Creighton hunched over and put his hands together, and he was back in character.

"Well, get on with it," Avalon said.

Creighton's catlike smile returned. "I just wanted to get your blessing. Young Taggerty has tasked me with administering your wedding vows."

They were married in the gorgeous candlelight. Avalon stared into Taggerty's eyes that seemed to beg her to say yes. And she did, of course. Avalon looked around the suite at her family, and she knew how lucky she was. She would miss Zaria and Kensington and Myra, but as much as she would miss them, she was happier than she'd ever been.

Counselor Creighton had joined their hands under her family's crest, and they said the words that would unite their lives together forever. He handed Taggerty the sprig of a walnut tree that they would plant together in Cormicks.

After dinner, the small party wound down and they said their tearful goodbyes. Avalon and Taggerty went back out through the small hidden gate to the Guide's village.

They bid their goodbye to Chylyn before sunrise, taking the horse and wagon slowly down the outer wall and onto the plains that led to the forest. The moon was almost full and it was easy for Taggerty to find his way through the hidden entrance in the outer wall.

Two more days of travel brought them to the elbagrass. It was dusk, and they didn't want to wait any longer to start their new life together. They ate the alleya leaf and slowly waded through the bright, blue elbagrass to the pond. Avalon and Taggerty stepped up to the pond together, and they each grabbed the sprig of the walnut tree between them. They looked down and saw each other's reflection in the water. Then Avalon took a deep breath and smiled, looking into her own eyes, and together, they vanished.

Thanks for reading! If you loved the book and have a moment to spare, I would really appreciate a short review as this helps new readers find my books.

Please go to anitarenaghan.com where you can find more titles and join the email list to receive a free ebook.

Thank you to my family and friends who support me endlessly and help in editing my work, especially you, Mom.

www.ingramcontent.com/pod-product-compliance
Lightning Source LLC
Chambersburg PA
CBHW071509110726
47908CB00003B/777